Modern Arabic Short Stories

MODERN ARABIC SHORT STORIES

Selected and translated by
DENYS JOHNSON-DAVIES

London
OXFORD UNIVERSITY PRESS
1967

Oxford University Press, Ely House, London W.1

GLASGOW NEW YORK TORONTO MELBOURNE WELLINGTON
CAPE TOWN SALISBURY IBADAN NAIROBI LUSAKA ADDIS ABABA
BOMBAY CALCUTTA MADRAS KARACHI LAHORE DACCA
KUALA LUMPUR HONG KONG TOKYO

PRINTED IN GREAT BRITAIN
BY WESTERN PRINTING SERVICES LTD. BRISTOL

Contents

v

Introduction

T HE ARAB genius for story-telling and romance expressed itself
from earliest recorded times; the desert campfire, after a hard
day's travelling and campaigning, by its intimacy encouraged the
flow of talk about past glories and present trials. These conversations have survived, albeit transformed and idealised, in much
of the poetry of ancient Arabia, and the narratives retold by later
writers to explain these verses. The most famous collections of the
old poetry, distinguished by a gift for minute observation which is
one of the most indispensable characteristics of artistic fiction, are
the *Mu'allaqāt*, the *Mufaddaliyāt*, and the *Hamāsa* anthologies.
The multi-volumed *Kitāb al-Aghāni* is the highest esteemed of the
repertories of tales.

Though the foregoing compositions began as popular diversions,
time and the revolutionary change of life from desert to city, tribe
to empire, converted them ultimately into schoolbooks, acceptable
arenas for the battles of grammarians and lexicographers. Now
there emerged a new creation of popular amusement, the inventions,
almost wholly legendary, of the *Arabian Nights* with their large
element of pure fantasy, the *Romance of Antar*, and similar cycles
of anonymous tales. These stories, originally oral of the market-
place, began to be written down probably from the tenth century
onwards, and accretions continued to flow in till in the early years
of the nineteenth century they were first committed irrevocably to
print. By the schoolmen and the religious these vulgar amusements
were austerely disdained, firmly excluded from the canon of classical Arabic literature.

During the nineteenth century, following the economic and
political penetration of the Arab lands by the European powers,
Arabs educated after the new, occidental pattern became conscious
of the attractions of Western literature, and not least (because these
were missing in Arabic) of the novel and the short story. Arabs, a

vii

small minority, educated abroad or in mission schools, enjoyed them in the original—French, English, more rarely Italian, German and Russian. The wider reading public, surely if slowly augmenting, made do very well with translation. Only during this twentieth century have Arab authors emerged able and willing to write original fiction.

Such in very brief is the background against which the achievements of Arab novelists and short story writers may be fairly assessed.

The present selection draws on contemporary authors from several Arab countries, especially Egypt, Lebanon, Syria and Iraq. These stories, cleverly chosen and admirably translated, represent a most interesting phase in the continuing renaissance of Arabic literature. Modern Arab authors are building upon the foundations laboriously laid by their predecessors, who accomplished painfully the several stages of transformation out of simple translation, through close imitation, to originality. But for the labours of authors such as Jurī Zaidān, Manfalūṭī, Māzinī, Haikal Jibrān Khalīl Jibrān, Raiḥānī, Ṭaha Husain and many others, not only would the Arabic language still have remained too stiff and inflexible to match the lightness and subtlety necessary in creative fiction; the transition from the Western or Western-dominated sociology to the portrayal of authentically Arab life could hardly have been accomplished. Meanwhile the varied influences of Dickens, Wells, Maugham, Victor Hugo, Anatole France, Maupassant, Mann, Kafka, Tolstoy, Chekov and the like had to be absorbed and, so to speak naturalised; together with, more recently, Joyce, Camus, Sagan, Steinbeck, Hemingway.

Denys Johnson-Davies, an excellent Arabic scholar with a wide knowledge of Arab life and ways, has here produced, in very readable translations, the first comprehensive anthology of contemporary Arabic short stories. His choice has been shrewdly varied to accommodate and illustrate many aspects of the Arab outlook and Arab sociology—the tragic, the tragico-comic, the lighthearted, the witty, the fantastic, the profound. Here in these pages Arab men, yes, and what is much more remarkable, Arab women too have become frankly articulate on their public and private aspirations and experiences. These enjoyable stories, throw a sudden flood of light on the Arab scene of today.

A. J. ARBERRY

Translator's Preface

THE PRESENT volume has been compiled in the belief that during the last two or three decades the Arabic short story has grown to manhood, that it now possesses a bulk of achievement that makes it of interest to readers outside the Arab world itself.

The twenty stories comprising the volume are—quite simply—twenty stories that I personally have enjoyed reading and which I believed would be read with interest and pleasure by the English reader. While feeling myself free in my choice of stories, one Arab author's name sounding much like another's to a public almost totally ignorant of modern Arabic writing, it has inevitably happened that for the most part my own preferences have coincided with the views of Arab critics and the reading public generally. Wishing the volume to contain samples of writing from as many authors as possible, and anxious not to make a distinction between those authors who are locally well known and those who are less known, by choosing two or more by the former and only one by the latter, I finally decided to represent each writer by a single story. Inevitably many writers whose stories I admire have not, for reasons of space, been included. (The extent of my own dilemma as to which writers and which stories to include can be measured from the fact that in the course of preparing this book I have translated more than fifty stories.)

I have not divided up the authors under countries but have regarded the whole of the Arab world as the cultural unity it is and these stories as the products of that culture. Although perhaps of general interest to the non-Arab reader, it is of little significance that one writer happens to have been born in Syria and another in the Sudan—though such information is given in the 'Notes on Authors' at the end of the book. The important thing, the common denominator possessed by each of the writers in this volume, is that his story has been written in the classical Arabic language, the factor upon which rests the unique linguistic unity of the Arab world. The classical Arabic in which the narrative portion, and in most cases the dialogue as well, of these stories is written is the language in which every Arab, be he from the town or the country, be he Moslem or Christian, monarchist or radical, reads his daily newspaper, comprehends the news bulletins on the radio, and writes his letters: when an Arab is literate he is literate in the classical language. The colloquial language, which may differ considerably from country to country, is used solely for the purposes of everyday conversation. Thus if Arabs from different parts of the world meet, though each may be ignorant of the other's particular brand of colloquial language, they possess in the classical language—provided they are both literate—a common medium in which they can make contact.

This, therefore, is a volume of *Arabic* short stories. I have therefore excluded from it the work of Arabs whose writings have been contributed to the literature of some other culture, as for instance the North African writers writing in French.

There are two main cultural centres in the Arab world—Cairo and Beirut—and most of the stories represented here, whatever the nationality of their authors, have originally appeared in one or other of the many literary magazines that are edited in these two capitals and enjoy a circulation wherever Arabic is read. It has so happened that half the stories I have chosen are by Egyptian authors, most of whom are household names throughout the Arab world; the non-Egyptian writers, however, are generally less widely known, particularly in Egypt.

It is my hope that these stories will be enjoyed by the English reader not only as works of fiction but as giving a picture of a culture and way of life different from our own. These stories give, as it were, an opportunity to eavesdrop on a part of the world and a people with whom the British have been very closely associated but with whose culture and literature only a few specialist scholars are familiar; they also provide us with the chance of comparing between how the Arabs see themselves and how they have been portrayed by non-Arab novelists and short story writers. I further hope that these stories will encourage the publication in English translation of more examples of fictional writing from modern Arabic.

I had better follow custom and admit that I have made no

attempt to follow any system of transliteration of Arabic proper names—my sole object has been to make them look as familiar and friendly as possible. Footnotes, it will be seen, I have kept to the minimum; readers will, for example, in due course come across *kunafa* and *taamiya*, but I do not think it necessary to provide them with a recipe for either of these delicious foods.

In conclusion, my thanks are due to the authors of these stories for giving me their permission to translate and publish them in this volume. It is a special pleasure to me, who studied Arabic at Cambridge, that Professor Arberry should have so kindly written the Introduction.

DENYS JOHNSON-DAVIES

Farahat's Republic

YUSUF IDRIS

No sooner had I made my way inside with the guard than I experienced an immediate feeling of depression. Though not the first time I had entered the police station, it was the first time I'd seen it at night. I felt, as I stepped across the threshold, that I was making my way into some underground trench utterly unconnected with the present or, indeed, the immediate past. The walls were covered half-way up with a blackness that resembled paint, while the other half was enveloped in a general gloom; white patches scattered here and there merely served to emphasize the ugliness of the rest. The floor was so slimy you couldn't tell if it was made of asphalt or just plain mud. The all-pervading smell, whose quintessence defied definition, gave one a sensation of nausea. From lamps of great antiquity on which the flies had settled and laid their eggs, lamps the greater part of whose light had been condemned to life imprisonment within themselves, a pale light emanated; the little that did succeed in escaping acted more as a protecting veil for the darkness than it dispelled, and when it did fall upon objects and people merely brought out their mournful and ugly aspects.

On being enveloped by all this, having become an inseparable part of it, with people around me wearing expressions of great gravity and going around as though under hypnosis, with the boxes of fruit and hand-carts, the café chairs confiscated by the Municipality police and stacked up in one corner, their owners strewn around the walls and corners, collapsed in exhaustion on the ground, heads lolling forward on to their laps, and the policemen in their black uniforms looking like *afreets* of the dead of night; while enveloped by all this I felt that I too must surely have committed some forgotten crime and I wished I might escape from the place as soon as possible. However, as I was to be detained at the police station for the night and sent up before the Parquet the following morning, I was unable to leave. They were at a loss where to put me, the detainment room being full, while the other room in which political prisoners were generally kept was a teeming mass of women under surveillance and ladies of easy virtue, so that in the end they could do no better for me than leave me, together with my guard, in the duty officer's room.

Despite its size the room was too small for the persons it contained. Of these the duty officer himself was the most striking. He was sitting at his desk like a commandant of police, on his right the muzzles of more than fifty stacked rifles, behind him a wooden board fixed to the wall and weighed down with every sort and kind of chain and fetter, shields, axes and helmets, while on his left stood the usual old iron chest. Seated thus, it seemed to me that there were no limits to his power and the awe he must inspire, that he would be capable of quite simply taking a bite out of my arm or gouging out my eye with a finger. I was certain, however, that he was no concern of mine nor I of his.

I found myself abandoning everything within me, everything with which I was preoccupied, and joining that army of eyes directed at him by the people crowded before him and separated from him only by a low wooden railing.

At first it seemed to me that he wasn't a living creature but merely a body fashioned from the black paint that had been used on the walls, his head one of the helmets hanging up behind him, his eyes rifle muzzles, his tongue most certainly a whip. But when I had calmed down a bit and got used to the place, I observed how he wore his cap at a most dignified yet fearsome angle, how his officer-type overcoat was buttoned right the way up—contrary to the usual practice—and how the skin of his face was drawn back so tautly, with such severity, that all the wrinkles in it disappeared and it became as smooth as the stretched skin of a drum. There was an intenseness about his gaze that made one feel that he not so much looked at people as pecked and stung them; his voice, required to perform feats of which it was incapable, snarled and roared, staccato as bullet shots, with unintelligible words.

Observing all this, he struck me as being like one of those prisoner-of-war Italian generals we used to see. Then it happened that a Sergeant or Master-Sergeant—I don't remember which—came and stood before him.

'Farahat,' he called out.

I was amazed how he addressed him with such informality. My amazement, however, disappeared when he again said:

'Farahat . . . Mister Farahat.'

The duty officer made no reply till the man had addressed him by 'Sergeant-Major . . . Sir!'

I had drawn close and was leaning, as were several others, on the wooden railing. I was thus able to hear his accent which contained faint traces of the countryside of Upper Egypt; his high-pitched voice betrayed the wide open spaces in which he had grown up, betrayed too the bellowing and barking required by his job: it had added to it the sort of grating rattle that befalls the local café wireless from having its volume turned up too high too often. The image of the genera_ went completely from my mind as his features took on an aura of awesome authority. I saw him then purely as Upper Egyptian: a nose as big as that of Rameses, a high angular brow like that of Mycerinus, and the imprint of his advancing years that indicated a crowded history in the service of the police, for he had inevitably spent whole decades in it to reach the rank of Sergeant-Major, having joined the force as a simple private. I saw his ageing body as it really was, straight in parts, twisted in others, forced into its uniform, heavy boots and leather belt, which had themselves imposed a shape upon his body in the same way as the iron gives shape and dimension to a tarboosh. It was quite apparent he enjoyed being duty officer and wanted people to treat him like a real honest-to-God officer, which no doubt he had been dreaming of becoming for three-quarters of his lifetime dreaming of the day when his shoulder would carry its one pip. It was clear, though, that his shoulder would be carrying nothing of the sort, for though he would sometimes undertake the role of duty officer, the time for his being pensioned off was imminent and for him the dawn star was more attainable than that of a second lieutenant. . . . And when my eyes moved away from him and I looked round the room I could see the empty desks vacated by their owners, the filing cabinet, the old fan placed above the safe, which looked as if it had not been used for at least ten years and over which the grime had made spidery tracings, and the electric lamp with its shade of sheet iron dangling down from the ceiling alongside Farahat's head bent over the papers before him. While the people crowding round the wooden barrier were a thoroughly mixed bunch, they were at one in their anxious, sadly angry looks and set, depressed expressions. Most of them, having been charged, were returning, joined together by a long chain, from being investigated at the Parquet.

After a while I realized that they attached no importance to their armed guard, the chain or to Sergeant-Major Farahat himself; his barkings were countered by bellows or sometimes with a riposte no less telling than his own. Then one of them exploded in rage because his identity and record cards had not yet arrived from the Identity Investigation Department and he was having to stay under detention till they did. He rained down curses on all and sundry, bewailing the unfairness of the world and his own accursed bad luck and poverty; if it had not been for some last vestige of respect for authority he would have heaped down curses on the duty officer too for good measure. I noticed that the officer in Farahat was undergoing extreme embarrassment as he listened to them ranting and raging while being unable—as real officers, in his view, should—to still the clamour because of their numbers, savagery, and defiance. When he had finished with them and they had gone off, a policeman at the head of the line and another bringing up the rear, the chain clinking and clanking and the prisoners still swearing and cursing, Farahat heaved the heavy sigh of someone at his wit's end.

When I again directed my attention to Farahat I found he was looking extremely old, so old you would have thought he was some item that had been lighted upon in a surprise police raid and, after being confiscated, had been sealed with a red tarboosh and uniform and had remained on in the government stores as an exhibit, deteriorating and growing more and more ragged, though without the seals themselves suffering any wear. His eye travelled over those present and he said:

'Ugh, I swear to God hard labour's easier than this lot.'

His eyes came to rest on me. They contained a clear invitation. I, who had been sitting for hours in silence listening, responded to it and found myself saying:

'Oh, is there so much work then?'

Like someone who has waited a long time for release he exploded: 'I should say there is, sir. This isn't a job, it's a circus, a madhouse. People have gone crazy. What are they up to? It's no skin off their noses! It all comes down on our heads. By the

Prophet, I'd prefer to work in irons for a hundred years than sit
around here for an hour. And what really drives you mad is that
it's all so much nonsense . . . it's all lies . . . all false allegations, I
swear to you. There's the fellow who's gone off and done himself
an injury, and the one who's lost his hammer, and the chap who
says he was fast asleep and his cap did a bunk. Why go any further?
Hasn't she been standing there since early morning? What's up
with you, girl? I'm not Sergeant-Major Farahat if she doesn't say
they beat her up and stole her jewellery. . . . What's up, girl?
What's the matter?'

The 'girl' was one of those standing in front of him. She was
wearing a black dress which the magician of poverty had changed
to a drab greyish colour; round her head she had wound a faded
handkerchief which hid but little of her short coffee-coloured,
kinky hair, the ends of which were twisted and ragged. Her face
was a dark brown and the *kohl* on her eyes had been smeared by
tears. 'Umm Sakeena', she said meekly, 'and the girl Ayyousha,
her niece Nabawiyya and the boy—'

'What of them? What of them?'

'They attacked me and hit me in the stomach,' and she began
sobbing.

In a flash she was in full flood. Her voice choked with tears, she
added, 'And Umm Sakeena . . . she bit me . . . here . . . in the
shoulder . . . and gave me a poke in the stomach. The girl
Ayyousha pinched my ear-rings.'

The Sergeant-Major's voice was thick and guttural from the
guffaws of laughter he gave vent to. 'See what I mean, sir?' he
said. 'D'you see? Didn't I tell you? I swear to you it's all a pack
of lies, an absolute fraud. I ask you, can you imagine her owning so
much as a brass button? What ear-rings are these, my girl, they've
taken? The crown jewels?'

'Gold ear-rings, Bey, and two bangles—'

The Sergeant-Major turned to me and said in a tone that reminded me of the comedian Nagib al-Rihani: 'Who d'you
honestly think is the victim in this story?'

'Who?'

'Me! It's me, sir. Such barefaced lying is worse than robbery
with violence. And the hell of it is that the report about it has to
be in two copies and what's more it's I who'll be writing out the
two copies.'

He faced round to the woman, piercing her with a searching look which contained a hint of fleeting laughter. He took hold of the pen and opened the large report ledger as though opening Mitwalli Gate. 'So . . . may the good God put an end to your life and mine that I may be spared all this.'

When he had finished writing the preamble to the report he asked her: 'What's your name, girl?'

He didn't wait for her to answer or concern himself with her reply when it came; facing round to me he continued with what he had to say, though I felt that he was talking more to himself than to me: 'By the Prophet, it's I who am the victim. And not only in this case, in a thousand cases, a billion. Perhaps you don't believe it. Then come and have a look at the day-book. We started off today with a rape on the highway and then following on that there's number 592, a pickpocketing of a wallet which was said to contain 147 pounds, 83 piastres and a couple of postage stamps. I swear by God, all that it had in it were the two postage stamps and being on oath as it were, two and a half piastres as well. The next case is the theft of some copper. They say in the statement that the copper weighed 50 pounds and they accuse the maid-servant, a mere chit of a girl who'd hardly herself be weighing more than ten pounds . . . and so on and so forth. From early morning I've had writer's cramp. And it's all just chickenfeed, rubbishy talk and lies. My dear chap, forget it.'

He turned to the woman.

'Why don't you say something, girl?' he asked. 'What's your name?'

Before she had answered he gave a laugh, like someone who has remembered a joke, and said: 'Or what about the body they found in the rubbish dump which didn't have an owner—or rather whose owner wasn't known? They found he'd given up the ghost just like that, without anyone saying so much as a harsh word to him. Tell me, though, why should he choose this particular rubbish dump to go and die on? D'you mean to say he had so little choice he couldn't have walked to Shobra for instance? God have mercy on his soul, he's dead when all's said and done, but why should it be I who suffers? Anyway, the long and short of it is that we're all destined for affliction and grief just as our ancestors were. . . .' He turned his head towards her.

'What's your name, woman?'

'Khadiga . . .'

'Khadiga what? Speak up.'

'Khadiga Mohamed . . .'

'Get a move on, woman . . . Mohamed what?'

But before she could give a reply he laid aside his pen and, resting his elbows on the page, placed his head between his hands. From under the brim of the cap, with the lamp in front of him swaying like a pendulum so that the shadow of his head moved along the wall behind him, backwards and forwards like a large monkey, he said:

'By the Prophet, I'm the victim, I swear it. It's not for nothing I've got old before my time! Thirty years' service, I tell you, and every day it's been just like this. I've been through it all, from Manzala to Uneiba, from Arish to Mersa Matrouh. I've seen men murder for a stick of sugar-cane, burn down a barn for a corn-cob. . . . People have gone crazy. It's not for nothing one goes grey.'

He stopped speaking suddenly and swooped down upon a hand that was gravitating towards the desk and gave it a violent, petulant thump.

'I've told you a hundred times to find yourself another blotter. Is this the only piece in the whole of the station? I take my refuge in God, are we at a gipsies' fair?'

Having said which he waited till the owner of the hand had disappeared discomfited, then turned on me his serious face with its tightly drawn features.

'One bursts a blood vessel and these sons of bitches don't give a damn and just fool around.'

As he talked he motioned with his eyes towards the telephone room where some policemen had gathered round a flaccidly corpulent colleague; some were holding his hands behind his back and the others were attempting to pull his trousers down, while the man panted and struggled with such strength as his obesity allowed.

Out of the corner of my eye I noticed that Sergeant-Major Farahat was smiling and chuckling; then, oblivious to everything else, he craned his neck forward so as to follow the battle. He looked really sorry when it ended with the victory and escape of the man with the large stomach. At this he raised his voice and spoke in his wholly Upper Egyptian accent:

'Ah, you set of old women—you couldn't even manage to deal with that flabby fellow.'

He had scarcely finished speaking when a side door opened and the Assistant Superintendent appeared in the courtyard. The station suddenly became deaf and dumb, everything was frozen over by the air of sternness that descended.

'You say your name is Khadiga Mohamed what?' the Sergeant-Major asked the woman gravely.

I left him to his questioning for I had become engrossed in the night patrol which had begun to collect in the courtyard. When duly gathered together it was a truly remarkable sight: two ranks of complete darkness with only a glimmer of yellow brass buttons and above the darkness a conflagration of bright-red tarbooshes. In front of each rank was another rank of hands stretched out dejectedly supporting rifles. Murmurings could be heard in the darkness and bursts of laughter that died with the speed of shooting stars. Occasionally an elbow would move out sideways from the outstretched hands and nudge its neighbour.

The Assistant Superintendent inspected them with his nose pointing skywards like a turkey cock and his eyes on the button that didn't shine, the boot which was not as black as it should be. To and fro he went, then entered his room. It appeared that he had just dined for when he came out again he was still chewing and there was a sheen on his lips. Once again he made his inspection, drying his hands which he had just washed. Boots and the butts of rifles crashed down on the ground several times. To some punishment was meted out, others were merely reprimanded. Then:

'Slope arms! Shoulder arms! Patrol, quick march.' And off went the night patrol, wheezing and reeling. Bringing up the rear was a corpulent policeman who was trying in vain to keep his ill-proportioned body in step.

On the departure of the patrol, the station courtyard became as empty as a coach on the night train approaching the terminus. Returning to Sergeant-Major Farahat, I found that he was still questioning the woman.

'And where did they attack you?'

'Inside the cinema.'

'And what made you go to the cinema, girl?'

'Mahmoud.'

'Mahmoud who?'

'Mahmoud!'

His Upper Egyptian origin was again in evidence as, with knotted brow and without writing in the report, he asked:

'And what, my girl, would this Mahmoud be?'

'My cousin.'

'Ah, what a cock-eyed country it is, you sons of bitches,' he said, putting down his pen. He extracted from his pocket an old metal box of the sort in which expensive cigarettes are sold. I saw that it contained two plain cigarettes and a cork-tipped one, also a packet of matches. He lit one of the plain ones and murmured one or two cryptic remarks about fathers and grandfathers. He dispelled any ambiguity when he said, speaking to himself: 'Cinema ... huh ... Cinema, they say, do they! What the hell would you be going to the cinema for? The likes of you don't go to the cinema!' Breaking off his conversation with himself, he leaned back, crossed his legs and asked the woman:

'And why should you be going to a cinema with a boy like that?' His eyes searched round in my direction, perhaps wanting me to bear witness to her answer. I therefore said to him:

'What, isn't the report done yet?'

'Not yet ... Will it ever be finished? I'll be right along, I know I've kept you waiting. Just a minute and I'll be free for you.'

It was clear he thought I was somebody with a complaint or an informer—most likely the latter. Perhaps, though, he found me well cast for the role of a listener to whom he could unburden himself on one of his long nights on duty and had thus decided to postpone my departure. Smiling, he wrote down something, then said:

'After all, you're being entertained. Honestly, isn't it better than the cinema?'

With a sigh he asked the woman:

'Huh, and why did your former husband plot against you? What's this rubbish about having gone off to the cinema? Come on, speak up, girl, why did your former husband plot against you?'

'The point is I had an order against him for maintenance.'

He jotted down a word or two and gave me a look of distaste.

'Stories! The cinema! What are these stories they make up? They might as well boil them up and make soup of them.'

'Why, don't you like it?'

'Like it? How can I like it? A film must be really interesting—

not all this clowning and dancing around that gets one nowhere.'

He took up the pen and rested the nib on the ledger. Instead of writing, however, he said listlessly:

'Once when I got fed up with stories I made a film.'

His lack of enthusiasm caused me not to listen all that carefully to him. His words, however, had an odd ring about them and I asked:

'You did what?'

'I made a film—a story.'

'How did you make it? You took part in it or what?'

'No, I made up a film specially for the cinema.'

I was about to dismiss the whole matter and laugh, thinking that he had no doubt been the witness of some incident or crime with which his life teemed and that he rather naïvely wanted to make it into a film.

'What sort of film would this be?' I asked, checking my laughter. Quite simply, without hemming and hawing or sitting upright or putting down the pen, or even paying attention to the woman and other people at the barrier, he said:

'There was an Indian came to Cairo, a very rich man, one of those who have as much money as we have poverty. The man came and put up in one of those terribly posh hotels, let's say Mena House or "Shabat"*, and there was some poor wretch like ourselves . . .'

Suddenly all my senses were wideawake. I leaned heavily over the barrier so as not to miss a word.

A woman came forward demanding help, half-screaming. She was fair-skinned and good-looking and her eyebrows were pencilled with exquisite care.

'What's up with you, woman?' Sergeant-Major Farahat growled at her. 'What's wrong—end of the world come or something?'

'Help! Help, the lad's beaten his mother to death.'

'What lad, woman?'

'Our neighbour's son.'

'And what's it got to do with us?'

'What . . .? Aren't you—may the Prophet protect you—the police?'

* An attempt at pronouncing the word 'Shepheard's'.

'Is it right for the police to come between the lad and his mother?'

'Eh!... And when the chap kills her brother?'

'That would be a different kettle of fish. In that case we'd be off and arrest him.'

The woman gave up in despair and retired into a far corner with the policeman who was guarding me. She began recounting the story to him in whispers, largely with the aid of her eyebrows. Then she left the station, with the policeman lost in amazement and delight at the whisperings of those eyebrows. Sergeant-Major Farahat again turned his attention to me.

'What a load of calamity it all is!' he said. 'Some lad I must say! Enough of that... This poor fellow was out of work, meaning, as the saying goes, that he was an employee of the Sun Company—packing sun into bottles all day and hawking them round at night. Ha ha! That's how it was. Yes, indeed! As I was saying, this Indian was once leaving the hotel when he dropped a diamond which today would be worth at the very least seventy or eighty thousand pounds. The Egyptian fellow, seeing it, picked it up and handed it to the rich Indian...'

'What diamond are you talking about, you old humbug?'

We turned round together to find that the person who had spoken was a tall sergeant carrying a file, who presently asked Farahat:

'What've you done about the deceased whose name's not known?'

'What d'you want me to do?' Farahat fired back. 'Walk round the streets saying "Anyone lost a body?"'

'I went to the hospital and saw him.'

'Happy to make your acquaintance.'

'Look here, old chap, his eyes are honey-coloured, his hair's grey and on his right temple—'

'What are you telling me all this for? Did I send you to ask his hand in marriage? You'd be better off getting on with your work. Honey-coloured indeed, you lanky oaf.'

Then he turned to me: 'When the Indian man came to give the Egyptian some money he swore by everything holy he wouldn't take a single *millieme*. In vain did he try to persuade him but there was nothing doing. He therefore went up enormously in the Indian's estimation, who was really won over to him. Well, the days came and went and the rich fellow went off to his country at a loss how to reward the Egyptian. He then decided that the best way was to buy him a lottery ticket. . . . Do you know how much the first prize was? But let's wait till we have a drink of tea.'

He went on clapping his hands till the boy from the canteen arrived. He asked for tea and had a lengthy argument as to the orders he had consumed that day, the boy saying three and he insisting that it was only two. But even when the tea had been brought the dispute remained unresolved.

We heard the Assistant Superintendent's door being opened. When he came out and stood stretching himself in the courtyard, Farahat resumed his questioning of the woman.

'Huh, what's it all about?'

'When I got the order against him, he came along wanting me to give it up. When I didn't agree he sent his mother, his sister and his cous—'

'Whoa . . . That's enough up to here. They attacked you in the cinema?'

'Yes, and they went on hitting me till I almost had a miscarriage . . .'

'What?'

'You see, I'm six months pregnant.'

Sergeant-Major Farahat, overcome by curiosity, laid aside the report. 'Good God! Who are you pregnant by, girl?'

'From him, Bey—from my divorced husband.'

'When?'

'Before he divorced me.'

'And why did your husband divorce you when you were pregnant?'

'Because he had sworn to.'

'Sworn to? And when did he divorce you?'

'The first day of Ramadan last. I broke his mother's water-jug when I got up to prepare the *sahour** and he made a triple oath that if he didn't break my arm in return, he'd divorce me.'

'And he broke your arm?'

'No, he divorced me.'

'By the Prophet, I felt in my very heart this would be it. . . . So, his mother's jug is the cause. So, because his mother's jug get's broken last Ramadan I get myself steamed up for the whole of today

* The daybreak meal during Ramadan.

—the victim of one piastre's worth of jug. Listen, my girl, have you any other statements to make? Anything else you'd like to say?'

'Yes, Bey, it was Ayyousha who pinched the ear-rings from me, while her mother . . .'

'Ugh! Anything more to say, apart from what you've already said?'

'But I haven't said anything yet.'

I was unable to refrain from laughing and Farahat's anger also turned into a loud guffaw. He finished off the report, gave a sigh and a yawn, and then shook his head.

The woman went out bearing a note sending her for a medical report. To my amazement all the people who were standing around went out with her.

'Huh, how much was the first prize?'

'You still remember? It was for a million pounds. After all, it too cost a lot of money!

'He bought a hundred tickets so as to make sure of winning, and when the draw came along one of them won the first prize—a million pounds free of tax. It never occurred to the man to be greedy and keep it for himself without anyone being any the wiser. Not a bit of it. What did he do? Off he went and bought an enormously big cargo-boat which he loaded up with the very best quality Indian silk, a bit of ivory, a few ostrich feathers, a bit of fine woollen cloth and Cashmere and classy furniture. Then he sent the ship complete with all its crew to Alexandria. After that, he sent the contract of sale and the bill of lading fully paid up to our friend in Egypt. That's to say he had nothing to do but take receipt of it.

'Then, lo and behold, the ship arrived at Alexandria—something absolutely out of this world. And who does it belong to, chaps? Why, so-and-so. Well, to cut a long story short, the fellow sold the goods on the ship and used the money to buy another ship. So he kept one ship going off overseas fully laden while the second was returning home also fully laden. Now, if a tiny parcel so big costs one so much to send by rail, you can see what a ship like this would make from a trip . . .'

At that moment a short, thin man came rushing in, wearing a *galabia* all covered in oil and stains, his head bare and his feet in wooden clogs that made a most excruciating sound. He darted in like an arrow, an expression of immense pain on his face.

'Effendi . . . Effendi . . .'

His entry irritated Sergeant-Major Farahat. As though someone had aimed a punch at the tip of his nose, he turned on the man
and thundered at him:

'What's up with you?'

'There's nothing up with me, Effendi. It's that bastard of a boy
who threw a brick which broke the pane of glass of the shop window, a pane of glass that you can't get these days, genuine Belgian
pre-war crystal. Three metres by three it was. May God bring about
your ruin as you've brought about mine, you bastard.'

'What shop's this?'

'The Friendship and Fraternity Grocery in the main street.'

'I know it—the one on the corner opposite the garage?'

'That's it, may God prosper you. May the Lord never bring
down upon you . . .'

'And which window was broken—the one on the street or the
other one on the lane?'

'The big one, Effendi, the one on the lane.'

'Then it's not ours,' said Sergeant-Major Farahat, dissociat-
ing himself from the matter and preparing to continue with his
story. 'It's Boulak's.'

'How's that, Bey, when the house is in your district?'

'The side that overlooks the lane is under Boulak.'

'Please, Effendi—'

'I've told you it's nothing to do with us. Go to Boulak station.'

'Ple—'

'Scram! A *khamsin* wind take you!'

The man darted out like an arrow, clip-clopping in his clogs.
Farahat waited till the hammering of the clogs had died away,
then endeavoured to recreate the atmosphere which had been disturbed by the grocer. He leaned far back, tilting his chair; then he
took off his cap and held it in his hand, twirling it round or fanning himself with it.

'The man was extremely fed up with all the European ships,
but in the space of a year God was good to him and he expanded
a lot. Bit by bit he began buying up all the ships of Alexandria so
that there wasn't a single one, English, Italian or what you will—
all were flying the green flag.'

I noticed that Sergeant-Major Farahat's features had relaxed;
they had shed all that sternness and distaste and had taken on an

expression that had about it the contentment of old age; his eyes wandered about in the sky of the room like two dreamy butterflies; his voice was free from all discordance and flowed with a sweet, casual elation, so that the words issued from his mouth as though sweetened with honey. You could not help loving them, loving their tremulous resonance as they stole forth unhurriedly into the lugubrious silence that reigned over the police station, giving it the air of a funeral marquee at the end of the night when nothing can be heard but the hissing of the pressure-lamps and the murmurings of people paying their last respects.

'The man came to have countless ships, the smallest of which would have been ten or fifteen times as large as this station. But was he satisfied with this? Not at all. The money didn't go to his head, so with the income from the ships he went off and bought an enormously large textile factory in which he employed about half a million workers. After one month the profits from the textile factory paid for a glass factory. The glass paid for flour mills—and rice-hulling works, then some cotton ginneries, a bit of sugar—a bit of gas—a bit of paper—a bit of machinery—a bit of steel— Anyhow, the day came when he owned all the factories in Egypt.

'But this untidy state of affairs didn't please him at all. So he gathered up all the factories and put them down in one place measuring a thousand feddans. No, what's a thousand? A thousand wouldn't be enough. More like ten thousand, of which five thousand were for the factories and the other five for the workers to live in. Not any sort of houses mind you. Oh no. Real homes they were with gardens and balconies and everything laid on —chicken coops, rabbit hutches, the lot. And that's not all! He didn't make any profit at all from workers' sweat. The man who did work worth five piastres got five piastres, the one who did work for ten got ten. Forgive my saying so, but a worker will put his heart and soul into his job when he's properly paid. We're a people who've had an inheritance of hard work handed down to us from father to son ever since the time of the Pharoahs. Instead of making a metre of cloth the worker would make two; instead of just one shoe he'd make a pair. That's how it was—give and take, give me my right and take yours. Also the worker himself was completely changed, with tip-top clean clothes, his overalls nicely ironed to go to work in, then returning in the afternoon to change into his best suit, 'Nisr' tarboosh and patent leather

shoes. And what cafés there were! What gardens! What casinos!
What splendour! And the people all looking nice and gay and
happy. There was no unpleasantness, no hard times, laughing
the whole day long and having fun. At night they'd go to the
cinema. These cinemas are terribly important. In every street there
was a cinema and by order everyone whoever he might be had
to go. And as for the films, they were absolutely tip-top. As for
police, there weren't any—just a constable who instead of having
to be out for eight hours on patrol would have a kiosk all made out
of glass, right in the middle of the street, and a small office, and
anyone who wanted anything would come to him. . . .

'Hang on, 'cos the vermin, begging your pardon, have arrived.
Let's see what today's catch is like.'

I had in fact heard a slight noise coming from the direction of
the door but had been too absorbed by what Farahat was saying
to pay any attention.

I turned towards the doorway and found it crammed with four
or five plain-clothes men, tall and broad, and all wearing felt skull-
caps, every one of whom held a fistful of unkempt children in
each hand and old beggars whom they dragged behind them,
the *galabia* of one child tied to that of the next. The plain-clothes
men looked like enormous giants and alongside them the children
were tiny and dwarfish, like frightened chicks. They crossed the
courtyard and the procession arrived at the wooden barrier; they
were accompanied by the din they were making, which Sergeant-
Major Farahat put a stop to with:

'Enough! Shut up, the lot of you! Line them up in front of me.
Stop that yattering, God strike you blind!'

The remainder of the plain-clothes men went off and the line fell
in quietly.

Sergeant-Major Farahat again leaned back in his chair, still in a
state of euphoria.

'And then?' I asked.

'Well, along came machinery from Germany right away and
engineers and workmen got busy and off they went cultivat-
ing the whole of the desert. Just imagine all this sand once it was
cultivated. An express train travelling for seven days wouldn't
reach the end of it! And the great thing was that there was
none of that nonsense called ploughs and water-wheels and such
rubbish. Everything was done by machinery—irrigation by

machinery, threshing by machinery, fertilizing by machinery. There were even machines for gathering up the cotton and cutting the clover. And the peasant who did the work didn't know any more about such things as *galabias*, skull-caps, yellow slippers and all that tomfoolery. Not on your life! It was all suits—khaki pants to the knees, clean white hats and shoes with double soles that never wore out. Off the peasants went to work in crocodile line, working up to noon only and coming back in line too. It was the same with the women, except that they were in one field and the men in another. And the houses were all of stone. Gas lamps were absolutely out—everything was electric and the cost of consumption was borne by the landlord. Every row of houses had its own canteen in which they all ate and then they'd all go home for a siesta and later they'd file off to school so as to learn to read and write and get to know their rights and duties. But, sir, not to make too long a story of it, the man, having so much money, lost all interest in it—it had become as common as dirt to him. The fellow who owns that sort of money can't help but get bored with it—like someone who eats apples every day. So one day he announced over the radio—oh yes, I forgot to tell you he'd made a radio station and linked it up with every single house; well, he announced into the microphone that he was giving it all up.'

Now Sergeant-Major Farahat was looking at me as though thinking about some other problem.

'Hey, you, what d'you think you're doing standing there?' he suddenly addressed himself to the constable. 'Haven't you got any work to do?'

'The fact of the matter is,' said the constable disjointedly, 'he was handed over to me.'

'Handed over? Why?'

'To guard him.'

Sergeant-Major Farahat turned and looked at me in a way he had not done before. He went on staring at me; no doubt he found that I did not lend myself to the role of a murderer, a thief, or a kidnapper. I don't know what he meant when he said, slowly and with a great deal of uncertainty:

'Oh, this gentleman. Are you one of them?'

'Of whom?' I said, smiling. 'Anyway, what did the man announce over the radio?'

He continued to gaze at me and then said absent-mindedly:

'Forget it—it's all just so many words. You don't really believe it, do you?'

The skin of his face tightened till it again became as taut as a drum; he pulled down his cap to its accustomed place over his forehead, and swooped down upon the old beggar who stood at the top of the queue, withering him with his gaze and then burst out in his customary bellowing:

'Say something, you animal! What's your name?'

The Dead Afternoon

WALID IKHLASSI

THE WALL-CLOCK struck five, filling the house with its ringing.
I was watching the swallows from my window as they crossed
the city sky; thousands of swallows, black moving specks.

The evening, meanwhile, prepared to occupy its place in a new
day.

'May they find favour with God,' I said to my grandmother,
who had finished her prayers.

'I was late performing the afternoon prayer,' she answered
sadly.

'Never mind, there will be other afternoons.'

My grandmother did not hear me.

I looked at an enormous fly squatting on the outside of the
window-pane: it seemed to be defying me, sitting there so close
to my nose.

'This fly has annoyed me all day,' I said, 'and I haven't been
able to kill it.'

My grandmother did not reply: she had started on a new
prayer.

I was not conscious of the passage of time: the fly had taken up
so much of it. I had threatened it by tapping on the glass, but
it had not stirred. Looking at my finger-nails and seeing that they
were long, I produced a pair of scissors and began to pare them.

The sky was being engulfed in soft darkness, and the only sound
to cut across my grandmother's voice as she recited her prayers,
seated in her gazelle-skin chair, was the clock striking six.

My young sister came in from the other room.

'Today we'll be eating *kunafa* with walnuts,' she announced.

'I don't like it.'

My sister laughed. 'This morning you said you wanted *kunafa*.'

'I just don't like it.'

19

Turning again to the window, I was surprised to find that the fly was still asleep.

My grandmother, caressing my young sister, said to her:

'Turn on the radio so we can listen to Feiruz.'

'We listened to her at midday,' I said firmly. The darkness outside prevented me from seeing the swallows. Even so, though, I liked Feiruz's voice.

'We'll listen to her again,' said my grandmother.

I did not reply: I was contemplating the sleeping fly.

A frightening thought occurred to me: what if one of them should watch me as I lay sound asleep?

I heard my sister asking my grandmother to tell us the story of *The Singing Nightingale* this evening and my grandmother saying, 'Didn't we finish it yesterday?'

The little girl cried out petulantly:

'Yesterday! Yesterday's over.'

'You won't hear the story of the singing nightingale any more,' I whispered to myself and I was filled with sadness.

'I'll tell you a new one today,' said my grandmother.

'We don't want a new story,' exclaimed my sister.

'But the old one's finished.'

'It's *not* finished,' shouted my sister.

I tried to excuse my sister, as she jumped off my grandmother's lap and hurried out of the room, but I too felt annoyed; I too wanted the old story.

After a while I complied with my grandmother's request to switch on the radio, and searched round for a station. I found one as the clock struck seven.

'This is Aleppo.'

I drew a veil of silence over the voice.

'Let's hear the news,' protested my grandmother.

Flicking through the pages of the morning paper, I said:

'It's stale news.'

'New things may happen, my son,' exclaimed the old lady, suddenly conscious of her age.

I began reading the headlines: having already done so at midday, they did not affect me.

All at once I wanted to get out of that room, but I had nowhere particular to go, so I changed my mind and stayed where I was.

The little girl returned with her large doll.

'Will you tell Suzanne a story?' she asked, looking at her grandmother with a challenge in her eyes.

The old lady laughed.

I went back to the window: the darkness had settled down completely in the vastness of the sky.

I felt a great desire to tease the sleeping fly coming over me. I no longer felt any resentment against it and had forgotten its impudence.

'Won't you tell Suzanne a new story?' asked my sister.

The fact was that I did not know any story. Then I remembered one I had heard on the radio at noon.

'I'll tell you the story of *The Bear and the Honey*,' I replied.

'But it's an old one,' cried my sister.

Confused, I returned to observing the fly.

'What is it?' asked the little girl, coming towards me as I sat by the window.

'A sleeping fly.'

'A sleeping fly?' my sister asked, knitting her brows. 'Is that a new story?'

'It's asleep, it's tired.'

'Will you tell it to Suzanne?' she said.

'All right, I'll tell it.'

My sister drew close to me.

'What are you looking at?' she demanded.

'I'm looking at the fly.'

She climbed on to a chair and stared at it. Then she proclaimed triumphantly in her shrill voice:

'But it's dead!'

I felt uneasy as I looked at the girl who was suddenly as tall as I was.

'It's asleep.'

'It's dead!' said my sister, amazed at my ignorance.

I opened the window cautiously and blew softly on the fly: it fell off like a wisp of paper.

I remembered it flying around me, remembered that I had hated it and then loved it.

'Won't you tell Suzanne the story of *The Sleeping Fly*?'

I didn't answer her: I was listening to the striking of the clock which reverberated through the house.

The Dream

ABDEL SALAM AL-UJAILI

IN HIS dream Mohamed Weess saw himself praying. There was nothing extraordinary in this for in his waking hours he was continually praying and never put off performing one of the obligatory prayers. He saw himself reciting out loud, during his first prostration, the *Sura* of *al-Nasr* from the Koran and on coming to the end of it he had woken up in a state of terror.

'God's word is the truth!' he had said, sitting up in bed and wiping his eyes.

Mohaméd Weess could not remember why it was that this of all his dreams should have fixed itself in his mind. However, when morning came he set off in search of Sheikh Mohamed Sa'id, the village elder. Around noon he ran him to ground and told him of his dream. The Sheikh, head lowered and with knotted brows, kept silent for a long time before asking:

'Are you sure that you were reciting the *Sura* of *al-Nasr*?'

'Absolutely,' replied Mohamed Weess. 'I recited it right through in full: "When there comes God's help and victory, and thou shalt see men enter into God's religion by troops, then celebrate the praises of thy Lord, and ask forgiveness of him, verily He is relentant!"'

'God's word is the truth!' said Sheikh Mohamed Sa'id. 'Celebrate the praises of thy Lord, O Mohamed Weess, and ask forgiveness of him, verily He is relentant.'

'O Sheikh, I trust that this bodes well for me. What do you make of my dream?'

Sheikh Mohamed Sa'id grasped hold of his thick, broad beard and ran his fingers through it. He appeared hesitant about bestowing his great learning on the mere interpretation of dreams.

'O Mohamed Weess,' he said eventually, 'ask forgiveness of thy Lord, verily He is relentant. The reciting of this *sura* in one's dream is a sign that one's end is near.'

Of a nervous disposition at the best of times, Mohamed Weess felt a shudder of dread course through his entire body.

'What are you saying, O Sheikh?'

'It pains me to face you with this,' replied the Sheikh. 'However, your consolation is that God's mercy will soon be yours and that death must come to us. No one who has this dream, Mohamed Weess, lives for more than another forty days.'

Having delivered himself of this pronouncement, the Sheikh hurried off to make his ablutions for the midday prayer, leaving Mohamed Weess seated on the ground in a daze, his legs completely incapable of bearing the weight of his body.

'Forty days,' he muttered through a parched throat. 'God give me strength!'

The village in which Mohamed Weess and Mohamed Sa'id lived was a small one and by evening everyone knew of Mohamed Weess's dream and of Sheikh Mohamed Sa'id's interpretation of it. The village was one whose people believed in the interpretation of dreams and so by the following evening everyone was firmly convinced that Mohamed Weess would be dead within forty days. Singly, then in groups, the men paid visits to Mohamed Weess; he was thus forced to keep to his house to receive those who came, in anticipation of his death, to enquire into his health, and to condole with him, during his lifetime, on his death. The womenfolk of Mohamed Weess's household came in search of news, casting telling glances at him. They found him in perfect health but with his features set in an abstracted air; mourning and wailing they beseeched God to intervene with the Angel of Death who was seeking to snatch him away while still as fit as ever. Though Mohamed Weess felt no pain or discomfort, the many precautions taken on his behalf, and the many tender enquiries made of him, induced in him an expectancy of pain and discomfort. He stuck it out for the first ten days and continued going and coming between his house and the cattle market. Soon, however, he was unable to hold out any longer; his nerves gave way and people began paying their visits to him during the daytime, whereas previously they had only found him at home in the evening. Twenty days from the date of his dream Mohamed Weess's family found that it was easier not to take up and remake his bed each night for the simple reason that he now remained in it night and day. When thirty days of the allotted period had passed, the various plates of his favourite foods, prepared specially for him by his family, accumulated at his bedside untouched. Dressed in an all-white garment and having let his beard grow, he spent his time in prayer. He wept, not from fear of death or in regret for life, but out of terror for the punishment that lay beyond the grave, and in dread lest God should not forgive him the many times he had taken His name in vain at the cattle market or had cheated the peasants from neighbouring villages. As the days melted away, drawing nearer to the fateful fortieth, so the store of fat which surrounded Mohamed Weess's stomach, empty with hunger, melted away and, in turn, through repentance, his past sins. People—those of his own village and those from round about—talked of the spiritual glow that emanated from his face and of the mystical and mysterious phrases which fell from his lips as he prostrated himself in prayer. Thirty-nine of the forty days passed, and on the evening of the thirty-ninth I made my appearance.

And who, you may well ask, am I?

I am the schoolmaster of the village in which Mohamed Weess works as broker at the cattle market and in which Sheikh Mohamed Sa'id is regarded as the holy man. I used to spend my summer vacations in Damascus and my return to the school coincided with the thirty-ninth day of the period granted to Mohamed Weess by Mohamed Sa'id. I was acquainted with Mohamed Weess in the same way as I knew all the inhabitants of the village and when Mohamed Atallah, the elderly school porter, informed me about him I was at a loss to know whether to laugh or feel sorry for him. I therefore set off with Mohamed Atallah to comfort him—or to condole with him on his impending death. The courtyard, usually filled with the livestock which Mohamed Weess bought from the market, was now crowded with people who had come to witness the slow creeping of death into his soul. In one corner were the men, in another the women, while in the third stood the sheep and goats which Mohamed Weess's friends had brought during his lifetime that they might be slaughtered on the morrow for the departure of his soul. On entering the room in which Mohamed Weess awaited the Angel of Death, I found him—Mohamed Weess, not the Angel—seated on his bed in a corner praying, while Mohamed Sa'id sat in another corner reciting the Koran in rolling tones. I was struck by the change that had come over the face of the Mohamed Weess I had known: his rounded, ruddy face had become long and pallid, the appearance of length being further increased by his beard, while his pallor was accentuated by his loose-fitting white garment. As he prayed he protracted his prostrations as though wishing that death might take him during one of them. There was no similarity between this saint of God whose whole face exuded a spiritual glow and that other Mohamed Weess whom I used to hear each morning under the school window swearing by all that was holy that if he hadn't lost three liras on the sheep he'd just bought he'd divorce his wife. I had visited Mohamed Weess in a mood of scepticism and curiosity, but the extreme change that had come over him brought me up with a start and persuaded me that he would in fact die on the morrow as fate had decreed. I was filled with anger as I listened to Sheikh Mohamed Sa'id loudly reciting the Koran and glancing sideways at me.

Between myself and this Sheikh, whose nature was compounded of simplicity, stupidity, and cunning, there existed an age-long enmity. I fought against the charlatanism and trickery with which he gained control of the souls of the ignorant villagers, while he never missed an opportunity to set them against me, accusing me of teaching blasphemy to my students and filling their minds with disobedience against God and His Prophet. His zeal in his attacks against me was no wit lessened on learning from people that I came of a family which traced back its ancestry to Zain al-Abidin, the grandson of the Prophet's son-in-law. On the contrary he made this a justification for being hostile to me and used to say, 'Look at this man, descended from Zain al-Abidin, who claims that the world turns round itself; yet,' he would say, 'I put it to you, has ever any one of you seen the door of his house which was facing east suddenly turn to the west?'

I was, as I said, filled with anger on seeing Sheikh Mohamed Sa'id. I almost shouted out that he was a murderer, that he was killing Mohamed Weess with his poison, the poison of implanting in his mind the thought that he would die within forty days. I recollected, however, that I had never succeeded in getting the better of Mohamed Sa'id by being annoyed or angry, for he was always able to win over the village folk by producing that perennial argument which in his view showed that the earth did not turn. Had it ever happened that a villager had seen the door of his house facing towards the west after it had faced eastwards? And

so, *ipso facto*, the earth did not turn. God have mercy on him for
his rancour against me, and God, too, have mercy on Mohamed
Weess should he remain under the crazy power of Sheikh
Mohamed Sa'id till tomorrow morning. Heavy of heart with
sorrow and anger, I went off to my room in the school building.

Mohamed Atallah, the school porter, woke me at dawn as I
had asked. I had placed three prickly pears, brought with me from
Damascus, under the water-jar which stood in the path of the
cooling breeze. I took one of these and hurried off to Mohamed
Weess's house. The courtyard was empty except for the sheep and
goats awaiting their owner's death and so, in turn, their own. The
women's quarters were lit up and a low sound of wailing issued
forth. The door of Mohamed Weess's room was shut, so I glanced
in through the closed window and saw that he was asleep, no
doubt exhausted after his long night of praying in readiness for
death. I knocked loudly several times, then pushed open the door
shouting:

'Give praise to God, Mohamed Weess.'

He started up from sleep in alarm. 'What is it?' he cried.

'I'm Naji the teacher. Don't be afraid, Mohamed Weess, and
listen to me.'

I saw the tears trickling down Mohamed Weess's cheeks as he
sat there tongue-tied with terror. Fearful that he would die of
fright before hearing me out, I said:

'I have come to you because I have just been awakened by my
ancestor Zain al-Abidin, God bless him, who said to me: "Go to
Mohamed Weess and tell him that God has tested him and found
that he is a repentant servant of His. Give him this, one of the
fruits of Paradise, and order him to pray with you and make two
prostrations before the rising of the sun; in the first of the prostrations he should recite the *Sura* of *al-Nasr* and God will so
extend his days that he shall live to see his children and his
children's children"'.

Mohamed Weess swallowed his spittle. It seemed to me that
his brain had not taken in all I had said to him as he gazed at the
prickly pear I held in my hand. (I was sure that no one in the
village had ever seen a prickly pear before.) I peeled it and stuffed
it in his mouth, inviting him to swallow it, seeds and all. I then
dragged him to a corner of the room.

'Prepare for prayers, Mohamed Weess, before day breaks.'

'But I haven't performed my ablutions, Mr. Naji.'

I recollected that I too had not performed my ablutions, but fearing that the effect of my suggestion would be lost, I exclaimed:

'Make a symbolical washing, O Mohamed Weess, as the Koran allows. Strike your hands upon the ground.'

I prayed standing behind Mohamed Weess. We made two prostrations, during the first of which he recited the whole of the *Sura* of *al-Nasr*. Then I went back to the school to await daybreak.

Within an hour the whole village had heard the new story about Mohamed Weess. All those people who had filled the courtyard of Mohamed Weess's house yesterday were now crowding the schoolyard, all tumbling over themselves to learn how it was that my ancester, Zain al-Abidin, had come to me bearing God's pardon for Mohamed Weess. At that moment I felt that here at last I had scored a decisive victory over Sheikh Mohamed Sa'id, for neither had Mohamed Weess died nor had the sheep and goats in his courtyard been slaughtered—they had been turned over to me, a present from Mohamed Weess's friends to that saint of God, schoolteacher Naji, the direct descendant of Zain al-Abidin!

But was it in fact a victory? In truth I am not sure. My doubts as to the value of this victory are increased by the fact that I have been unable to reduce by one single person the number of those who take part in communal prayers behind Sheikh Mohamed Sa'id; on the contrary, I have increased his congregation by one: the village teacher, which is to say myself! To preserve the honour of my forefather, about whom I had fabricated my dream, I am obliged to attend in person behind Sheikh Mohamed Sa'id at all prayers—with ablutions performed, not symbolically but in full!

The Death of Bed Number 12

GHASSAN KANAFANI

D^{EAR AHMED,}

I have chosen you in particular to be the recipient of this letter
for a reason which may appear to you commonplace, yet since
yesterday my every thought has been centred on it. I chose you in
particular because when I saw him yesterday dying on the high
white bed I remembered how you used to use the word 'die' to
express anything extreme. Many is the time I've heard you use
such expressions as 'I almost died laughing', 'I was dead tired',
'Death itself couldn't quench my love', and so on. While it is
true that we all use such words, you use them more than anybody.
Thus it was that I remembered you as I saw him sinking down in
the bed and clutching at the coverlet with his long, emaciated
fingers, giving a convulsive shiver and then staring out at me with
dead eyes.

But why have I not begun at the beginning? You know, no
doubt, that I am now in my second month at the hospital. I have
been suffering from a stomach ulcer, but no sooner had the surgeon
plugged up the hole in my stomach than a new one appeared in
my head, about which the surgeon could do nothing. Believe me,
Ahmed, that an 'ulcer' on the brain is a lot more stubborn than one
in the stomach. My room leads on to the main corridor of the Inter-
nal Diseases Wing, while the window overlooks the small hospital
garden. Thus, propped up by a pillow, I can observe both the continuous flow of patients passing the door as well as the birds which
fly past the window incessantly. Amidst this hubbub of people who
come here to die in the serene shadow of the scalpel and whom I
see, having arrived on their own two feet, leaving after days or
hours on the death trolley, wrapped round in a covering of white;
in this hubbub I find myself quite unable to make good those holes

28

that have begun to open up in my head, quite incapable of stop-ping the flow of questions that mercilessly demand an answer of me.

I shall be leaving the hospital in a few days, for they have patched up my insides as best they can. I am now able to walk leaning on the arm of an old and ugly nurse and on my own powers of resistance. The hospital, however, has done little more than transfer the ulcer from my stomach to my head, for in this place, as the ugly old woman remarked, medicine may be able to plug up a hole in the stomach but it can never find the answers required to plug up holes in one's thinking. The day she said this the old woman gave a toothless laugh as she quietly led me off to the scales.

What, though, is such talk to do with us? What I want to talk to you about is death. Death that takes place in front of you, not about that death of which one merely hears. The difference between the two types of death is immeasurable and cannot be appreciated by someone who has not been a witness to a human being clutching at the coverlet of his bed with all the strength of his trembling fingers in order to resist that terrible slipping into extinction, as though the coverlet can pull him back from that colossus who, little by little, wrests from his eyes this life about which we know scarcely anything.

As the doctors waited around him, I examined the card that hung at the foot of his bed. I had slipped out of my room and was standing there, unseen by the doctors, who were engaged in a hopeless attempt to save the dying man. I read: 'Name: Mohamed Ali Akbar. Age: 25. Nationality: Omani.' I turned the card over and this time read: 'Leukaemia.' Again I stared into the thin brown face, the wide frightened eyes and the lips that trem-bled like a ripple of purple water. As his eyes turned and came to rest on my face it seemed that he was appealing to me for help. Why? Because I used to give to him a casual greeting every morn-ing? Or was it that he saw in my face some understanding of the terror that he was undergoing? He went on staring at me and then —quite simply—he died.

It was only then that the doctor discovered me and dragged me off angrily to my room. But he would never be able to banish from my mind the scene that is ever-present there. As I got on to my bed I heard the voice of the male nurse in the corridor alongside my door saying in a matter-of-fact voice:

'Bed number 12 has died!'

I said to myself: 'Mohamed Ali Akbar has lost his name, he is Bed number 12.' What do I mean now when I talk of a human being whose name was Mohamed Ali Akbar? What does it matter to him whether he still retains his name or whether it has been replaced by a number? Then I remembered how he wouldn't allow anyone to omit any part of his name. Every morning the nurse would ask him, 'And how are you, Mohamed Ali?' and he would not reply, for he regarded his name as being Mohamed Ali Akbar —just like that, all in one—and that this Mohamed Ali to whom the nurse was speaking was some other person.

Though the nurses found a subject for mirth in this insistence on his whole name being used, Mohamed Ali Akbar continued to demand it; perhaps he regarded his right to possessing his name in full as being an insistence that he at least owned something, for he was poor, extremely poor, a great deal more so than you with your fertile imagination could conceive as you lounge around in the café; poverty was something engraved in his face, his fore-arms, his chest, the way he ate, into everything that surrounded him.

When I was able to walk for the first time after they had patched me up, I paid him a visit. The back of his bed was raised and he was sitting up, lost in thought. I sat on the side of the bed for a short while, and we exchanged a few brief, banal words. I noticed that alongside his pillow was an old wooden box with his name carved on it in semi-Persian style writing; it was securely tied with twine. Apart from this he owned nothing except his clothes, which were kept in the hospital cupboard. I remembered that on that day I had asked the nurse:

'What's in the old box?'

'No one knows,' she answered, laughing. 'He refuses to be parted from the box for a single instant.'

Then she bent over me and whispered:

'These people who look so poor are generally hiding some trea-sure or other—perhaps this is his!'

During my stay here no one visited him at the hospital. As he knew no one I used to send him some of the sweets with which my visitors inundated me. He accepted everything without enthu-siasm. He was not good at expressing gratitude and his behaviour over this caused a certain fleeting resentment in me.

I did not concern myself with the mysterious box. Though Mohamed Ali Akbar's condition steadily worsened, his attitude towards the box did not change, which caused the nurse to remark to me that if there had been some treasure in it he would surely have given it away or willed it to someone, seeing that he was heading for death at such speed. Like some petty philosopher I had laughed that day saying to myself that the stupidity of this nurse scarcely knew any bounds, for how did she expect Mohamed Ali Akbar to persuade himself that he was inevitably dying, that there was not a hope of his pulling through? His insistence on keeping the box was tantamount to hanging on to his hope of pulling through and being reunited with his box.

When Mohamed Ali Akbar died I saw the box at his side, where it had always been, and it occurred to me that the box ought to be buried unopened with him. On going to my room that night I was quite unable to sleep. While Mohamed Ali Akbar had been deposited in the autopsy room, wrapped up in a white covering, he was, at the same time, sitting in my room and staring at me, passing through the hospital wards and searching about in his bed; I could almost hear the way he would gasp for breath before going to sleep. When day dawned across the trees of the hospital garden, I had created a complete story about him for myself.

Mohamed Ali Akbar was a poor man from the western quarter of the village of Abkha in Oman; a thin, dark-skinned young man, with aspirations burning in his eyes that could find no release. True he was poor, but what does poverty matter to a man if he has never known anything else? The whole of Abkha suffered from being poor, a poverty indentical to Mohamed Ali Akbar's; it was, however, a contented poverty, a poverty that was deep-seated and devoid of anything that prompted one to feel that it was wrong and that there was something called 'riches'. And so it was that the two water-skins Mohamed Ali Akbar carried across his shoulders as he knocked on people's doors to sell them water, were the two scales which set the balance of his daily round. Mohamed Ali Akbar was aware of a certain dizziness when he laid down the water-skins, but when taking them up again the next morning he would feel that his existence was progressing tranquilly and that he had ensured for himself a balanced, undeviating journey through life.

Mohamed Ali Akbar's life could have continued in this quiet and ordered fashion, had fate emulated civilization—in not reaching faraway Oman. But fate was present even in far-off Oman and it was inevitable that Mohamed Ali Akbar should suffer a little from its capricious ways.

It happened on a scorchingly hot morning. Though the sun was not yet at the meridian, the surface of the road was hot and the desert blew gusts of dust-laden wind into his face. He knocked at a door which was answered by a young, brown-skinned girl with wide black eyes, and everything happened with the utmost speed. Like some clumsy oaf who has lost his way, he stood in front of the door, the water-skins swinging to and fro on his lean shoulders. Abstractedly he stared at her, hoping like someone overcome with a mild attack of sunstroke that his eyes would miraculously be capable of clasping her to him. She stared back at him in sheer astonishment, and, unable to utter a word, he turned his back on her and went off home with his water-skins.

Though Mohamed Ali Akbar was exceptionally shy even with his own family, he found himself forced to pour out his heart to his elder sister. As his mother had died of smallpox a long time ago and his father was helplessly bedridden, it was to his sister that he turned for help, for he had unswerving confidence that Sabika possessed the necessary intelligence and judgement for solving a problem of this sort. Seated before him on the rush mat, shrouded in her coarse black dress, she did not break her silence till Mohamed Ali Akbar had gasped out the last of his story.

'I shall seek her hand in marriage,' she then said. 'Isn't that what you want?'

'Yes, yes, is it possible?'

Removing a straw from the old rush mat, his sister replied:

'Why not? You are now a young man and we are all equal in Abkha.'

Mohamed Ali Akbar spent a most disturbed night. When morning came he found that his sister was even more eager than himself to set off on her mission. They agreed to meet up at noon when she would tell him of the results of her efforts, and from there they would both make the necessary arrangements for bringing the matter to completion.

Mohamed Ali Akbar did not know how to pass the time wandering through the lanes with the water-skins on his shoulders. He kept looking at his shadow and beseeching God to make it into a circle round his feet so that he might hurry back home. After what seemed an eternity, he made his way back and was met at the door by his sister.

'It seems that her mother is agreeable. But it must all be put to her father, who will give his answer in five days.'

Deep down within him Mohamed Ali Akbar felt that he was going to be successful in making the girl his wife. As far as he was able to imagine he began from henceforth to build up images of his future with this young and beautiful brown-skinned girl. His sister Sabika looked at the matter with a wise and experienced eye, but she too was sure they would be successful, for she was convinced that her brother's name was without blemish among the people of Abkha; she had, in addition, given a lot of attention to gaining the approval of the girl's mother, knowing as she did how a woman was able to put over an idea to her husband and make him believe that it was his own. Sabika, therefore, awaited the outcome of the matter with complete composure.

On the fifth day Sabika went to the girl's house in order to receive the answer. When she returned, however, her disconsolate face showed that she had failed. She stood in a corner of the room, unable to look Mohamed Ali Akbar in the eye, not knowing how to begin recounting what had happened.

'You must forget her, Mohamed Ali,' she said when she had managed to pluck up her courage.

Not knowing what to say, he waited for his sister to finish.

'Her father died two days ago,' continued Sabika, finding an opportunity in his silence to continue. 'His dying wish to his family was that they should not give her to you in marriage.'

Mohamed Ali Akbar heard these words as though they were addressed to someone else.

'But why, Sabika—why?' was all he could ask.

'He was told that you were a scoundrel, that you lived by stealing sheep on the mountain road, trading what you steal with the foreigners.'

'I?'

'They think you are Mohamed Ali,' said Sabika in a trembling voice she was unable to control. 'You know—the scoundrel Mohamed Ali? Her father thought that you were he . . .'

'But I am not Mohamed Ali,' he replied, palms outstretched like a child excusing himself for some misdeed he has not committed. 'I'm Mohamed Ali Akbar.'

'There's been a mistake—I told them at the beginning that your name was Mohamed Ali. I didn't say Mohamed Ali Akbar because I saw no necessity for doing so.'

Mohamed Ali Akbar felt his chest being crushed under the weight of the blow. However, he remained standing where he was, staring at his sister Sabika without fully seeing her. Blinded by anger, he let fly a final arrow:

'Did you tell her mother that I'm not Mohamed Ali but Mohamed Ali Akbar?'

'Yes, but the father's last wish was that they shouldn't marry her to you.'

'But I'm Mohamed Ali Akbar the water-seller, aren't I?'

What was the use, though, of being so stricken? Everything had, quite simply, come to an end, a single word had lodged itself in the gullet of his romance and it had died. Mohamed Ali Akbar, however, was unable to forget the girl so easily and spent his time roaming about near her house in the hope of seeing her once again. Why? He did not know. His failure brought in its wake a savage anger which turned to hate; soon he was no longer able to pass along that road for fear that his fury would overcome him and he would pelt the window of her house with stones.

From that day onwards he refused to be called by anything but his name in full: Mohamed Ali Akbar, all in one. He refused to answer to anyone who called him Mohamed or Mohamed Ali and this soon became a habit with him. Even his sister Sabika did not dare to use a contracted form of his name. No longer did he experience his former contentment, and Abkha gradually changed to a forbidding graveyard in his eyes. Refusing to give in to his sister's insistence that he should marry, a worm called 'wealth' began to eat its way into his brain. He wanted to take revenge on everything, to marry a woman with whom he could challenge the whole of Abkha, all those who did not believe that he was Mohamed Ali Akbar but Mohamed Ali the scoundrel. Where, though, to find wealth? Thus he decided to sail away to Kuwait.

The distance between Abkha and Ras al-Khaima is two hours by foot, and from Ras al-Khaima to Kuwait by sea is a journey of three days, the fare for which, on an antiquated boat, was seventy rupees. After a year or two he would be able to return to Oman and strut about proudly in the alleyways of Abkha wearing a snow-white *aba* trimmed with gold, like the one he had seen round the shoulders of a notable from Ras al-Khaima who had come to his village to take the hand of a girl the fame of whose beauty had reached all the way there.

The journey was a hard one. The boat which took that eager throng across the south and then made its way northwards to the corner of the Gulf was continually exposed to a variety of dangers. But ebullient souls accustomed to life's hardships paid no heed to such matters; all hands co-operated in the task of delivering safely that small wooden boat floating on the waves of the great sea. And when the sails of the ships lying in Kuwait's quiet harbour came into view, Mohamed Ali Akbar experienced a strange feeling: the dream had now fallen from the coloured world of fantasy into the realm of reality and he had to search around for a starting-point, for a beginning to his dream. It seemed to him that the fantasies nourished by his hate for Abkha and for which he now sought vengeance were not of sufficient moment. As the frail craft approached, threading its way among the anchored boats, he was slowly drained of his feeling and it appeared to him that his long dreams of wealth were merely a solace for his sudden failure and that they were quite irrational. The packed streets, the buildings with their massive walls, the grey sky, the scorching heat, the warm air of the north wind, the roads crammed with cars, the serious faces, all these things appeared to him as barriers standing between him and his dream. He hurried aimlessly through this ocean of people, conscious of a deep feeling of loss which resembled vertigo, almost convinced that these many faces which did not glance at him were his first enemy, that all these people were the walls obstructing the very beginning of the road to his dream. The story was not as simple as in Abkha. Here it was without beginning, without end, without landmarks. It seemed to him that all the roads along which he walked were endless, that they circuited a rampart that held everything—every single thing—within its embrace. When, at sunset, a road led him to the sea-shore and he once again saw the sea, he stood staring across at the far horizon that joined up with the water: out there was Abkha, enveloped in tranquillity. It existed, every quarter had its beginning and its end, every wall carried its own particular lineaments; despite everything it was close to his heart. He felt lost in a rush of scalding water and for the first time he had no sense of shame as he lifted his hand to wipe salty tears from his cheeks.

Mohamed Ali Akbar wept without embarrassment, perhaps for the first time since he grew up, involuntarily, he had been overcome by a ferocious yearning for the two water-skins he used to carry across his shoulders. He was still staring out at the horizon while night gradually settled down around him. It made him feel in a way that he was present in a certain place at a certain time and that this night was like night in Abkha: people were sleeping behind their walls, the streets bore the lineaments of fatigue and silence, the sea rumbled heavily under the light of the moon. He felt relief. Wanting to laugh and yet unable to, he wept once again.

Dawn brought him an upsurge of fresh hope. He rose and went running through the streets. He realized that he must find someone from Oman with whom he could talk and that he would, sooner or later, find such a person, and from there he would learn where he was destined to proceed, from where to make a start.

And so Mohamed Ali Akbar attained his position as errand boy at a shop and was provided with a bicycle on which to carry out his duties. It was from this bicycle that the features of the streets, the qualities of the walls, registered themselves in his head. He felt a certain intimacy with them, but it was an intimacy imposed upon a background of a forbidding impression that he was being dogged by the eyes of his sister Sabika, the chinks in the girl's window, and Mohamed Ali the scoundrel who, unwittingly, had caused such dire disaster.

Months passed with the speed of a bicycle's wheels passing over the surface of a road. The wealth he had dreamed of began to come in and Mohamed Ali Akbar clung to this tiny fortune with all his strength, lest some passing whim should sweep it away or some scoundrel lay his hands on it. Thus it was that it occurred to him to make a sturdy wooden box in which to keep his fortune.

But what did Mohamed Ali Akbar's fortune consist of? Something that could not be reckoned in terms of money. When he had collected a certain amount of money he had bought himself a diaphanous white *aba* with gold edging. Every evening, alone with his box, he would take out the carefully folded *aba*, pass his thin brown fingers tenderly over it and spread it before his eyes; on it he would spill out his modest dreams, tracing along its borders all the streets of his village, the low, latticed windows from behind which peeped the eyes of young girls. There, in a corner of the *aba*, reposed the past which he could not bring himself to return to but whose existence was necessary in order to give the *aba* its true value. The thin fingers would fold it gently once again, put it safely back in its wooden box, and tie strong cord round the box. Then, and only then, did sleep taste sweet.

The box also contained a pair of china ear-rings for his sister Sabika, which he would give her on his return to Abkha, a bottle of pungent perfume, and a white purse holding such money as God in His bounty had given him and which he hoped would increase day by day.

As for the end, it began one evening. He was returning his bicycle to the shop when he felt a burning sensation in his limbs. He was alarmed at the thought that he had grown so weak, and with such speed, but did not take a great deal of notice, having had spells of trembling whenever he felt exceptionally homesick for Sabika and Abkha; he had already experienced just such a sensation of weakness when savagely yearning for all those things he hated and loved and had left behind, those things that made up the whole of his past. And so Mohamed Ali Akbar hastened along the road to his home with these thoughts in mind. But his feeling of weakness and nostalgia stayed with him till the following mid-day. When he made the effort to get up from bed, he was amazed to find that he had slept right through to noon instead of waking up at his usual early hour. What alarmed him even more was that he was still conscious of the feeling of weakness boring into his bones. Slightly afraid, he thought for a while and imagined himself all at once standing on the sea-shore with the glaring sun reflected off the water almost blinding him, the two water-skins on his shoulders, conscious of a sensation of intense exhaustion. The reflection of the sun increased in violence, yet he was unable to shut his eyes—they were aflame. Abruptly he slid back into sleep.

Here time as usually understood came to an end for Mohamed Ali Akbar. From now on everything happened as though he were raised above the ground, as though his legs were dangling in mid-air: like a man on a gallows, he was moving in front of Time's screen, a screen as inert as a rock of basalt. His part as a practising human had been played out; his part as a mere spectator had come. He felt that there was no bond tying him to anything, that he was somewhere far away and that the things that moved before his eyes were no more than fish inside a large glass tumbler; his own eyes, too, were open and staring as though made of glass.

When he woke up again he realized that he was being carried by his arms and legs. Though he felt exhausted, he found the energy to recall that there was something which continued to be necessary to him and called out in a faint voice:

'The box . . . the box!'

No one, however, paid him any attention. With a frenzied movement he rose so as to get back to his box. His chest panting with the effort of getting to his feet, he called out:

'The box!'

But once again no one heard him. As he reached the door he clung to it and again gasped out in a lifeless voice:

'The box . . .'

Overcome by his exertions, he fell into a trance that was of the sea-shore itself. This time he felt that the tide was rising little by little over his feet and that the water was intensely cold. His hands were grasping a square-shaped rock with which he plunged downwards. When he awoke again he found himself clasping his old box tied round with cord. While spectres passed to and fro in front of him, a needle was plunged into his arm, and a face bent over him.

Long days passed. But for Mohamed Ali Akbar nothing really happened at all. The mercilessness of the pain continued on its way, and he was not conscious of its passing. He was conscious only of its constant presence. The sea became dissolved into windows behind wooden shutters low against the side of the street, a pair of china ear-rings, an *aba* wet with salt water, a ship suspended motionless above the waves, and an old wooden box.

Only once was he aware of any contact with the world. This was when he heard a voice beside him say:

'What's in the old box?'

He looked at the source of the voice and saw, as in a dream, the face of a young, clean-shaven man with fair hair who was pointing at the box and looking at something.

The moment of recollection was short. He returned to gazing

silently at the sea, though the face of the clean-shaven, blond young man also remained in front of him. After this he felt a sudden upsurge of energy; for no particular reason things had become clear to him. He distinctly saw, for the first time since he had collapsed, the rising of the sun. It seemed to him that he was capable of getting up from his bed and returning to his bicycle. Everything had grown clear to him: the box was alongside him, bound round as it had always been. Feeling at peace, he moved so as to get up, when a crowd of men in white clothes suddenly descended upon him, standing round him and regarding him with curiosity. Mohamed Ali Akbar tried to say something but was unable to. Suddenly he felt that the tide had risen right up to his waist and that the water was unbearably cold. He could feel nothing. He stretched out his arms to seize hold of something lest he should drown, but everything slid away from under his fingers. Suddenly he saw the clean-shaven face of the blond young man again; he stared at him, somewhat frightened of him on account of his box, while the water continued to rise higher and higher until it had screened off that fair, clean-shaven face from his gaze.

'Bed number 12 has died.'

As the male nurse called out I was unable to free myself from Mohamed Ali Akbar's eyes staring out at me before he died. I imagined that Mohamed Ali Akbar, who refused to have his name mutilated, would now be satisfied at being merely 'Bed number 12' if only he could be assured about the fate of his box.

This, my dear Ahmed, is the story of Mohamed Ali Akbar, Bed number 12, who died yesterday evening and is now lying wrapped round in a white cloth in the autopsy room—the thin brown face that shifted an ulcer from my intestines to my brain and who caused me to write to you, so you don't again repeat your famous phrase 'I almost died laughing' in my presence.

Ever yours,

I haven't yet left the hospital. My health is gradually getting back to normal and the method by which I gauge this amuses me. Do you know how I measure my strength? I stand smoking on the balcony and throw the cigarette end with all my strength so that it falls along the strips of green grass in the garden. In past weeks the cigarette would fall just within the fourth strip, but today it was much nearer the sixth.

From your letter I understood you to say that you were in no
need of being a witness to Mohamed Ali Akbar's death to know
what death is. You wrote saying that the experience of death
does not require the tragic prologues with which I described
Mohamed Ali Akbar's life and that people die with far greater
matter-of-factness: the man who fell down on the pavement and
so let off the loaded pistol he had with him, whose bullet ripped
open his neck (he was in the company of a strikingly beautiful
girl), or the one who had a heart attack in the street one April
evening, having become engaged to be married only a week before.
Yes, that's all very true, my dear Ahmed, all very true, but the
problem doesn't lie here at all, the problem of death is in no way
that of the dead man, it is the problem of those who remain, those
who bitterly await their turn so that they too may serve as a
humble lesson to the eyes of the living. Of all the things I wrote
in my last letter what I want to say now is that we must transfer
our thinking from the starting-point to the end. All thinking must
set forth from the point of death, whether it be, as you say, that
of a man who dies contemplating the charms of the body of a
wonderfully beautiful girl, or whether he dies staring into a newly-
shaven face which frightens him because of an old wooden box
tied round with string. The unsolved question remains that of the
end; the question of non-existence, of eternal life—or what? Or
what, my dear Ahmed?

Anyway, let's stop pouring water into a sack with a hole in it.
Do you know what happened after I sent you my last letter? I
went to the doctor's room and found them writing a report about
Mohamed Ali Akbar. And they were on the point of opening the
box. Oh, Ahmed, how imprisoned we are in our bodies and minds!
We are always endowing others with our own attributes, always
looking at them through a narrow fissure of our own views and
way of thinking, wanting them, as far as we can, to become 'us'.
We want to squeeze them into our skins, to give them our eyes to
see with, to clothe them in our past and our own way of facing up
to life. We place them within a framework outlined by our present
understanding of time and place.

Mohamed Ali Akbar was none of the things I imagined. He was
the father of three boys and two girls. We have forgotten that over
there men marry early. Also, Mohamed Ali Akbar was not a
water-seller, water being plentiful in Oman, but had been a sailor

on one of the sailing ships that ply between the ports of the south and the Gulf, before settling down here quite a time ago.

It was in fact four years ago that Mohamed Ali Akbar arrived in Kuwait. After unimaginably hard effort he managed—only two months ago—to open what passed for a shop on one of the pavements of New Street. As to how he provided for his children in Oman, we simply don't know.

I read in the doctor's report that the patient had lost his sight six hours before death and so it would seem that Mohamed Ali Akbar had not in fact been staring into my face at the moment of his death as he was then blind. The doctor also wrote that as the address of the patient's family was not known, his burial would be attended solely by the hospital grave-diggers.

The doctor read out the report to his colleague. It was concise and extremely condensed, merely dealing in technical terms with the man's illness. The doctor's voice was lugubrious and colourless. When he had finished reading he proceeded to untie the string round the box. At this point I thought of leaving the room, for it was none of my business: the Mohamed Ali Akbar I knew had died and this person they had written about was someone else; this box, too, was some other box. I knew for certain what Mohamed Ali Akbar's box contained. Why should I bother myself about some new problem?

And yet I was unable to go to the door, but stood in the corner, trembling slightly.

The box was soon opened and the doctor quickly ran his fingers through the contents. Then he pushed it to one side.

Fearfully I looked into the box: it was filled with recent invoices for sums owed by the shop to the stores which supplied it; in one corner was an old photo of a bearded face, an old watch strap, some string, a small candle and several rupees among the papers.

I must be truthful and say that I was sadly disappointed. Before leaving the room, though, I saw something that stunned me: the nurse had pushed aside Mohamed Ali Akbar's invoices and revealed a long china ear-ring that glittered. In a daze I went to the box and picked up the ear-ring. I don't know why it was that I looked at the nurse and said:

'He bought this ear-ring for his sister Sabika—I happen to know that.'

For a brief instant she stared at me in some surprise—then she laughed uproariously. The doctor, too, laughed at the joke.

You are no doubt aware that nurses are required to humour patients with stomach ulcers in case they should suffer a relapse.

Yours ever—

Sundown

SHUKRI AYYAD

FOR THE twentieth, the seventieth, the hundredth time, he read through the same piece of news. This time the letters drilled themselves into position with superb precision, some moving forward, others taking a step back, while yet others had disappeared completely, had fled the field; some were as big as walking sticks, others as small as ants; some a mere whisper, others a bugle blast. The item of news, scattered over the page of the newspaper, now read approximately as follows:

Tewfik Hussein Baligh
one of the passengers of the ill-fated plane
on a mission connected
with the organization he represents
had put forward the time of his departure in order
to be beside his eldest daughter
who is expecting a happy event

The sun was flooding the balcony. A beautiful warm day. His wife appeared, wearing a pink-coloured knitted house-coat. Her body looked as though it had been stuffed with numerous articles of clothing; on her feet she wore a pair of his old socks and shabby slippers. He almost let out a short childish laugh but managed to stifle it. What did it matter? She sat down beside him on the other cane chair, the one with arms, and busied herself with her knitting-needles, without saying anything. Her face was still, still as a tranquil pool, though wrinkles had begun to make their incursions upon it. She was followed by the maid who placed the tray on the table, and then passed him his unsugared cup of tea. The newspaper was now on the table in front of him; the words had disappeared, had sneaked away in indifference between the lines of the newspaper as though some secret pact existed between them and

43

him. She thrust the needles into the ball of wool, put it on the table and took up her tea which had become tepid. This was what she always did. He felt his heart thumping. These were the minutes during which she would take up the newspaper and start commenting. He was longing for the secret to come to light. It had to do so. He would have to speak. If only she remembered the name! If only she would prompt him into speaking!

'Good heavens, what a terrible accident! Sixty-three passengers. The plane must have been full—did you read about the accident?

'I wonder how it crashed. They say here that the exact reason isn't known. These aeroplanes are really frightful. This poor family —the husband, wife, and three sons. God bring comfort to their relatives.'

She put the paper down on her lap and went into a day-dream. Perhaps she had read enough, perhaps the tranquil pool had been sufficiently disturbed. He almost despaired. She glanced at the paper once more before throwing it on to the table.

'Did you read the story of this man? He put forward his departure so as to be with his daughter when she was having her child. What an ill-omened birth! Look how they wrote up the news in the paper: "Because his daughter was expecting a happy event." Happy!?'

'Don't you know this man?'

Again she gazed at the name, then looked up at him perplexed.

'I mean—don't you remember the name?'

She shook her head and he experienced a feeling of resentment towards her. He felt obscurely that her having forgotten the name was a neglect of himself. In exasperation he muttered:

'Tewfik Hussein Baligh—don't you remember him?'

A certain worried irritation, as though the surface of a pond had become muddied, appeared in her eyes. It was of no avail, though.

'Don't you remember the case I once brought, the case I brought in the Supreme Administrative Court, because they promoted someone over my head?'

She bit her lower lip.

'Of course. You wore yourself to shreds over it; for years you wore us all out too, and then you lost it.'

He gave a wan smile.

'This Tewfik was the colleague of mine they promoted over my head. God rest his soul. He was hasty in everything.'

'Even in death.'

'Even in catching the plane.'

His eyes suddenly sparkled.

'Can you imagine, it might have been I who died in that blazing plane. Didn't we compete for one and the same place our whole lives? Do you see where this haste has taken him? To the seat in the aeroplane. Don't be alarmed. Always it seemed to me that he took my place, so much so that many a time I forgot that there was a place for me apart from the one Tewfik occupied. Yet here I am sunning myself on this balcony, while Tewfik is over there, a charred corpse on the mountain.'

She pursed her lips and returned nervously to her knitting. No doubt she was remembering bitter conversations that had taken place in the middle of the night and had brought him to early diabetes and blood pressure.

'I haven't told you much about Tewfik,' he said with sudden tenderness. 'We were fellow students at secondary school. He wasn't my friend. No, he was never once my friend, though we were always mentioned in the same breath. As for him, no one knows where he came from. His father was a government official or something of the sort. He was a lovable, soft person who after a while made friends with all his class-mates. As for myself, I was always accused of being a bit snobbish and mixed with the boys from my own village, a few of whom were my particular friends. He and I were rivals, in continual competition in the various subjects we were taking.'

He was silent for a moment; his face was slightly flushed and he looked younger. She placed the two knitting needles and the wool in her lap, tilting her head slightly as she listened to him.

'We joined the College of Engineering together and were in the same class. We went up together year by year, remaining rivals at the top of our year. Coming out first was now regarded by the students as of more importance, not like at secondary school where leadership generally went to the tallest student or to the captain of the basket-ball team. The rivalry between us became sharp and bitter though we were polite enough when meeting face to face. Though he remained pleasantly friendly, he now began to employ his talents with the teaching staff; he made himself known to them from the very first day, after which he went on to ingratiate himself with them. Even so, though, I often beat him to first place. And so came the year for taking our finals.

'The country was boiling with revolution and among those who met their deaths in the streets were colleagues of ours. Even so an English lecturer ventured, within the hearing of us all, to make a remark insulting to Egypt. Finding myself unable to disregard it, I insulted him back. The man kept silent and didn't react at all. The emotional coldness of the English! At the end of the year, though, I found that I had failed in his subject. This was unbelievable. Who knows, I might well have been failed again had not the lecturer left the Faculty and returned home. This put me a year behind Tewfik and he was therefore ahead of me, both in being sent abroad to complete his studies and in taking up his first appointment. Yet I still did everything I could to establish my superiority over him by putting more into my work.'

She gave a deep sigh; she tried to return to her knitting but found that she had miscounted. She knew well what had happened after that. He had no longer tried to talk to her about his work and achievements which meant his having to use long English words which had been meaningless to her; instead he talked about his work in a bitter, resentful manner. Later, when the other man was chosen for the important post, his zeal had cooled off completely. And what a post it was! From what he had to say it had seemed to her that the person occupying it was all-powerful. And so the legal case had been brought and replaced work as a subject of conversation. She had listened and had then tried to amuse him, to distract him with other things.

He looked at her. Her face had begun to fade with age, yet it gazed at him imploringly, like the face of a child. Had she gazed at him like this in the old days?

'But he was always smooth as a snake. I never knew how he managed to twist his bosses round his little finger. I used to hear about some frightful things, though, some filthy things that went on between them. I wasn't able to mention everything when the case was brought as I lacked evidence.'

Was he able to mention everything to her now? Had he ever talked to anyone about his dreams, strange dreams that he still remembered whenever he looked at his wife? When he remembered them he would turn away his head to escape from himself.

But what dreams were these? Dreams without meaning, night-mares. Was it possible that these dreams were at all connected with those 'filthy things' he had heard? But what connection had these dreams got with his wife? Why, for nights on end, did he dream that Tewfik had come and taken his wife away from him, his wife who was still a bride, sweet and good, and whom he loved most dearly? He had heard people saying behind his back that she was the most marvellous choice he'd made in his life, and the funny thing was that after these dreams of his he found himself incapable of loving her as he should. He would also feel fear of Tewfik, to-gether with extreme hatred. No, Tewfik had not known Hana, had perhaps never seen her in his life. But this was not at all the crux of the matter. Besides, he had never doubted his wife. Yet, even in his waking hours the dream did, sometimes, appear pos-sible, and he would release his closely-guarded secret to twist about like a worm in his bosom, careful to appear outwardly calm and strong.

'Five years you wasted on that case. How you burnt yourself up over it and lost it in the end!'

Yes, he had lost the case, as well as the work which he loved. He had lost life itself because he had been unable to stand his colleagues seeing him defeated and had therefore asked to be trans-ferred. Eventually he had come to rest at his present desk, where he would sit through the morning hours scarcely doing any work. The case had become his one amusement all these years, a bitter amusement of which his wife was not aware, nor yet his colleagues in the office; it was like an addiction, a fell disease. He would search through the papers for news of Tewfik, reading and re-read-ing each item till he found that its words and letters often became so engraved upon his mind that when he was sitting by himself on the balcony or lying stretched out on his bed he was able to recall it. At first this had happened by chance; he had not been looking for news of Tewfik when, amusing himself as was his wont by reading the newspaper at the office, his eye had alighted on the name. It was nothing of any importance, merely the reporter asking him, among a number of other people, about some project, and the space given to what he had to say occupied no more than a few lines following on from a brief description of who he was. But reporters, as is their wont, once having got to know someone, begin writing more and more about him for no apparent reason. Also there was no doubt that Tewfik was past master at making reporters welcome. In any event, the items of news became both longer and more frequent. At first the reading of them had been a bitter, joyless experience and had stirred up feelings of resentment and opened old wounds. Soon, though, it no longer did so; the bitterness became pleasurable in the same way as when one gets used to bitter sugarless coffee and finds any other sort completely insipid. And so he began to look around for news and stories about Tewfik, and when he found them he would feel as though he had read something of real interest.

Year after year he followed Tewfik on his upward path. When he left government service and became a director of an important organization there was a noticeable shift in the attention accorded to him in the press: his name no longer appeared in items of news and stories but in paid announcements. Such announcements, however, had an advantage, which was that his picture would appear in them so that it was possible to ruminate over his expensive clothes, his body which had filled out slightly, and his shining hair now grey around the temples. Apart from this, though, he did not differ greatly from the young Tewfik returned from abroad, or Tewfik the student at college, or even Tewfik the secondary schoolboy.

One day he found himself feeling he would like to meet him again. It was a strange wish, for he didn't imagine that he would really enjoy the meeting, neither did he know how he would behave at such a moment. Anyway, where could they meet? His activities had dwindled considerably and he no longer went to his professional association, even on election day. But conjuring up pictures of this encounter had become something else on which to spend time at his office, or when sitting on the balcony, or stretched out on his bed.

'What hours I spent with him,' he thought. 'All this will now come to an end.' Perhaps a news item or two—the fortieth day after his death and the first anniversary, on that back page. Tewfik would move from the front page to the back before finally withdrawing. The newspaper would lose its interest and flavour.

'Aren't you going inside? It gets cold on this balcony, I tell you.'

'H'm, h'm. I'll be coming in soon.'

The sun had grown decidedly pale as though it had become

chilly; its rays gave out light without heat, and from time to time it was covered over by a small cloud seeking warmth. A slight wind rustled the dry leaves. Now he was alone on the balcony. Though he had begun to feel the cold he put off the moment for getting up. He was at the climax of his discussion with himself and didn't want to abandon it without reaching a conclusion. It was as though his eyes had looked down on a minute, wondrous spot which would be lost to him if he shifted to either right or left; as though he were balanced precariously on the side of a ship: he had only to move a hair's breadth and he would fall.

Admit it! Admit it! What were you doing all these years? This man ruined your life, and now that he is dead, what will you do? Nothing, of course, your life will merely become more empty. Why don't you admit it? As time went on he became your main concern, and life seems wholly trivial without him. What irony! Some people have a love story in their lives, others a story of strife, while your whole life has been made up of a story of hatred.

The girl handed him a blanket. 'Madam says you should put this round your feet.'

'Where is she?'

'In her room, sir.'

'Listen, Hamida—tell your mistress—or—never mind.'

His was a love story he had failed to make anything of, like a book that has fallen apart before its pages are cut. How sweet and full of vitality she had been as a young woman! Now nothing mattered to her at all: her two children had grown up and gone away and nothing remained but the two of them face to face and the long lonely nights of winter.

The time for love had passed. Had he tried to inspire any feelings in her now she would have experienced nothing but distress. Such affection as existed between them was shown by the blanket she had sent to him on the balcony to protect him from the cold.

If only he could see his children now!

Tewfik came so as to be with his daughter while she was having her baby. What an affectionate father he was! We regard our children as being what we have made them; we do not know what life will make of them later.

Could his son become like him, he asked himself, and his daughter like her mother? God forbid! Were his children beside him now he would give them some sound advice. He would have so much to say to them.

Are you happy or sad at Tewfik's death? I find you neither happy nor sad. The time for happiness and sadness has passed too. But do you think that he was happier than me? It's funny that I should never have thought about this question before. I had imagined that it required no thought. I always imagined him as being happy—merely because I was miserable. Yet I know nothing of his life. I wish I had met him, if only just once during all these years. Oh, how bound up our lives were! More than with a wife or children! Is it possible for us to love our enemies so? Strange! It seems to me now that we were never enemies. If only Tewfik hadn't been so hasty, if only he hadn't put forward the time of his departure—God rest his soul, he was a pleasant fellow. Do you remember how you used to tease him with:

> Tewfik they called you, a flop you are,
> Who named you thus from truth were far?*

Had he been successful or a flop? When the sun sets all colours are reduced to the same level. I feel something pressing down on my chest. I am calling to them but they don't seem to hear. . . .

His wife called to him to come inside so that she could close the balcony door, but he didn't answer. When she went out to him she found he was dead, his eyes staring out at the setting sun while the sparrows still chirruped noisily among the trees.

* The Arabic contains puns on the names Tewfik and Baligh.

The Dying Lamp

FOUAD TEKERLI

THE BLACK screen hung motionless; the other section of the hut remained in silence. Outside, the wind blew violently and raindrops beat on the roof made of matting. Within the damp hut the silence was stifling. For a long while he had listened to them talking, his father and mother, and was hazily but painfully conscious that what he feared would soon happen. He was squatting on his bed, with his knees drawn up, cradling his legs with trembling arms. Above him the heavens roared; raising his eyes, he saw the small lamp with its contorted red glow and the smoke spiralling up to a corner in the roof. For the past five nights his mother had filled the lamp with oil and lit it after sunset and thus it had remained, high up in its corner until, during the night, it had died. Four times he had seen it die, the wick shuddering slightly and then expiring in a thick trail of white smoke.

Tonight, too, he would see it die. For three consecutive nights Heela had stayed up with him but in the end she had been unable to hold out against sleep. Perhaps she sensed that there was some obscure reason preventing her bridegroom from fulfilling the course of action expected of a man. Pallid of face, she lay covered up to her neck by the dark red bedspread. During these nights he had not spoken a word to her, representing as she did a disquieting mystery that filled his heart with dread. He had heard his mother tell his father that she was only thirteen years old. For an hour he had heard his parents talking together. His arms trembled as he imagined seeing the black curtain stir, the lamp dyeing it with the redness of its glow, its folds swaying under his gaze. His mother, in a choked voice, had tried to dissuade his father from what she suspected he had in mind: 'Would you betray our honour, Abu Jabbar?'

Jabbar, too, suspected that his father was about to perpetrate something terrible. He heard him answering his mother: 'You stupid woman, didn't we agree that I should have her? Didn't we go and ask for her hand in marriage?' To which his mother shrieked hoarsely: 'And they didn't give her to you. You took my money to buy yourself a woman, but they wouldn't give her to you, Abu Jabbar. Aren't I your wife?'

Jabbar had been stretched out on his bed; now he sat up to listen. The mumbling voice of his father reached his ears mingled with the thunder and he was unable to make out his father's reply. The wind roared like raging waters and the sky went on rumbling. A deadly silence reigned between his parents, a silence which intensified his vague forebodings. Would his father carry out tonight the intent which lurked behind his bright narrow eyes? They had not exchanged a word since Heela had come to their hut. Jabbar had glanced at him furtively, puckering his thin brown face, and his heart trembled at his father's great size. Were he to enter now he would have to bow his head. But would he? Suddenly he became aware of the lamp quivering violently high up in its corner and he gazed at it steadfastly.

Heela's breathing was deep and regular; he could hear it despite the drumming of the rain and the roaring wind. Thirteen years old? What would he do with this child? He had not wanted her. His father had gone to betroth her for himself and when her parents had refused he had taken her for his son Jabbar. She was sleeping, her eyes firmly closed and her face intensely pale under its brownness. How frail she looked, though she was a mere two years younger than he himself! In the other section of the hut something fell to the ground and his muscles tensed as he wheeled round towards the black curtain; its swathed folds were motionless. He heard the soft tread of footsteps, but they soon stopped. The thunder cracked violently, more lightning rolled then exploded with awesome noise, and all the while the wind roared and roared. Were some ghastly thing to happen no one would hear on such a stormy night. A shudder ran through Jabbar's body and he clasped his knees to his chest. Was he going to be killed?

Feet, barefoot like a thief's, could again be heard. His heart pounded and his breathing quickened each time he strained to listen. There was no escape. What would happen now? Was it reasonable to suppose that his father would dare to . . . ? Ah, the black curtain was stirring. A long wave of shuddering seized him and he pressed down strongly against his shins. He could feel his bladder almost bursting. Was his father going to kill him? The flame of the lamp writhed alongside him and the folds of the black curtain rippled before his fixed gaze. The left-hand corner of the curtain shifted slightly. Was he going to be killed?

A dark, yellowish face came into view: his father's face, deeply lined, scarcely the visage of a living human, the eyes small and intensively bright. His father had come to do away with him. The face continued to stare into Jabbar's eyes, like nails boring into his head; then, like a spectre, it disappeared and once again the black curtain swung to and fro before Jabbar's gaze. He wanted to shout out to wake up his mother, the neighbours, the whole world. He moaned, and Heela turned over on to her right side, the ends of her hair showing red from under her head-scarf. The day before they had dyed their hair with henna; she, his mother, and his sister.

He heard a thudding noise outside. Despite the uninterrupted drumming of the rain on the matting, he could distinguish the thuds clearly—the wind must have knocked something over, or was it perhaps *he* searching round for something with which to smash in Jabbar's head? His mouth and throat felt dry and he kept swallowing in vain. Just one gulp of water might bring him back to life. He looked all round him: the mud walls of the room were dark and turbid and directly under the lamp it was pitch black. He saw that there was a gap in the roof from which water was leaking slowly; the floor under it was bare except for Heela's iron box which stood there with its lid open like the jaw of some wild beast.

Next door all was quiet. Had his father gone back to bed? There was a pain in his stomach as though someone were pricking him with pins. He had not supped, but had contented himself with watching the others as they ate, by lamplight, the scraps sent in to them by the neighbours. Despite his hunger he had not felt able to join them. As night came on he had lost his desire for food. It was futile to search for something to eat now for no food was ever left over till the morning. He gripped his belly, squeezing it violently. His mother used to bind a piece of rag round his waist whenever he wanted food and there wasn't any, permeating his body with a sense of relief as she tightened it round him. His legs were stiff and once again he cradled them with his arms. He glanced at the black curtain. Where was his father now? Heela's breathing was soft, inaudible; in the light of the flame, calm and erect like a luminous minaret, her cheek and ear looked smooth. After several long hours the lamp would die. He felt his eyelids growing heavy as he looked at it. How weary and strained he was with this meaningless vigil! His head resounded with the booming noise of the wind. Was it the wind that was causing the luminous minaret to stir?

Suddenly the flame twisted and dimmed. Would it go out? He felt the touch of cold air against his face as the curtain was drawn back and an immensely tall man stood before him. He glanced up quickly. What would he do to him? Merciful God, would he kill him?

'What are you sitting about for, you dog?'

His ears heard nothing but the pounding of his heart. The voice that spoke to him was strange, unfamiliar. It wasn't his father; no, it couldn't be his father. This person carried a long stout stick in his right hand and his eyes shone as bright as lightning. He wanted to speak to him, to grovel imploringly at his feet, but his lifeless tongue would not come to his aid. He saw the stick raised up high—it was the one he used for driving off dogs—and then descend, cleaving the air silently.

His head exploded like a crack of lightning and his eyes were blinded. A moment later he felt his body collapsing in a heap on the damp, bare floor near the iron box. He had struck him but one blow with the stick he used for driving off dogs. He, too, was like those stray dogs: a small, filthy, abject dog, a dog one has only to throw a shoe at in order to be able to take away the bone it doesn't really want. His head ached all over like an enormous boil, while his arm lay twisted under his back, supine on the soaking floor. What was happening, there in that dark cave? He felt as though he were in another world, his eyes closed, his ears hearing nothing. Was it, perhaps, that the lamp had gone out? The pain in his arm sent a stinging numbness into every part of his body. Making a great effort to drag it from under him, he felt his numbed fingers pass across his face, rubbing his eyes and then his forehead. His hands were cold and streaked with mud. He waggled a finger in his ear, which buzzed and roared, and then was silent.

Imagining he heard a violent movement close by him, he thought that he was going to be struck again, that this time it was going to be the end. Gathering his strength, he drew his limbs together and found himself sitting upright on the ground. He rubbed his eyes frenziedly and then looked about him. The red glow from the lamp lit up the bed. He saw them there, a rumpled heap of clothes. The man was lying on top of her and Heela, with her last vestiges of strength, was uttering short agonized screams through her savagely closed mouth.

The bed was shaking violently, its creaks mingling with a strange and unfamiliar grunting noise.

An overwhelming terror suddenly flooded through him. Dizzy, his body trembling, he wanted to scream. He was aware of nothing but the hideousness of what was being enacted before his gaze. He quickly braced his legs, stood up and backed against the wall, his heart pounding with fear. Directly he stood up he felt a warm wetness on his thighs. Yet despite the terror that set his heart pounding, he was unable to shift his gaze from them. The glow from the lamp was as darkly red as congealed blood. The heap of clothes moved rapidly, subsided for a moment then took up its crazed heaving again. Amidst the violent agitation of the clothes, Heela's screams, and the bestial grunting, he saw a leg raised high like some skinned carcass. There followed a high-pitched, animal shriek. Behind him the wall was cold and muddy, and the rain still drummed on the roof. He tried to scream, and the wind roared and roared from afar.

The Man and the Farm

YUSUF SHAROUNI

AT TEN o'clock in the evening Munira felt the first twinges of pain and at eleven her husband, Badawi Effendi, went off at a run—in spite of his size—to call the doctor.

Badawi Effendi's luck was in: the doctor had no other delivery to deal with that evening, though he was not in his clinic when Badawi got there. One of the nurses telephoned him at the club where he was on night call, playing Coon-can with his friends. So he told the nurse to go and find out how urgent it was and to judge for herself as to when he would be required.

Panting, Badawi Effendi got back to the house with the nurse to find that his mother-in-law—whom he had sent for—had come to sit through the hours of labour with her daughter. At midnight the doctor arrived.

It was a somewhat cold March night, with the moon not yet up. The doctor and Badawi Effendi sat on the balcony which was just above ground floor level, sipping coffee, gazing at the stars, and listening to the rustling of the trees in front of them. Spring had covered their branches with green and the wind carried the scent of blossom which had not yet revealed its fruit. Meanwhile the two men strained their ears towards the woman within who was suffering the pangs of childbirth. The doctor had given her some drops of medicine to assist her during labour and an injection to guard against the risk of haemorrhage; after that he had left it to nature to complete her work while he merely acted as watchman and assistant. The woman herself gave out an almost continuous low moaning sound which was intensified from time to time.

Though the first experience of its kind in the lives of Badawi Effendi and his wife Munira, it was one that was being continually repeated in the life of the doctor. While for him cases of childbirth —like the human creatures he treated—possessed a certain similarity, each none the less possessed its own uniqueness.

56

Badawi Effendi and Munira were no newly-weds, however: they had been married for seven long years without having either sons or daughters and during these years they had come to feel that their marriage was like a barren fruit tree.

Badawi Effendi was a farmer or, to put it more exactly, the owner of a market garden near the city of Cairo. On marrying he had left the market garden to his brother and had settled with his bride in one of the suburbs of the capital. Though Munira was his cousin, she had spent her life in the city. She was as white as milk, as plump as a duck, and rather short of stature, especially when measured against the tall, hefty frame of her husband. Quite possibly she herself would not have objected to living in the country, but Badawi Effendi, ever-watchful for her comfort (a feeling resembling love had existed between them since childhood) had moved to a small modern home. His share of the work consisted of looking after the transportation of the produce and selling it by auction to the traders in the city markets; from time to time he also advised his brother about bringing on a certain crop so as to make it available before the market became glutted, or keeping back some other produce so that it could be sold out of season at double the price. Badawi Effendi's spare-time hobby was reading: papers, magazines, and the occasional book, for he had had the opportunity of studying up to secondary school level and had also learnt how to sport a European-type suit; his brother's education, on the other hand, did not extend beyond the village school and he continued to wear either *galabia* or *jubba*.

One month of their marriage, then another, passed in expectancy. The earth had taught Badawi that he should wait, that he should allow time, after sowing and watering, for it to produce its first small green shoots in due course; these shoots too, should be given time in which to grow and flower, and these blossoms in their turn should be accorded time to wither and give place to fruit.

They began to be perturbed. Badawi Effendi did not wish to upset his bride, though he knew she was in fact already apprehensive and that her mother—who was now standing beside her as she suffered her labour—had also begun to share their concern. Their need for a child was an instinctive one, the need for the next step in the natural order of things. Each began wondering: Is there something abnormal in this? Which of us is it—the seed or the soil?

A year passed, a second year began. Whenever night came and bed brought them together, Badawi Effendi would feel that the spark of passion within him burnt as brightly as ever. Before marrying he had heard from certain of his friends that this spark would wane, that frequency, habit, and the ease with which it could be satisfied would all serve to quench the flames of passion. But he had found that the opposite was true, and that sex was like food: no sooner had one had one's fill at one meal than one was looking forward greedily to the next.

Badawi Effendi was by nature skilled in the ways of love. He knew how, little by little, to awaken in his wife the deepest of her dormant emotions so that she responded to and with him, while he rejoiced in his manhood and the passionate desire it kindled within her. Why, though, was it, he continually asked himself, that each failed to give the other a proof that they had done all in their power, that they had both played their parts to perfection, he as a complete man and she as a complete woman. These poignant moments passed, yet the seed did not grow, the vegetation did not flower, the blossoms bore no fruit.

It is not, however, in the make-up of a farmer to resign himself to the infertility of his land. The soil which Badawi Effendi and his brother now cultivated had been regarded as barren more than fifty years ago. His grandfather, buying it for next to nothing, had begun to till it, at first planting it with rice, then with lucerne and beans. Then his father had taken over and, doubling his efforts, had treated it with chemical fertilizers until he managed to make it yield a fine crop of vegetables both summer and winter. And thus it was that the idea began, little by little, to grow in Badawi Effendi's mind, timorously at first, yet with ever-growing insistence.

Munira's sister had married several months after them and not a year had passed before she was delivered of a child who had filled the house with his crying. His mother had told Badawi Effendi, just before she died, that one shouldn't let such matters rest without doing something, while his mother-in-law had pointed out to her daughter that children gave a wife a certain standing in the home, that they were a comfort in one's loneliness and gave an atmosphere of warmth and gaiety to a house.

And thus Badawi Effendi and his wife came to have experience of doctors as they went from clinic to clinic, from laboratory to laboratory, being examined and analysed. They came to know other childless couples, entering a world of doctors, of women and men and their troubles, a world in which women struggled to attain the pangs of childbirth. Badawi Effendi felt that he was like the branch of a tree and that he did not want this tree to be felled; he wanted it to be handed on after his death in the same way as he had taken it over from those before him.

They went away from the doors of these clinics and laboratories with a verdict of 'not guilty': the seed was fertile, the soil was fertile, yet somehow no plant grew. And so they abandoned medicine, more bewildered than ever, feeling as though accursed by some unknown hand.

For a little while Badawi Effendi considered the suggestion, made by one of the doctors, that his wife should have recourse to artificial insemination. However, he rejected this idea absolutely; in fact he expressed such disgust at it that the doctor, who had suggested it in a most delicate and indirect way, felt quite embarrassed. Badawi Effendi wanted to have a son of his own, a sprig that would grow from his own branch; he wanted to enjoy seeing his own features coming to life in the growing child. He wanted him to be sturdy, intelligent, and full of energy like his father. He had no desire to import the seed—he wanted to till his own farm by himself, otherwise it might as well remain barren.

Two years passed, and his mother-in-law insisted more and more that medicine was nothing but humbug and robbery. Otherwise why did they not have children when neither of them was in any way to blame? Despite the fact that Badawi Effendi had studied up to secondary school level, despite his reading of the magazine *The Doctor* and his being well aware that it was chemical fertilizers which gave life to the land and not charms, magic, or incense, he still fell back on a childhood filled with superstition in his moments of despair. So he left the whole thing to his mother and mother-in-law, between whom there had been a kind of reconciliation when they received the doctors' reports, where before there had been something closely akin to furtive recrimination, as though each was responsible for her son or her daughter. The two of them agreed that the spirits, who were clearly casting their spells between Munira's thighs, preventing her from becoming pregnant, must be placated.

And so it was that the outside lavatory—where the spirits had their home—was thoroughly cleaned, sprinkled with sand, and adorned with roses and other flowers; at the same time a bottle of sherbet, another of rose water, and several pounds of sweets were strewn on the ground. Incense was burnt, drums were beaten, and no one was allowed inside; Badawi Effendi, Munira, or any others in the house had to use the neighbours' lavatory. These rites were carried out for a whole twenty-four hours. The old woman who had been called in also ordered that a sheep be slaughtered and that by dawn no single piece of it should be left; every scrap of meat had to be eaten before midnight and the bones buried before daybreak.

Badawi Effendi and his wife were told to wait for a month for the results of these endeavours. The month duly passed and there was indeed a pregnancy. The trouble was, though, that it wasn't Munira who became pregnant but her mother, who was nearly forty-five and whose youngest child was ten years old. In explaining this away it was said that the spirits must have lost their way.

This disaster had a bad effect on Badawi Effendi and his wife, for having previously tried out scientific methods with scientific calm they now took to superstitious methods with superstitious zeal. It came as a terrible shock to Badawi Effendi to see his mother-in-law's stomach swell up when she already had no less than seven children—it was as if she had stolen his child from him. From the very beginning Badawi Effendi had not seen eye to eye with his uncle's wife; when, therefore, she became pregnant in place of his wife, his hatred of her grew only too evident and the mere sight of her irritated him. As for Munira, she felt real jealousy of her mother. It was as though she faced one of Fate's enigmas: why should it bestow something on someone who didn't want it while denying it to someone who yearned for it?

An atmosphere of tragedy settled on the house. The hot weather had spoilt the tomato crop of which Badawi Effendi had had high hopes. Though Munira was in no way responsible for this, her husband became sullen, quick-tempered, and rude towards her. Sometimes Munira would bend to the storm, at others she would flare up. When at her wit's end she would burst into heart-rending tears and say: 'I know the reason, it's because I haven't given you children. You know it's not my fault, though!' to which he would reply furiously:

'Well, it certainly isn't mine.' But before long, little by little, his heart would relent and he would wipe away her tears. It was no easy task to calm her, and he would have to fondle and caress her, draw his big fingers through her soft, flowing hair, and over the uncovered parts of her body and kiss her as she lay in his strong arms, supine as a frightened cat, and all too soon, like the most passionate of lovers, their bodies would be joined and serenity would reign.

The previous summer Badawi Effendi's mother had died at the farm. She had been brought up there, and had seldom left it, though she would pay visits of several days to her son Badawi when she would ask how they were getting on and deliver herself of advice to both sides. After hearing the news of her death Badawi and his wife were obliged to attend the funeral and receive the usual condolences. On the night of the funeral ceremony, after the flood of wailing and weeping had died down, Munira learned from the women who came to pay their condolences that a strange bedouin woman had arrived at the village three days earlier. This woman claimed to have the power of finding lost things, curing the sick, and quickening the barren. Though Munira's faith in such matters had diminished considerably since the episode of the spirits, she was like a drowning person clutching at any straw. On the following day, therefore, she sent for the bedouin woman and told her of the thing for which she yearned. The woman asked for a gold ornament of hers on which, as she expressed it, 'she could pass the night', and said she would return it at dawn the following morning. She also gave Munira two small rolls of wool, telling her to place one of them between her thighs; at midnight she was to substitute the other one and keep it there till morning and, with the help of God the One, she would become pregnant.

In an agony of hope Munira had given the bedouin woman one of her gold bracelets—worth no less than twenty pounds—and had then carried out her instructions to the letter. The next morning she had waited for the woman to return with her bracelet as promised. But the woman never came back, and on enquiring about her Munira was told that she had left the village on the previous evening for an unknown destination. Realizing that the whole business was a sheer swindle, Munira opened the two rolls of wool and found that one contained what looked like lucerne seeds together with some white powder, while in the other there was a

piece of paper written on in such a small and poor hand that she
was only able to make out a few words such as 'At your service . . .'
Bemoaning her bad luck more than the loss of the bracelet,
Munira threw the lot away. Some women who heard her weeping
came to console her, thinking that she was crying for the old
woman who had departed this life—and who had also been her
uncle's wife—and were both surprised and impressed at such
loyalty.

The days of mourning passed and Munira returned to Cairo
with her husband. On one of their nights together, outwardly
laughing at her stupidity but with the heaviest of hearts, she told
her husband of the story of the bedouin woman. Despite this un-
fortunate experience, Munira's period was overdue. She waited a
few more days in disbelief and then informed her husband.

Badawi Effendi had toyed with the idea of divorce but had
found it distasteful and had therefore rejected it, just as he
had rejected the suggestion of artificial insemination. Munira was
his cousin; she had become a habit and he was not one to change
his habits. Besides, they loved one another, and just as the fault
was not his so, too, it was not hers. More than once he had been
told that if he were to marry some other woman children would
be born to him, while she, by marrying someone else, would bear
children. His feelings on the matter were those of a peasant who
refuses to sell any of his land however hard pressed he may be.
More than once his friends had urged him to take a second wife.
This, too, he knew was impossible, for it would hurt Munira to her
very depths. Moreover this would be a new departure in his family,
neither his father, grandfather, nor—he had heard—his great-
grandfather ever having taken more than one wife.

These thoughts had given place to even more dangerous ones.
At a certain period a desire for death had stirred within him—the
death of one of them so that he could marry someone else and have
children, or she some other man and bear him children. These
sombre thoughts did not come to him merely as a wish but in the
form of an obituary, of people offering their condolences, of
funeral rites. He would imagine one of them mourning the other,
and many other details came to him with the utmost clarity.
Badawi Effendi did not allow such pictures to take root in his
mind but fought against them, thrusting them away from him one
by one, believing—as did his wife—that everything was ordained

by fate. This faith of his brought Badawi Effendi to a state of mind not far removed from mysticism.

When his wife, who was determined to continue the struggle, informed him of her state of health, a ray of hope sprang up within him, but most warily, for this was not the first time her period had been delayed. Once, in fact, it had stopped altogether for two months, at which they had gone off to a famous woman doctor who had advised them to have an analysis made at a cost of two pounds. The victim of this analysis was a rabbit which was injected with some of Munira's urine and was then slaughtered on the following day for an examination of its ovaries. On returning to the doctor to learn the result of the analysis she informed them that there was no pregnancy. They didn't believe this doctor and accused her of not knowing what she was talking about, though it was not long before the truth of her words became apparent. And so it was that this time Badawi Effendi waited in trepidation for several more days.

Eventually, Munira confirmed the good news, for she and her mother had gone to a doctor who assured her that this time she really was pregnant—after six years and three months of marriage. Badawi Effendi, in spite of his huge size, had literally danced with joy; he had caressed her stomach, fondling it with fingers and lips; he had placed his ear against it as though to hear the pulse beats of the embryo which was as yet no more than a mere sperm. Now Badawi Effendi's manhood was fulfilled: the barren land had been fertilized just as his grandfather before him had made fruitful the waste land he had bought. Now it was up to him to guard it, nurture it, care for it, until in the fullness of time its fruit was born, live, warm, real.

Arrangements for welcoming the baby were begun and the two of them gave much thought to the question of a suitable name. Would it be a boy or a girl? Munira started to make baby clothes, a small mattress, a small pillow, a small coverlet—everything small became a part of their world.

But still Badawi Effendi was nagged by a slight feeling of doubt. He had often heard (especially in his bachelor days) of women with husbands who, deprived of their most cherished dreams, nevertheless continued to love their wives more than their dreams and thus found themselves torn between two conflicting desires: love for the wife who existed and for the dream which did not. Torn between love and sympathy for her husband and the desire to fulfil herself as a woman and a mother, such a woman would go with some young man just once, so that she might experience motherhood and her husband fatherhood; having achieved this, she would never see the young man again. Badawi remembered that Munira had become pregnant during the days of his mother's funeral and had come to him with the story of the bedouin woman at that time. Could it be that she had been preparing the way for what happened later? Could it, for instance, have been his own brother? His brother was the one who actually cultivated the farm, while he merely had the job of selling the produce. Could it be that his brother had cultivated his farm for him in another fashion? He banished the ridiculous idea from his mind, knowing full well that neither his wife nor his brother was capable of perpetrating such a thing—it was merely a stupid thought that had come to him in a moment of weakness, just as other stupid thoughts had done in the past. Perhaps those two rolls of wool, with that white powder in one of them, had been responsible after all? Perhaps one of them had contained the seed of some other man?—No, it was his own seed, he was sure of it. After all, he was not the only man to whom such a thing had happened. It had, for instance, occurred in the case of the former *omda* of their village after ten years of marriage, and to Sheikh Maihoub after no less than twelve, and both their wives were above suspicion.

He remembered the first night of the funeral when all the mourners had left and Munira, in the living-room on the flat roof of the house, had exhausted herself with weeping and wailing, while he, too, despite the fact that his mother had been a lady of advanced years, had been much saddened by her departure from this life. It had been a chokingly hot, clammy July night and each of them had gone to sleep without feeling desire. At dawn, though, he had woken up and left the room to relieve nature; he had felt the early breezes on his face, had breathed in the odour of the countryside, a mixture of earth, greenery, and animals, and it was as though this smell, charged with the memories of childhood and youth, had revitalized him and kindled within him a flame of desire. He had returned to the room on tiptoe, but his movements must have disturbed her, for she opened her eyes momentarily as he drew near to her. It was as though he wanted to bury his sorrows within her body, and the desire that burned between them had never been stronger.

Now here she was—nine months later—suffering the pangs of labour. Being his first experience of such matters, it was quite impossible for him to know whether the sufferings of his wife were peculiar to her or were in fact experienced by every woman in such circumstances. Several times he had looked for the answer in the doctor's eyes, unwilling to reveal his fear and feeling of helplessness. Six hours had elapsed and the cocks had begun to call like muezzins from the neighbouring roof-tops as his wife continued her cries and groans. He had slipped into her room for a moment and had been confronted with the frightful spectacle of her lying there bathed in sweat in spite of the cold weather, moaning softly. The six years' struggle had become focused into these hours. He said a few tender words of encouragement before being ordered out by the doctor who saw no point in allowing him to witness such a scene.

Badawi Effendi had the highest respect for the doctor, for his calmness, gentleness and experience; he was like some small deity, holding in his hands the keys of life for his wife and child. Badawi was also struck by the doctor's great humanity; and the fee he would be getting seemed to Badawi quite inadequate for being kept up so late and for all the care and attention he was giving. Furthermore, the doctor's cheerful manner and smiling face inspired boundless confidence in Badawi.

They were of similar age, each being about thirty-five. The night, the solitude, and the silence had created a sort of friendship between them. Badawi Effendi knew certain facts about the doctor, for instance that he was a government doctor by day and that he had his own private clinic in the evenings. He both earned and spent a great deal, his spending being largely at the gambling table and on his mistress, despite the fact that he had a wife who was an object of desire to others.

The doctor talked to him about his two children, a boy and a girl. The girl, though the younger of the two, was the cleverer and was in a higher form than her brother. Badawi Effendi talked to him about his farm, methods of fertilization, the seasons for the various vegetables, and the way prices rise and fall. The doctor spoke about the government hospitals, their lack of equipment, and the general muddle they were in, and about a woman who had come to him at the government hospital with a haemorrhage: no sooner had they put her on the operating table than she had died and an investigation had been made to determine the extent of his responsibility. Badawi Effendi told him about his long struggle to produce a child, about the doctors he had met, and the data he possessed about the pregnancy, as though wishing to make quite sure that it was genuine.

Once again, as a faint sickle moon appeared in the east, they drank down a couple of cups of coffee. While the doctor reassured Badawi Effendi about his wife, the first light of dawn unfolded, the first early morning breeze stirred. The doctor then went inside to see how things were progressing. A matter of minutes before sunrise—at seven-thirty a.m.—Badawi Effendi heard the crying of his newborn child and was himself moved to silent tears.

The Lost Suitcase

ABDEL-MONEIM SELIM

I BEGAN hunting round for my black suitcase but couldn't find it. While the other cases rested one on top of the other by the door of the flat—one, two and the little one—the black suitcase was nowhere to be seen.

I remembered well that I had had it with me in the train, that the porter at Cairo station had charged me for three suitcases and that I had carried the fourth, the small one, myself. After that I had taken a taxi and had placed three of the suitcases beside me, while the largest had stood alongside the driver. On leaving the cab the driver had carried the large suitcase, while I had taken two of the small ones. This meant that I must have left the black one inside the cab.

I dressed hastily in order to report the loss of the suitcase; then I started thinking: was it possible that the driver had not yet discovered the suitcase? Finally I decided to wait until morning; if the driver had not returned the case by then I would take apropriate action.

As the driver had not made his appearance by morning, I quickly got dressed and took myself off to Roda police station. I went into the duty officer's room, went up to him with extreme politeness and said:

'Good morning.'

'Good morning.'

As the officer was writing in a ledger I remained standing in silence.

'Yes,' he said, looking up at me.

'Please, I'd like to report something,' I said with the same politeness.

'Next door,' he said abruptly.

'Who to?' I asked.

67

'The duty sergeant,' he said, equally abruptly; 'Sergeant Abdul Basit.'

'Thanks', I said, and went into the other room where I saw Sergeant Abdul Basit seated at a table, his tarboosh in front of him. On seeing me he put on the tarboosh and looked at me enquiringly.

'Good morning,' I said to him.

'Good morning.'

'You're Sergeant Abdul Basit?'

'Yes, I'm the duty sergeant.'

'Please, I've got something to report.'

'What—a theft?'

'Yes, a theft.'

'Certainly, sir, we'll make out a report,' and he took up a piece of paper and began to write.

I asked him if I could sit down and without raising his head he answered, 'Go ahead.'

I sat down to his right and glanced at what he was writing. I read:

This report was made out on today's date at 9.30 a.m. by me, Sergeant Abdul Basit Abu Hassanein, Duty Sergeant. Whereas there attended before us—

Glancing up at me he asked: 'What's your name?'

'Ahmed Shefik Lutfi.'

He wrote: *Ahmed Shefik Lutfi.*

'What's your job?'

'I work at the Raml Company.'

He wrote: *Employee at the Raml Company.*

'Age?'

'Thirty-two.'

He wrote: *Age thirty-two.*

'Where were you born?'

'In Edfiena.'

'Edfiena? Where's this place Edfiena?'

'In the Rosetta district.'

'What province?'

'Beheira.'

He continued by writing: *Born in Edfiena, district of Rosetta, province of Beheira.*

'And where do you live?' he asked.

'At No. 28 al-Malik al-Salih Street,' I answered.

He wrote down: *Resident at No. 28 al-Malik al-Salih Street, district of Roda.*

'It is in Roda, isn't it?' he queried.

'Yes,' I answered.

'H'm—Well, sir, and what do you want to report? Briefly.'

'Briefly I would like to report in the following terms—'

'Let's just have it in your own words.'

'Certainly. Yesterday—'

'Not so fast,' he interrupted, 'so I can keep up with you—fine. Yesterday . . . Yesterday what?'

'Yesterday I was coming back from Alexandria with four suit-cases, a large one, one for papers, and two medium sized ones—'

'And two medium sized ones—H'm?'

'I took a taxi from the station and when I arrived home I searched around for the black case, couldn't find it and—

'Hang on a moment for Heaven's sake . . . you didn't find the black one? And then?'

'I remembered I'd left it in the taxi.'

'H'm.'

'That's it.'

'That's all?'

'Yes.'

'What sort of a report do you think that is?'

'Yes?'

'Where are you from?'

'I'm from Edfiena, district of Rosetta, province of Beheira.'

'Yes, yes, I know—And I, let me tell you, am from Gharbiyya —meaning what? Meaning that we're neighbours and naturally, being neighbours, I've got your interests at heart.'

'Yes.'

'You believe in God?'

'There is no god but God.'

'Then let me tell you that this report is worthless.'

'Why?'

'Why? You may well ask. And how do you think we're going to be able to find the case? We, that is the police—let me tell you—perhaps—maybe, somehow or other—who knows. Tell me about it, sir,' and he got ready to write.

'When did you return from Alexandria ?'

'I returned on the four p.m. train.'

'Can you describe to me the cases you brought back with you?'

'Yes.'

'Then go ahead and do so.'

'The first suitcase was of a dimension of—'

'Let's have it in your own words.'

'All right. The first case, the large one, measured about a metre and a half by a metre and was brown; the second was one metre by three-quarters, also brown; the third was half a metre by half a metre, and was black, and the small brief-case was brown.'

'And which was the case that was lost?'

'The black one.'

'Did it contain clothes?'

'Yes.'

'Why not say so? All we're doing is wasting time.'

'It contained a thick suit, four shirts, five ties, and some personal papers.'

'Bit by bit if you don't mind. What colour were the suit, shirts, and ties?'

'The suit was a plain light grey, the shirts were white, and the ties were of various colours.'

'What do you mean by "various colours"? We must know.'

'One was plain red; the second red with a blue pattern; the third grey; the fourth yellow and brown with a green pattern, the fifth white.'

'White!'

'Yes, white. Well, a sort of off-white.'

'Fine, it's fine so far. Now let's get down to brass tacks. You took a taxi?'

'Yes.'

'Do you know the make and number of the taxi and the driver's name?'

'The taxi was a Ford.'

'Ford?'

'Yes.'

'How do you know?'

'I can tell easily.'

'And I, my dear fellow, can't . . . how do you know?'

'I read it on the front.'

'I see. And the number?'

'4646.'

'And how do you know the number?'

'I always note the numbers of the taxis I ride in.'

'Whatever for?'

'For fun.'

'What sort of fun's that? My dear sir, let's have a sensible reply which we can put down in the report.'

'It's just a habit I've got into.'

'Have it your own way. This reply isn't in your interests, but have it your own way. And what was the driver's name?'

'I didn't ask him.'

'H'm, good. Are you sure that when you left the train you had four cases with you?'

'Yes, I am.'

'Did anyone see you with these cases?'

'The station porter carried three of them and I took the small one.'

'Do you know this porter?'

'No, but I'd know him if I saw him.'

'Good, we'll see about that later. Where did you put the cases?'

'In the car.'

'Yes, I know, but where? In the boot? On the roof? Where?'

'I put the big case next to the driver and the three other ones beside me.'

'Not so quick—the big case you put next to the driver and the three other ones—h'm—where?'

'On the seat beside me.'

'And then?'

'And then I arrived home. The driver took the big case, while I carried two and forgot about the last one.'

'H'm, and when did you realize you'd forgotten the case?'

'About an hour after getting home.'

'Isn't it possible that you forgot the case somewhere else?'

'No.'

'H'm, and what else is there to ask? Oh yes—how much do you reckon the things lost were worth?'

'The case I bought for three pounds and the things in it were practically all new. The suit cost me twenty pounds, the four shirts were a pound and a half each, while the ties were a pound each—thirty-one pounds altogether.'

'It's quite unreasonable to write down such a sum—thirty-one pounds is too much. Let's say fifteen.'

'What! Only fifteen, officer?'

'Let's at least hope we'll find the things. Don't upset yourself. What's it matter—fifteen, twenty, or even more?'

I looked at him without saying a word.

'Well, that's it,' he said.

'Can I go then?'

'What do you mean "go"? You've still got to sign the report. I'll complete it and you can sign.'

He wrote: *With this the report was completed at today's date the time being 12.30 p.m. and it was duly signed by the complainant.*

'Please sign here.'

I took up the pen and signed.

'No, write your name, don't sign. I mean, just write your name.'

I wrote my name a second time, then asked him: 'Is that it?'

'That's it.'

As I got up to leave I asked: 'Tell me, Sergeant Abdul Basit—I mean to say, is there any hope that anything'll turn up?'

'Of course, why shouldn't it? Directly anything happens we'll let you know immediately. Let's all hope that God will be helping.'

I thanked him and left. On returning to the Company the manager called for me. I apologized for being late and told him the story. He showed some concern for what had happened to me but did not consider it sufficient reason for my being absent a whole morning. As for my colleagues in the office, they agreed that, as the saying goes, my sole consolation lay in God and that I should expect never to see my suitcase again.

A week passed, then two, and I began to be resigned to the loss of the suitcase. But one morning the manager summoned me to his office. Without so much as a good morning he held out a small slip of paper. I looked at him in astonishment.

'Go on, read it,' he said.

I took the paper and read:

Mr. Ahmed Shefik Lutfi is required to attend at the police station for questioning re Offence No. 215. Signed: The Super-intendent of Abbasiyya police station.

I read through the paper a second time but was unable to make anything of it. As I began to read it yet again I became aware of the manager's voice.

'And what offence might this be, Mr. Ahmed?'

'Really, sir, I'm quite at a loss—I don't know what it's all about.'

'Well, I certainly don't know. Take yourself off to the police station and come and see me directly you get back. Off you go now. All this nonsense about an offence—off you go.'

I left the manager's office, walked glumly to my own, locked it and went off to Abbasiyya police station. Was I being accused of having committed some offence? I asked myself on the way there. I stopped a taxi and told the driver to take me quickly to Abbasiyya.

On arriving at the police station I jumped out of the cab and hurried into the duty officer's room. I produced the letter summoning me there at which he politely indicated a chair.

'Take a seat.'

I sat down while the officer busied himself with an enquiry into a case of assault and battery.

I asked him hastily: 'If you could just let me know what it's all about—'

'Certainly, I'll tell you right away—just let me finish what I'm doing.'

I fell silent and began watching the scene being enacted before me without understanding it. I heard the officer ask if anybody had anything more to say, after which those present proceeded to sign, and then left the room with one of the policemen. I thus found myself alone with the officer.

Turning over the papers which lay before him, he addressed me with formidable calm:

'The question, my dear sir, is one of great simplicity and relates to a complaint lodged by you in regard to the suitcase you lost last month.'

'Ah, the suitcase! You've found it?'

'No.'

'Then, what?'

'The owner of taxi Number 4646 lives here in Abbasiyya and

so Roda police station has transferred the case to ourselves for action.'

'And so?'

'So the first thing we must do is ask you some questions.'

'Right. Go ahead.'

The officer took up his pen.

'Your name, sir?'

'My name is Ahmed Shefik Lutfi, I am thirty-two years of age. I am an employee of the Raml Company. I was born in Edfiena, district of Rosetta, province of Beheira, and I live at 28 al-Malik al-Salih Street which is in the district of Roda.'

'What is the subject of your statement?'

'But, officer, I've already given all this information.'

'Never mind. Everybody has his own way of going about things and I'd like to look into the matter for myself.'

'All right, go ahead,'

'What's the subject of your complaint?'

'The subject of my complaint is that I was returning from Alexandria about three weeks ago with four suitcases of different sizes, the largest being brown in colour and measuring a metre and a half by a metre, the second a metre by three-quarters and also brown, the third half a metre by half but black, and the fourth being a briefcase.'

'A little slower, if you'd be so good.'

'Certainly.'

'All right, let's hear the rest.'

'I took a taxi from the station and put three of the suitcases beside me and the fourth alongside the driver and on arriving home I discovered that I had forgotten the black one. The taxi was a Ford and its number 4646. The missing case contained a grey woollen suit which cost twenty pounds, four white shirts costing one pound fifty piastres each, and five ties of which one was a plain red, the second blue on red, the third pale grey, and the fourth green on yellow and brown, and the fifth white. The ties cost a pound each.'

'You're going too fast.'

'The fact of the matter is I haven't got all that amount of time, besides which the whole thing's most annoying.'

'I appreciate your position and I also appreciate the considerable loss you've had.'

'Thanks very much.'

'I'd just like to ask you something else.'

'Do.'

'Why didn't you report the loss of the suitcase on the same day?'

'The fact is I thought that maybe the driver wasn't free to bring it back to me, that perhaps he was busy taking people about or something. I thought I'd give him till next day.'

'Are you certain that the taxi you took from Cairo station to Roda on the day of your return from Alexandria with four suitcases was a Ford?'

'I'm absolutely certain.'

'Are you certain that the number of the Ford taxi you took from Cairo station to your home in Roda on the day of your return from Alexandria was 4646?'

'Yes, absolutely certain.'

'How can you be?'

'I'm certain because I read the number.'

'Have you any other statements to make.'

'No, thank you.'

I signed and hurried out, jumped into a taxi, and told the driver: 'As quick as you can please to Mazloum Street.'

Back at the office I rushed off to see the manager.

'Can you imagine, sir, what it was all about?' I said.

He looked at me coldly without answering.

'About the business of the suitcase,' I went on.

'What suitcase, Mr. Ahmed?'

'The suitcase I forgot in the taxi—the report has been transferred from the Roda police station to Abbasiyya police station because the driver lives there.'

But the manager made no reply and returned to his papers. I left the room despondently and went back to my office where I threw myself down into the chair feeling utterly miserable.

A week later the manager called me to his office again and handed me two letters, the first of which read:

Please bring to the notice of Mr. Ahmed Shefik Lutfi that his attendance is required at the police station in order to complete the enquiry into the offence concerning which he was previously questioned.

The Superintendent of Abbasiyya police station

The second one read:

Please inform Mr. Ahmed Shefik Lutfi that his attendance is urgently required at the police station.

The Superintendent of Roda police station

I looked at the manager, who was turning over some papers in front of him. I left his room quietly, returned to my desk and locked the drawers, and went out into the street. There I stood outside the main door to the company's offices, not knowing what to do. I held the two letters in my hand; I had in any case to go both to the Abbasiyya police station and the Roda police station.

I walked to the bus stop, telling myself that I should go to the Roda police station first in the hope that they had found the suitcase, which would then make it unnecessary for me to go to Abbasiyya.

I arrived at Roda police station and went straight to Sergeant Abdul Basit. After wishing him good morning I said to him, 'I've come.'

'Yes, sir.'

I took the summons to attend from my pocket and handed it over to him.

'Don't you remember me?' I asked. 'I'm the suitcase man.'

He stretched out his hand, read the paper and said:

'Ah—ah—please sit down.'

'I hope everything's all right,' I said, sitting down quickly. 'What do you want me for?'

'It's all right, just take it easy.'

'Actually, I've got work to do and still have to go to Abbasiyya.'

'Why Abbasiyya?'

'No reason except that the report was transferred there—I've very little time.'

'Ah, certainly—our detectives have found a few stolen articles—among them a pale grey suit like yours.'

'In a suitcase?' I asked eagerly.

'Eh? That's hardly reasonable, is it? You don't honestly think the thief would sell the thing with the suitcase. That doesn't make much sense.'

'Quite—never mind—can I see these things?'

'Why not? After all, what did we send for you for? Come along.'

He got up and went to a cupboard on his right, opened it, and produced a suit.

'Take a look and see if it's yours—no, wait a bit.'

He put the suit back in the cupboard, locked it again, and hurried back to his desk.

'Before you see it,' he said, taking out his pen, 'I must ask you about the cut.'

'What cut?'

'The cut of the suit. Not all suits are cut the same way. Just a couple of words will do—your name, sir?'

'My name is Ahmed Shefik Lutfi, I am thirty-two years of age and was born in Edfiena, in the district of Rosetta, province of Beheira.'

'Yes, yes, that's right. What sort of cut was it?'

'Single-breasted.'

'Single-breasted?'

'Single-breasted—like the one I'm wearing now.'

'H'm and its pockets?'

'Also like these.'

'H'm . . . All right, come along and have a look at the suit.'

He got up again, opened the cupboard and took out the suit. He began turning it this way and that, but from the first glance I could tell it wasn't mine. I didn't get up from my seat.

'So it's not your suit,' said the Sergeant. 'That's so, isn't it?'

'No, it's not my suit.'

'Right, then let's finish the report.'

He returned to his desk and began writing:

The report was begun at the date and time hereof when Mr. Ahmed Shefik Lutfi, employee at the Raml Company, was summoned to attend and after the suit previously acquired was shown to him he stated that it was not the suit he had lost.

With this the report was concluded and he duly signed it.

'Please sign it.'

I got up, took the pen, and signed.

'Is that all?' I asked.

'That's all. Sorry to have troubled you. I'm sure we'll find your things, though.'

I bade him farewell as I hurried out. 'Peace be upon you.' But I stopped suddenly.

'Tell me, Sergeant Abdul Basit, wouldn't it be possible to send notices to my home?'

'Of course, why not?'

'Good, in future always send them to my home.'

'The fact is one gets a bit lazy and the Raml Company's nice and easy to write and it's a large company and well known.'

It was now twelve o'clock, which meant that I would not be able to return to work that day; this also meant a further humiliating encounter with the manager. In any case I had to hurry off to Abbasiyya police station so as to catch the officer before he went off to lunch and yet another day was wasted.

I got on to a bus, arrived at the station and went into the duty-room, where the officer met me with a genial smile which boded well. I greeted him and asked permission to sit down.

'Please do,' he said.

'You remember me of course?' I asked him.

'Of course.'

'And what's it all about this time, I wonder?'

'The thing's got into a bit of a muddle.'

'How's that?'

'I'll tell you.'

He pulled a file towards him and extracted the report relating to myself.

'It's like this. We summoned the driver of Taxi 4646 who stated that he hadn't been working that day and forwarded a certificate from a repair shop to the effect that his vehicle had been out of service on the day when your suitcase was lost.'

'And the upshot?'

'I don't know.'

'Isn't it possible that this certificate was sort of forged?'

'To tell the truth it's possible, but it'd be hard to prove.'

'And now what?'

'Well, I've an idea.'

'What is it?'

'I really do appreciate your position—your loss, so to speak, and I'd naturally like to help you.'

'I'm most grateful.'

'What I want to say is, isn't it possible that you—muddled up the number?'

'Muddled up the number? Out of the question! I remember distinctly that it was 4646.'

'All right, sir, but what I mean is, instead of being 4646, couldn't the number be 6464 or 4664 or 6446 or some such combination of fours and sixes?'

'Impossible. For a start I remember clearly that each four had a six next to it.'

'All right, this means that just as the number could be 4646 it might equally well have been 6464.'

I kept silent and began to think.

'What do you think?'

'I don't know,' I said. From that moment the numbers had in fact begun to get mixed up in my brain.

'It's possible,' I said.

'What's possible?'

'What you say's possible.'

'Which is the most likely number?'

'I don't know anything any longer. Let's say 6464 and try it out.'

'All right, I'll take down these statements from you and we'll look into it all. After that certificate forwarded by the driver I'm really supposed to close the report and file it away. However, I appreciate your position so I'll open it again on the basis that you want to amend your statements in respect of the number of the vehicle.'

'Fair enough. It's possible—it's possible I really did make a mistake.'

The officer began to write.

'What statement do you wish to make?'

'With regard to the number of the vehicle which I took on the evening of my return from Alexandria and which I previously said was Number 4646, I would like to state that I have remembered that the correct number of the vehicle was 6464.'

'Is there any further statement you wish to make?'

'No.'

I left. The time was past two o'clock, which meant that the Company had closed its doors and there was nothing for me to do but go home.

I woke early next morning wanting to arrive at the office in good time so as to get through some of my work which was in arrears. All day long I succeeded in avoiding the manager. Neither did I meet the manager during the following week nor did he send for me. Gradually I dismissed the business of the suitcase from my mind.

However, one morning he did call for me.

When I entered his office I found him standing in front of his desk. At once he burst out angrily:

'What I want to know, Mr. Ahmed, is where all this is going to end!'

I looked at him mutely.

'Where are all these police stations, questionings, and offences going to end!'

In dread I asked: 'What police stations, sir?'

'Read it,' he said and handed me a small slip of paper. I stood rooted to the spot, too scared to step forward and take it from him.

'Go on, read it!'

I stretched out my trembling hand and took the piece of paper without looking at it.

'Read what it says—go on.'

At last I read:

Imbaba police station.

Please note that Mr. Ahmed Shefik Lutfi is requested to attend urgently at the police station for questioning in Offence Number——

I was unable to go on. I stood up, not knowing what to do and looked beseechingly at the manager.

'What about it?' he asked sharply.

'I don't know,' I answered.

'How do you mean you don't know? The suitcase was said to be at the Roda police station, then at Abbasiyya and now it's found its way to Imbaba.'

'But, sir, it's not as if I've been a thief or done anything wrong!'

'You'd better go off to the police station. I'd dearly like to know where it's all going to end. Everything must have an end somewhere. Off you go.'

With difficulty I dragged myself back to my office and sat down at the desk. I felt unable to move, unable to think intelligently. I then became aware of the piece of paper in my hand. Imbaba police station—Roda police station—whatever police station it might be at, I no longer wanted the suitcase.

However, there was nothing to do but get up and go to the police station. It was ten a.m. and I had a mass of work in front of me. It was a long way to Imbaba. What had I to do with Imbaba police station?

I left my office and, feeling that I shouldn't waste any time, I signalled a taxi.

'Imbaba—the police station—as quick as you can, please.'

When I got there I dashed into the duty officer's room and silently handed over my piece of paper.

'You're Ahmed Shefik?' he asked me.

'The very same.'

'Please sit down.'

I sat down and waited.

Opening the file in front of him, the officer said:

'Last month you made a statement at Roda police station?'

I was getting impatient.

'Yes! What else?'

'And you said that the number of the taxi was 4646?'

'H'm,' I said quietly, looking at him.

'And then at Abbasiyya station, the station for the district in which the taxi driver lived, you said that the number of the taxi was not 4646 but 6464?'

'H'm.'

'The driver of that taxi's called Mustafa Humeida and he lives here in Imbaba.'

'Yes.'

'That's why I've got you to come along, so that I could ask you about the whole business.'

'I've told it all before.'

'Never mind. The thing's now in our court and I'm never happy about an investigation unless I've done it myself.'

'H'm, and what would you like to ask me about? Shouldn't you question the taxi driver first?'

'Look here, my dear fellow, I can't ask him till I've made sure.'

'Made sure of what?'

'Once you said the number of the vehicle was 4646 and on another occasion you said it was 6464. I must make sure. Maybe you'll be saying yet some other number.'

'So you want to ask me about that?'

'I'm going to start from the very beginning. I always like to do all my own investigations.'

'Right. Go ahead. And what would you like to ask me about?'

'I'll tell you right away.' He produced several sheets of paper from the drawer of his desk and began to write:

On today's date there appeared before us, the Duty Officer, Mr. Ahmed Shefik Lutfi who stated—

The officer leafed through the previous reports, and then went on writing.

My name is Ahmed Shefik Lutfi, I am thirty-two years of age and was born at Edfiena in the district of Rosetta, province of Beheira. I am an employee of the Raml Company and live at 28 al-Malik al-Salih Street in Roda.

He turned to me. 'What exactly was the subject of your statement?'

I sat up straight and said, 'Officer.'

'Yes?'

'Officer, I have lost nothing.'

'What's that?'

'I haven't lost any suitcases.'

'What do you mean?'

'What I mean is that I returned from Alexandria with all my suitcases complete and intact. I lost nothing.'

'I don't understand what it's all about.'

'I am telling you that I haven't lost a thing.'

'Not quite so fast, my dear fellow! First of all, your name is Ahmed Shefik Lutfi, is it not? And you were born in Edfiena, district of Rosetta, province of Beheira, were you not? And you are, are you not, an employee of the Raml Company?'

'Exactly.'

'What then are you talking about? Previously you made certain statements in a police report at Roda and Abbasiyya to the effect that you had lost a suitcase on—'

'It isn't true.'

'What? Isn't this your signature?' He thrust the reports I had previously signed into my hand.

'Yes, that's my signature,' I said.

'Then the suitcase was stolen from you?'

'And I, as owner of the suitcase, tell you that nothing was stolen from me.'

'And these statements?'

'A mistake.'

'Forged?'

'No, a mistake.'

'Didn't you read them before you signed them?'

'Yes, I did.'

'Sir—officer, my four suitcases are all safely at home and no-body's stolen anything from me.'

'Fine, we'll just write a couple of words to that effect.'

The officer began to write. In complete silence I watched the pen racing across the paper. At last he looked up at me and said:

'Please sign here.'

I signed.

'Well, that's it,' I said, getting to my feet. 'If you'll excuse me.'

'Where do you think you're going?' the officer asked.

'To my work. That's the end of the matter, isn't it?'

'The end of the matter? What do you mean? Sergeant Mah-moud!' he shouted at the top of his voice. 'Hey, you standing by the door!'

The policeman appeared and saluted.

'Take this gentleman away,' the officer told him.

'Take me where?' I asked in alarm.

But the officer was again writing in the report. I glanced at the policeman standing behind me; straining forward as far as I could I managed to read:

The said person is to be transferred back to the police station at Roda where he is resident so that he may be questioned in respect of a charge of being a nuisance to the authorities and dealt with under Section 135 of the Criminal Code.

The Doum Tree of Wad Hamid

TAIEB SALIH

WERE YOU to come to our village as a tourist, it is likely, my son, that you would not stay long. If it were in winter time, when the palm trees are pollinated, you would find that a dark cloud had descended over the village. This, my son, would not be dust, nor yet that mist which rises up after rainfall. It would be a swarm of those sand-flies which obstruct all paths to those who wish to enter our village. Maybe you have seen this pest before, but I swear that you have never seen this particular species. Take this gauze netting, my son, and put it over your head. While it won't protect you against these devils, it will at least help you to bear them. I remember a friend of my son's, a fellow student at school, whom my son invited to stay with us a year ago at this time of the year. His people come from the town. He stayed one night with us and got up next day, feverish, with a running nose and swollen face; he swore that he wouldn't spend another night with us.

If you were to come to us in summer you would find the horse-flies with us—enormous flies the size of young sheep, as we say. In comparison to these the sand-flies are a thousand times more bearable. They are savage flies, my son: they bite, sting, buzz, and whirr. They have a special love for man and no sooner smell him out than they attach themselves to him. Wave them off you, my son—God curse all sand-flies.

And were you to come at a time which was neither summer nor winter you would find nothing at all. No doubt, my son, you read the papers daily, listen to the radio, and go to the cinema once or twice a week. Should you become ill you have the right to be treated in hospital, and if you have a son he is entitled to receive education at a school. I know, my son, that you hate dark streets and like to see electric light shining out into the night. I know, too, that you are not enamoured of walking and that riding donkeys gives you a bruise on your backside. Oh, I wish, my son, I wish— the asphalted roads of the towns—the modern means of trans- port—the fine comfortable buses. We have none of all this—we are people who live on what God sees fit to give us.

Tomorrow you will depart from our village, of this I am sure, and you will be right to do so. What have you to do with such hardship? We are thick-skinned people and in this we differ from others. We have become used to this hard life, in fact we like it, but we ask no one to subject himself to the difficulties of our life. Tomorrow you will depart, my son—I know that. Before you leave, though, let me show you one thing—something which, in a manner of speaking, we are proud of. In the towns you have museums, places in which the local history and the great deeds of the past are preserved. This thing that I want to show you can be said to be a museum. It is one thing we insist our visitors should see.

Once a preacher, sent by the government, came to us to stay for a month. He arrived at a time when the horse-flies had never been fatter. On the very first day the man's face swelled up. He bore this manfully and joined us in evening prayers on the second night, and after prayers he talked to us of the delights of the primi- tive life. On the third day he was down with malaria, he con- tracted dysentery, and his eyes were completely gummed up. I visited him at noon and found him prostrate in bed, with a boy standing at his head waving away the flies.

'O Sheikh,' I said to him, 'there is nothing in our village to show you, though I would like you to see the doum tree of Wad Hamid.' He didn't ask me what Wad Hamid's doum tree was, but I presumed that he had heard of it, for who has not? He raised his face which was like the lung of a slaughtered cow; his eyes (as I said) were firmly closed, though I knew that behind the lashes there lurked a certain bitterness.

'By God,' he said to me, 'if this were the doum tree of Jandal, and you the Moslems who fought with Ali and Mu'awiya, and I the arbitrator between you, holding your fate in these two hands of mine, I would not stir an inch!' and he spat upon the ground as though to curse me and turned his face away. After that we heard that the Sheikh had cabled to those who had sent him, saying: 'The horse-flies have eaten into my neck, malaria has burnt up my skin, and dysentery has lodged itself in my bowels. Come to my rescue, may God bless you—these are people who are in no need of me or of any other preacher.' And so the man departed and the government sent us no preacher after him.

But, my son, our village actually witnessed many great men of power and influence, people with names that rang through the country like drums, whom we never even dreamed would ever come here—they came, by God, in droves.

We have arrived. Have patience, my son, in a little while there will be the noonday breeze to lighten the agony of this pest upon your face.

Here it is: the doum tree of Wad Hamid. Look how it holds its head aloft to the skies; look how its roots strike down into the earth; look at its full, sturdy trunk, like the form of a comely woman, at the branches on high resembling the mane of a frolic-some steed! In the afternoon, when the sun is low, the doum tree casts its shadow from this high mound right across the river so that someone sitting on the far bank can rest in its shade. At dawn, when the sun rises, the shadow of the tree stretches across the cultivated land and houses right up to the cemetery. Don't you think it is like some mythical eagle spreading its wings over the village and everyone in it? Once the government, wanting to put through an agricultural scheme, decided to cut it down: they said that the best place for setting up the pump was where the doum tree stood. As you can see, the people of our village are concerned solely with their everyday needs and I cannot remember their ever having rebelled against anything. However, when they heard about cutting down the doum tree they all rose up as one man and barred the district commissioner's way. That was in the time of foreign rule. The flies assisted them too—the horse-flies. The man was surrounded by the clamouring people shouting that if the doum tree were cut down they would fight the government to the last man, while the flies played havoc with the man's face. As his papers were scattered in the water we heard him cry out: 'All right—doum tree stay—scheme no stay!' And so neither the pump nor the scheme came about and we kept our doum tree.

Let us go home, my son, for this is no time for talking in the open. This hour just before sunset is a time when the army of sand-flies becomes particularly active before going to sleep. At such a time no one who isn't well-accustomed to them and has become as thick-skinned as we are can bear their stings. Look at it, my son, look at the doum tree: lofty, proud, and haughty as though—as though it were some ancient idol. Wherever you happen to be in the village you can see it; in fact, you can even see it from four villages away.

Tomorrow you will depart from our village, of that there is no doubt, the mementoes of the short walk we have taken visible upon your face, neck and hands. But before you leave I shall finish the story of the tree, the doum tree of Wad Hamid. Come in, my son, treat this house as your own.

You ask who planted the doum tree?

No one planted it, my son. Is the ground in which it grows arable land? Do you not see that it is stony and appreciably higher than the river bank, like the pedestal of a statue, while the river twists and turns below it like a sacred snake, one of the ancient gods of the Egyptians? My son, no one planted it. Drink your tea, for you must be in need of it after the trying experience you have undergone. Most probably it grew up by itself, though no one remembers having known it other than as you now find it. Our sons opened their eyes to find it commanding the village. And we, when we take ourselves back to childhood memories, to that dividing line beyond which you remember nothing, see in our minds a giant doum tree standing on a river bank; everything beyond it is as cryptic as talismans, like the boundary between day and night, like that fading light which is not the dawn but the light directly preceding the break of day. My son, do you find that you can follow what I say? Are you aware of this feeling I have within me but which I am powerless to express? Every new generation finds the doum tree as though it had been born at the time of their birth and would grow up with them. Go and sit with the people of this village and listen to them recounting their dreams. A man awakens from sleep and tells his neighbour how he found himself in a vast sandy tract of land, the sand as white as pure silver; how his feet sank in as he walked so that he could only draw them out again with difficulty; how he walked and walked until he was overcome with thirst and stricken with hunger, while the sands stretched endlessly around him; how he climbed a hill and on reaching the top espied a dense forest of doum trees with a single tall tree in the centre which in comparison with the others looked like a camel amid a herd of goats; how the man went down the hill to find that the earth seemed to be rolled up before him so that it was but a few steps before he found himself under the doum tree of Wad Hamid; how he then discovered a vessel containing milk, its surface still fresh with froth, and how the milk did not go down though he drank until he had quenched his thirst. At which his neighbour says to him, 'Rejoice at release from your troubles.'

You can also hear one of the women telling her friend: 'It was as though I were in a boat sailing through a channel in the sea, so narrow that I could stretch out my hands and touch the shore on either side. I found myself on the crest of a mountainous wave which carried me upwards till I was almost touching the clouds, then bore me down into a dark, fathomless pit. I began shouting in my fear, but my voice seemed to be trapped in my throat. Suddenly I found the channel opening out a little. I saw that on the two shores were black, leafless trees with thorns, the tips of which were like the heads of hawks. I saw the two shores closing in upon me and the trees seemed to be walking towards me. I was filled with terror and called out at the top of my voice, "O Wad Hamid!" As I looked I saw a man with a radiant face and a heavy white beard flowing down over his chest, dressed in spotless white and holding a string of amber prayer-beads. Placing his hand on my brow he said: "Be not afraid," and I was calmed. Then I found the shore opening up and the water flowing gently. I looked to my left and saw fields of ripe corn, water-wheels turning, and cattle grazing, and on the shore stood the doum tree of Wad Hamid. The boat came to rest under the tree and the man got out, tied up the boat, and stretched out his hand to me. He then struck me gently on the shoulder with the string of beads, picked up a doum fruit from the ground and put it in my hand. When I turned round he was no longer there.'

'That was Wad Hamid,' her friend then says to her, 'you will have an illness that will bring you to the brink of death, but you will recover. You must make an offering to Wad Hamid under the doum tree.'

So it is, my son, that there is not a man or woman, young or old, who dreams at night without seeing the doum tree of Wad Hamid at some point in the dream.

You ask me why it was called the doum tree of Wad Hamid and who Wad Hamid was. Be patient, my son—have another cup of tea.

At the beginning of home rule a civil servant came to inform us that the government was intending to set up a stopping-place for the steamer. He told us that the national government wished to help us and to see us progress, and his face was radiant with enthusiasm as he talked. But he could see that the faces around him expressed no reaction. My son, we are not people who travel very much, and when we wish to do so for some important matter such as registering land, or seeking advice about a matter of divorce, we take a morning's ride on our donkeys and then board the steamer from the neighbouring village. My son, we have grown accustomed to this, in fact it is precisely for this reason that we breed donkeys. It is little wonder, then, that the government official could see nothing in the people's faces to indicate that they were pleased with the news. His enthusiasm waned and, being at his wit's end, he began to fumble for words.

'Where will the stopping-place be?' someone asked him after a period of silence. The official replied that there was only one suitable place—where the doum tree stood. Had you that instant brought along a woman and had her stand among those men as naked as the day her mother bore her, they could not have been more astonished.

'The steamer usually passes here on a Wednesday,' one of the men quickly replied; 'if you made a stopping-place, then it would be here on Wednesday afternoon.' The official replied that the time fixed for the steamer to stop by their village would be four o'clock on Wednesday afternoon.

'But that is the time when we visit the tomb of Wad Hamid at the doum tree,' answered the man; 'when we take our women and children and make offerings. We do this every week.' The official laughed. 'Then change the day!' he replied. Had the official told these men at that moment that every one of them was a bastard, that would not have angered them more than this remark of his. They rose up as one man, bore down upon him, and would certainly have killed him if I had not intervened and snatched him from their clutches. I then put him on a donkey and told him to make good his escape.

And so it was that the steamer still does not stop here and that we still ride off on our donkeys for a whole morning and take the steamer from the neighbouring village when circumstances require us to travel. We content ourselves with the thought that we visit the tomb of Wad Hamid with our women and children and that we make offerings there every Wednesday as our fathers and fathers' fathers did before us.

Excuse me, my son, while I perform the sunset prayer—it is said that the sunset prayer is 'strange': if you don't catch it in time it eludes you. *God's pious servants—I declare that there is no god but God and I declare that Mohamed is His Servant and His Prophet—Peace be upon you and the mercy of God!*

Ah, ah. For a week this back of mine has been giving me pain. What do you think it is, my son? I know, though, it's just old age. Oh to be young! In my young days I would breakfast off half a sheep, drink the milk of five cows for supper, and be able to lift a sack of dates with one hand. He lies who says he ever beat me at wrestling. They used to call me 'the crocodile'. Once I swam the river, using my chest to push a boat loaded with wheat to the other shore—at night! On the shore were some men at work at their water-wheels, who threw down their clothes in terror and fled when they saw me pushing the boat towards them.

'Oh people,' I shouted at them, 'what's wrong, shame upon you! Don't you know me? I'm "the crocodile". By God, the devils themselves would be scared off by your ugly faces.'

My son, have you asked me what we do when we're ill?

I laugh because I know what's going on in your head. You townsfolk hurry to the hospital on the slightest pretext. If one of you hurts his finger you dash off to the doctor who puts a bandage on and you carry it in a sling for days; and even then it doesn't get better. Once I was working in the fields and something bit my finger—this little finger of mine. I jumped to my feet and looked around in the grass where I found a snake lurking. I swear to you it was longer than my arm. I took hold of it by the head and crushed it between two fingers, then bit into my finger, sucked out the blood, and took up a handful of dust and rubbed it on the bite.

But that was only a little thing. What do we do when faced with real illness?

This neighbour of ours, now. One day her neck swelled up and she was confined to bed for two months. One night she had a heavy fever, so at first dawn she rose from her bed and dragged herself along till she came—yes, my son, till she came to the doum tree of Wad Hamid. The woman told us what happened.

'I was under the doum tree,' she said, 'with hardly sufficient strength to stand up, and called out at the top of my voice: "O Wad Hamid, I have come to you to seek refuge and protection— I shall sleep here at your tomb and under your doum tree. Either you let me die or you restore me to life; I shall not leave here until one of these two things happens."

'And so I curled myself up in fear,' the woman continued with her story, 'and was soon overcome by sleep. While midway between wakefulness and sleep I suddenly heard sounds of recitation from the Koran and a bright light, as sharp as a knife-edge, radiated out, joining up the two river banks, and I saw the doum tree prostrating itself in worship. My heart throbbed so violently that I thought it would leap up through my mouth. I saw a venerable old man with a white beard and wearing a spotless white robe come up to me, a smile on his face. He struck me on the head with his string of prayer-beads and called out: "Arise."

'I swear that I got up I know not how and went home I know not how. I arrived back at dawn and woke up my husband, my son, and my daughters. I told my husband to light the fire and make tea. Then I ordered my daughters to give trilling cries of joy, and the whole village prostrated themselves before us. I swear that I have never again been afraid, nor yet ill.'

Yes, my son, we are people who have no experience of hospitals. In small matters such as the bites of scorpions, fever, sprains, and fractures, we take to our beds until we are cured. When in serious trouble we go to the doum tree.

Shall I tell you the story of Wad Hamid, my son, or would you like to sleep? Townsfolk don't go to sleep till late at night—I know that of them. We, though, go to sleep directly the birds are silent, the flies stop harrying the cattle, the leaves of the trees settle down, the hens spread their wings over their chicks, and the goats turn on their sides to chew the cud. We and our animals are alike: we rise in the morning when they rise and go to sleep when they sleep, our breathing and theirs following one and the same pattern.

My father, reporting what my grandfather had told him, said: 'Wad Hamid, in times gone by, used to be the slave of a wicked man. He was one of God's holy saints but kept his faith to himself, not daring to pray openly lest his wicked master should kill him. When he could no longer bear his life with this infidel he

called upon God to deliver him and a voice told him to spread
his prayer-mat on the water and that when it stopped by the shore
he should descend. The prayer-mat put him down at the place
where the doum tree is now and which used to be waste land.
And there he stayed alone, praying the whole day. At nightfall a
man came to him with dishes of food, so he ate and continued his
worship till dawn.'

All this happened before the village was built up. It is as though
this village, with its inhabitants, its water-wheels and buildings,
had become split off from the earth. Anyone who tells you he
knows the history of its origin is a liar. Other places begin by being
small and then grow larger, but this village of ours came into being
at one bound. Its population neither increases nor decreases, while
its appearance remains unchanged. And ever since our village has
existed, so has the doum tree of Wad Hamid; and just as no one
remembers how it originated and grew, so no one remembers how
the doum tree came to grow in a patch of rocky ground by the
river, standing above it like a sentinel.

When I took you to visit the tree, my son, do you remember the
iron railing round it? Do you remember the marble plaque standing on a stone pedestal with 'The doum tree of Wad Hamid'
written on it? Do you remember the doum tree with the gilded
crescents above the tomb? They are the only new things about
the village since God first planted it here, and I shall now recount
to you how they came into being.

When you leave us tomorrow—and you will certainly do so,
swollen of face and inflamed of eye—it will be fitting if you do not
curse us but rather think kindly of us and of the things that I have
told you this night, for you may well find that your visit to us was
not wholly bad.

You remember that some years ago we had Members of Parliament and political parties and a great deal of to-ing and fro-ing
which we couldn't make head or tail of. The roads would sometimes cast down strangers at our very doors, just as the waves of
the sea wash up strange weeds. Though not a single one of them
prolonged his stay beyond one night, they would nevertheless bring
us the news of the great fuss going on in the capital. One day they
told us that the government which had driven out imperialism
had been substituted by an even bigger and noisier government.

'And who has changed it?' we asked them, but received no

answer. As for us, ever since we refused to allow the stopping-place to be set up at the doum tree no one has disturbed our tranquil existence. Two years passed without our knowing what form the government had taken, black or white. Its emissaries passed through our village without staying in it, while we thanked God that He had saved us the trouble of putting them up. So things went on till, four years ago, a new government came into power. As though this new authority wished to make us conscious of its presence, we awoke one day to find an official with an enormous hat and small head, in the company of two soldiers, measuring up and doing calculations at the doum tree. We asked them what it was about, to which they replied that the government wished to build a stopping-place for the steamer under the doum tree.

'But we have already given you our answer about that,' we told them. 'What makes you think we'll accept it now?'

'The government which gave in to you was a weak one,' they said, 'but the position has now changed.'

To cut a long story short, we took them by the scruffs of their necks, hurled them into the water, and went off to our work. It wasn't more than a week later when a group of soldiers came along commanded by the small-headed official with the large hat, shouting, 'Arrest that man, and that one, and that one,' until they'd taken off twenty of us, I among them. We spent a month in prison. Then one day the very soldiers who had put us there opened the prison gates. We asked them what it was all about but no one said anything. Outside the prison we found a great gathering of people; no sooner had we been spotted than there were shouts and cheering and we were embraced by some cleanly-dressed people, heavily scented and with gold watches gleaming on their wrists. They carried us off in a great procession, back to our own people. There we found an unbelievably immense gathering of people, carts, horses, and camels. We said to each other, 'The din and flurry of the capital has caught up with us.' They made us twenty men stand in a row and the people passed along it shaking us by the hand: the Prime Minister—the President of the Parliament—the President of the Senate—the member for such and such constituency—the member for such and such other constituency.

We looked at each other without understanding a thing of

what was going on around us except that our arms were aching
with all the handshakes we had been receiving from those Presi-
dents and Members of Parliament.

Then they took us off in a great mass to the place where the
doum tree and the tomb stand. The Prime Minister laid the foun-
dation stone for the monument you've seen, and for the dome
you've seen, and for the railing you've seen. Like a tornado blowing up for a while and then passing over, so that mighty host disappeared as suddenly as it had come without spending a night in
the village—no doubt because of the horse-flies which, that particular year, were as large and fat and buzzed and whirred as
much as during the year the preacher came to us.

One of those strangers who were occasionally cast upon us in the
village later told us the story of all this fuss and bother.

'The people,' he said, 'hadn't been happy about this government since it had come to power, for they knew that it had got
there by bribing a number of the Members of Parliament. They
therefore bided their time and waited for the right opportunities
to present themselves, while the opposition looked around for something to spark things off. When the doum tree incident occurred
and they marched you all off and slung you into prison, the news-
papers took this up and the leader of the government which had
resigned made a fiery speech in Parliament in which he said:

"To such tyranny has this government come that it has begun to
interfere in the beliefs of the people, in those holy things held most
sacred by them." Then taking a most imposing stance and in a
voice choked with emotion, he said: "Ask our worthy Prime Minister about the doum tree of Wad Hamid. Ask him how it was that
he permitted himself to send his troops and henchmen to desecrate
that pure and holy place!"

'The people took up the cry and throughout the country their
hearts responded to the incident of the doum tree as to nothing
before. Perhaps the reason is that in every village in this country
there is some monument like the doum tree of Wad Hamid which
people see in their dreams. After a month of fuss and shouting and
inflamed feelings, fifty members of the government were forced
to withdraw their support, their constituencies having warned
them that unless they did so they would wash their hands of them.
And so the government fell, the first government returned to
power and the leading paper in the country wrote: "The doum

tree of Wad Hamid has become the symbol of the nation's awakening." '

Since that day we have been unaware of the existence of the new government and not one of those great giants of men who visited us has put in an appearance; we thank God that He has spared us the trouble of having to shake them by the hand. Our life returned to what it had been: no water-pump, no agricultural scheme, no stopping-place for the steamer. But we kept our doum tree which casts its shadow over the southern bank in the afternoon and, in the morning, spreads its shadow over the fields and houses right up to the cemetery, with the river flowing below it like some sacred legendary snake. And our village has acquired a marble monument, an iron railing, and a dome with gilded crescents.

When the man had finished what he had to say he looked at me with an enigmatic smile playing at the corners of his mouth like the faint flickerings of a lamp.

'And when,' I asked, 'will they set up the water-pump, and put through the agricultural scheme and the stopping-place for the steamer?'

He lowered his head and paused before answering me, 'When people go to sleep and don't see the doum tree in their dreams.'

'And when will that be?' I said.

'I mentioned to you that my son is in the town studying at school,' he replied. 'It wasn't I who put him there; he ran away and went there on his own, and it is my hope that he will stay where he is and not return. When my son's son passes out of school and the number of young men with souls foreign to our own increases, then perhaps the water-pump will be set up and the agricultural scheme put into being—maybe then the steamer will stop at our village—under the doum tree of Wad Hamid.'

'And do you think,' I said to him, 'that the doum tree will one day be cut down?' He looked at me for a long while as though wishing to project, through his tired, misty eyes, something which he was incapable of doing by word.

'There will not be the least necessity for cutting down the doum tree. There is not the slightest reason for the tomb to be removed. What all these people have overlooked is that there's plenty of room for all these things: the doum tree, the tomb, the water-pump, and the steamer's stopping-place.'

When he had been silent for a time he gave me a look which I don't know how to describe, though it stirred within me a feeling of sadness, sadness for some obscure thing which I was unable to define. Then he said: 'Tomorrow, without doubt, you will be leaving us. When you arrive at your destination, think well of us and judge us not too harshly.'

Mother of the Destitute[*]

YAHYA HAKKI

PRAISED BE He whose dominion extends over all creatures and who knows no opposition to His rule. Here I have no wish but to recount the story of Ibrahim Abu Khalil as he made his way down the steps of life, like the leaves of spring, which, though lifted a little by the wind, contain, even at their height, their ineluctable descent until at last they are cushioned and trampled down into the earth. I was a witness to his descending the last steps of the ladder, but I only learnt later that he was an orphan and had been cast out upon the world at an early age; as to whether he came from the town or the country I know not, though my belief is that he was a city creature born and bred. His life of misery started with being a servant, and then a vendor of lupine on a hand-cart hung round with earthenware water-coolers from Kena, their necks decorated with flowers and sweet basil. I heard that later he had opened a small herbalist's, after which he had gone back again to being a street-vendor, jumping from tram to tram with his pins, needles for primus stoves, and clothes-pegs. His life contained sporadic periods about which I have no information, though I am inclined to think that during his roving existence he must at times have known the sting of asphalt in the Kora Maidan penitentiary.

Just before I got to know him he used to occupy the triangular corner of pavement in the Square facing the shop of the Turk who sold *halva*. There he would sit with a basket containing radishes, watercress, and leeks. His cry was simply, 'Tender radishes, fine watercress!' His face told of none of the various upheavals he'd been through or the buffetings he had had in his innumerable occupations. Such people take life as it comes; each day has its individual destiny, each day passes away and dies—like them—

---

[*] The name given to Sayyida Zeynab, the grand-daughter of the Prophet, who is buried in Cairo and after whom a district is named.

97

without legacy. They enter life's arena with their sensitivity already dead—has it died from ignorance, from stupidity, or from contentment and acceptance? Their eyes do not even blink at the abuse showered down at them. Yet you must not be too hasty in judging in case you should be unfair; had you known him as I did you would have found him a simple-hearted person—genial, polite, and generous.

In spite of the efforts he expended in his search for sufficient food to keep himself alive, his heart knew neither envy nor rancour. His rheumy eyes hinted that in his heart there was a latent propensity for joking and being gay. He had a most captivating way of looking at you; his smile seemed to emerge through veil after veil—just like watching a slow-motion picture of a smile of the eyes being born. When he raised his face, sheltering his eyes with his hand, it would seem to me as if the world had shrunk to this small frame containing just the two of us and that his words were a communion, subdued and private.

Abu Khalil would take up his accustomed place shortly before noon. When afternoon came and the morning basket was sold out, or almost so, he would get up and walk off in his languid way; wandering round the Square, he would pass by many of the shopkeepers, lingering with this one and that as they asked each other how they were getting on, and swapping anecdotes and jokes with some of them. He had a friend from whom he would buy a loaf stuffed with *taamiya* and carry it off tucked under his arm, and another friend from whom he bought the cheapest kind of cigarettes, which he kept in a metal tin above his belt, between his naked body and his outer garment. Then he would leave his friends for the pavement outside the Mosque where (as he put it) he'd enjoy a breath of fresh air—and meet the newcomers of the day. When the novelty had worn off he would return to his place, seat himself, mutter a grace, and eat his meal. Having finished it he would kiss the palm and back of his hand in gratitude, give thanks to God and, settling his body into a relaxed position, light up a cigarette and smoke it with great delight, for he was a man who took his pleasures seriously. Then he would disappear from the Square and not return until just before sunset when he would lay out the evening basket. As for his supper, it consisted of a loaf of bread and a piece of *halva* which he would buy from his neighbour whose shop lay north of his pitch; after which he would vanish from the Square as it became empty of passers-by. I don't know where he slept, though I did hear that he shared a mat with a toothless, bedridden hag in a small room under the curve of some steps at the furthermost end of a steep lane.

Had he ever married? Did he have any children or relations? I don't know. Because of my liking for Abu Khalil I have no wish to talk here of the things I've heard about his strange relationship with that bedridden, evil-smelling old woman (Ibrahim has a kindly heart), nor do I want to talk about the way he was unfaithful to her from time to time, when God provided him with the necessary money and vigour on a hill close by Sayyida, for there is nothing I am more reluctant to do than speak evil of this holy quarter and its inhabitants.

One clear, radiant day Abu Khalil arrived at his customary place on the pavement to find that the far corner was occupied by a woman surrounded by three young children, with a fourth at her breast, its eyes closed in swooning ecstasy as though it were imbibing wine. The catastrophic thing about it was that she was sitting in front of a basket filled with radishes, watercress, and leeks, and when she began calling out, 'Sun-kissed radishes, a *millieme* the bundle!' her piercing voice rang out through the whole Square. O Provider, O Omniscient! For a while Abu Khalil sat watching her in silence, then he sighed and took himself a little way off. He, too, began to call his wares, trying to raise his voice above hers, but he could not do it and broke into a fit of coughing. He wanted to speak to her, to ask her where she came from and why she had chosen this particular place, but she paid no attention to him. With one hand she sold her wares, with the other she managed her children, transferring the drugged infant with a mere bend of her knee from one breast to the other, and then moving towards her water-cooler like a cripple, so that a little of her thigh showed naked. But this had no effect—Abu Khalil's heart was so incensed against her that he was not in an affectionate mood. No doubt, he assured himself, this was but a fleeting intrusion and everything would be all right the next day.

But the following morning he found her there before him as large as life. He began turning his gaze towards her, towards the passers-by and his neighbours, getting up and sitting down again, leaving his basket and going off to tell his friends this depressing piece of news. Then he would return only to find her voice ringing through the Square as though calling together her kin on the fateful Day of Resurrection.

During these days Abu Khalil bought five cigarettes instead of his usual ten.

He was at his wit's end and sought to dispel his anxiety by watching this brazen woman who had trespassed on his pitch and was competing with him in the earning of his daily bread. The strange thing was that he started to become interested in her and tried to exchange smiles with her on one occasion. Days went by and his basket crept closer to Badr's; it was as though he wanted to say to her, 'Come, let's go into partnership together'; but he didn't do it.

Badr felt that she was firmly established and that Ibrahim was powerless against her; she realized that she had gained some sort of hold over him. So, one day, she deigned to reply to him and it was not long before she was bidding him keep an eye on the children when, at a call from nature, she had to go off to the plot of waste land close by the public fountain.

For a long time Abu Khalil neglected his own basket and gave up loafing round with his friends or standing at the door of the Mosque, whether a breeze was blowing or not. A secret hope lay in his heart. Perhaps Badr would prove to be his share of good fortune, rained down unexpectedly upon him by the heavens. Nothing would he love better than to hand over the leading-rein of his life to this resolute woman and to live under her protecting wing. She was a woman (although so much like a man) of whom he would have every reason to boast to all and sundry. He would ingratiate himself with her, would make her laugh so that he might laugh with her, and would wait till she first bit off a mouthful or two from the loaf before she passed it to him and he would eat from where her mouth had been, possibly receiving a taste of her spittle; she it would be who would wake him in the morning and cover him up at night; and when he behaved badly and stayed on with his friends and the shopkeepers, she would search him out and drag him back to where he ought to be. It was thus that he talked to himself. But would he ever broach the matter to her? He wouldn't dare, for he knew nothing about her and there was no one in the Square who knew her.

At this time Abu Khalil bought the *taamiya* for his lunch on credit.

One evening when his basket had drawn so close to hers that they were touching, Badr—without being asked—told him about her life. And thus it was that she too became one of the problems which it had been decreed should fall to Ibrahim's lot in this world. She told him that she was free yet not divorced, married yet living as a widow, for she had a husband of whose whereabouts she was ignorant, a man from Upper Egypt who used to carry a large bundle of vests, socks, and towels on his back, hawking them round the cafés. He would stay with her for a time and then suddenly disappear; on one occasion she had heard that he had gone to Lower Egypt, on another to the south, not knowing whether he was running away from her or from the fear of an old blood-feud, or whether he himself had a blood-feud which honour forced him to pursue. Almost a year and a half having passed since his last disappearance, she did not know whether he was dead or alive—though the odds were that he was alive and well, because the news of his death would have reached her, as he had his name and that of his village tattooed on his arm. Or had they perhaps skinned his body? Was he a murderer lingering in prison, or had he been murdered and was lying in some grave unknown to her? He had just disappeared, leaving her with her children. She had gone out in search of her daily bread and chance had led her to a good man like Ibrahim Abu Khalil.

More days passed and they grew closer. Badr began to feel tenderly for Ibrahim and would buy him food without asking for money, for she had amalgamated their baskets, while both their earnings had landed up in her pocket. She felt that her life had finally taken on this particular form. One day, accepting her position (and don't ask if it was from choice or necessity, it being no easy matter to find another Upper Egyptian to replace the absent man), she said to Ibrahim, 'Your *galabia* is dirty. Come with me tonight and I'll wash it for you.'

Abu Khalil was sitting in front of her, his back to the road. He began talking to her, oblivious of the passing of people and of time. Could he believe his eyes or were they playing him tricks? It seemed to him that her lips suddenly trembled, her teeth gleamed and her eyes, wide open, were sparkling. Her glance was glued to a spot behind him. He turned and found an Upper Egyptian, his back bowed under a large bundle, coming towards them with measured gait. It needed but one glance to tell him that this was a hard and merciless man, one who couldn't be trifled with. The man lowered his burden, squatted down, and wiped away the sweat from his brow.

'How are you?' was all he had to say to Badr.

'Everything is well,' she answered. 'Thank God for your safe return!'

The young Upper Egyptian was silent for a while. Then, turning his head, he directed but one glance at Abu Khalil. Reassured, he turned to his wife and said:

'Everything comes to pass in time, but patience is good.'

Poor Ibrahim rose, shaking the dust from his backside, and disappeared from their sight, swallowed up by the crowds in the Square.

Many days passed during which I didn't see him. Some say that he was taken ill with fever, others that the old bedridden woman had learnt about Badr and had put something into his food—something which she had had to wait for till nature took its course with a woman younger than herself—and that this had caused him grievous harm.

For a long time I was absent from the Square and its inhabitants. When I returned and passed by the pavement facing the Turk who sold *halva*, I found neither Badr of the many offspring nor Ibrahim.

Then one day it chanced that I went out early on some business or other and entered the Square before the shops had opened. My teeth were chattering with the cold, for we were then in the Coptic month of Touba which is proverbially the peak of winter. Barefooted beings thrust their swollen fingers under their armpits and walked as though treading on thorns; from time to time a harsh, raucous cough rang through the Square, followed by silence; then muttered scraps of conversation could be clearly heard from voices still heavy with sleep and phlegm. In spite of all the people to be seen coming and going, one couldn't help having the sensation of being in a deserted city, which neither knew, nor was known by, those passers-by. Suddenly I bumped into Ibrahim Abu Khalil: his clothes were tattered and torn, his head and feet bare, his walk a sort of totter, though his sombre manner of looking at one was the same as ever, and his smile unchanged.

He had gone out at this early hour to do his job, which had to be finished before traffic unfolded in the Square. He had a new occupation: providing incense—a job requiring no more than a pair of old scales, a thick chain, sawdust, and a few bits of frankincense and wormwood. These, together with chunks of bread, he would put into a nose-bag slung round his shoulder, into which some *millieme* and *half-millieme* pieces had perhaps also been thrown.

The moment I saw him I realized that this was the occupation to which Abu Khalil had been born. I should have expected him to have ended up in it, for it suited his temperament admirably, being an easy job that provides its practitioners with the pleasures of loafing about and coming across all kinds and descriptions of people. Besides which the earnings were steady—being in the form of subscriptions—and there was no fixed price. He was his own master and there was no fear of his goods spoiling in case business was bad. While a man in such an occupation would admit that he does not attain the status of those pedlars who gain their livelihood with the sweat of their brow, he cannot on the other hand be accused of mendicancy, for there he is in front of you, going off to work with the tools of his trade in his hand.

If this was how this occupation was regarded by the majority of those practising it, it was something altogether different in Abu Khalil's view. He had tired of trade in its various forms, having found it to be a tug-of-war of deceit, calculation, and endless haggling over *milliemes*. The incense business, however, was based solely on emotion, and he was confident that his greeting, with which shopkeepers would begin their day, was bound to be auspicious, emanating from a heart which was pure, devout, and affectionate. Poor Abu Khalil! he understood neither life nor the nature of human beings.

For many days after this I was often in his company, and saw with my own eyes Master Hassan the barber (who was no simpleton!) unwilling to pay him his *millieme* until he'd dragged him into the shop to fumigate the chair, the mirror, and the small brass basin with its edge cut away to allow for the customer's neck; I also saw the owner of *The National Restaurant* pick him out a single *taamiya* left over from yesterday or the day before; as for the Turk he would give him a *millieme*, irritated and resentful, and send him packing. When most of the shopkeepers had got used to him, they would give him the *millieme* whether there was any incense floating upwards or not, and so Abu Khalil became negligent about his business and his coals were dead for the greater part of the morning; or, if there was a faint glow, all that issued forth was an evil-smelling black smoke repellent to the nostrils.

One clear, radiant day I was walking beside Ibrahim when I felt a sudden hush descend on the Square, just as the weather grows calm before the advent of a cyclone and the eye imagines that the sky is quivering like a bat's wing. Then a man with hawk-like eyes approached from Marasina Street, wearing a garment made up of seventy patches, a green turban on his head, and with a brisk, determined, indefatigable gait; his body erect, his tongue unceasingly chanting prayers and supplications, holding a brazier from which rose beautifully fragrant smoke, the brazier's chain sparkling yellow. O Provider, O Omniscient!

On the first day the shopkeepers sharply repulsed this newcomer, for they were Abu Khalil's customers and it wasn't reasonable to buy two blessings, one of which might spoil the other, on the same morning. But when he returned on the second, the third, and the fourth day, he received his first *milliemes*. Then he did the rounds of all the shops once again, whether the owner had had pity on him or not. I was fascinated by this man's perseverance and strength of purpose. Leaving my bleary-eyed friend, I went off after this extraordinary newcomer and found myself being dragged along at a brisk pace from Sayyida Zeynab to Bab al-Khalk Square, to the Citadel and thence to Sayyida A'isha and across the Cemetery to Sayyida Nafisa and so to Suyoufiyya and Khayamiyya and Mitwalli Gate. Then he went to a small café in Sayyida Hussein where he took off his green turban and sat down to smoke a *narghile*. Breathless and dripping with sweat, I sat down beside him, having seen how he had walked for a whole hour to get one customer. Never in my life have I met anyone who strove to earn his living with the perseverance, patience, and energy of that man.

Poor Ibrahim left his brazier and began to content himself with passing by the shopkeepers empty-handed, in the hope that they would remember him and dispense their usual charity. His income decreased and he was sometimes forced to stand in the middle of the Square, or at the Sayyida Zeynab Gate, so that some visitors might press their charity into his hand, taking him for a beggar too shy to ask for alms. The strange thing was that after a while Abu Khalil worked up a clientele of a few faithful customers who would search him out to give him what they could. Poor Abu Khalil! he understood neither life nor the nature of human beings.

One clear, radiant day as poor Ibrahim sat in his accustomed place, a loud shout rang out close by him which echoed through the whole Square: 'The Everliving! The Eternal!' People gathered round a man who had fallen down in a trance, seized by religious ecstasy. A woman, dressed in a black gown, yellow mules, and a necklace of large amber beads, stood at his head and broke out into trilling cries. The stricken man came to, but his mouth was closed and he uttered not a word; his squinting eyes, darkened with kohl, stared round at the faces of those gathered about him and filled with tears. Then he raised his hands, loaded with blue, green, and red rings, wiped his face, and prepared to gather up the money.

When Abu Khalil heard that very same scream at the very same hour on the second and third day, he left his place and turned towards the Mosque, mumbling:

'O Mother of the Destitute! Give me succour!'

He had tired of life; illness and weakness held him in their grip. The film on his eyes had grown worse, and his back was bowed. With heavy steps he moved towards the shrine of the Mother of the Destitute; around it were ranks of squatting beggars—it seemed as though they had been created like that, their backs propped against its wall, making a circle like lice round a poor man's collar. Little hope for him to find himself a place in the 'first-class' by the door! So he left and went round the Mosque till he came to the place of ablution, where he sat himself down by its door. Those who had come before him and had seniority turned and gave him a withering look: nobody hates a beggar like a beggar.

Here I left Abu Khalil and dissociated myself from him, for he had joined the people of a world which is not our world. He was in a world from which there was no exit; it had but one entrance and above it was written—'The Gate of Farewell'.

The Picture

LATIFA EL-ZAYAT

AMAL'S EYES came to rest on the spray that left behind it, against the horizon, a zigzag thread of sunrays in the colours of the rainbow: a marvellous spectrum which could scarcely be seen unless one tilted one's head at a particular angle and looked hard. She pointed it out to her husband facing her across the table in the Casino overlooking the meeting-place of sea and Nile at Ras al-Barr. He could not see it. If only he could have. The spectrum disappears when it's really there, then one imagines it to be there when in fact it has disappeared with the waves rolling away from the rocks of the promontory known as *The Tongue* which juts out at this spot. The waves of the sea start butting against the rock once more and the spray resumes its upward surge.

'There it is, Izzat,' Amal shouted in her excitement, and her son Midhat grasped the hem of her dress and followed her gaze.

'Where?—Mummy—where?' he said in disjointed words that didn't ripen into a sentence.

The look of boredom faded from Izzat's eyes and he burst out laughing. An effendi, wearing a tarboosh and suit complete with waistcoat, shouted: 'Double five, my dear sir, double five,' and rapped the board with the backgammon pieces, at which the fat man swallowed his spittle and pulled aside the front of his fine white damascene *galabia* to mop away the sweat. An old photographer wearing a black suit jogged his young assistant, who was taking a nap leaning against the developing bucket. The seller of tombola tickets, brushing the sand from his bare feet, called out: 'Couldn't *you* be the lucky one?' Amal gave her shy, apologetic smile and then she was overcome by infectious laughter so that she burst out laughing without knowing why. Suddenly she stopped as she realized she was happy.

'Daddy—food—Mummy—ice cream!'

Izzat turned round in search of the waiter. His gaze became riveted to the Casino entrance and he smiled, turning down his thick, moist lower lip. His hand stretched out mechanically and undid another of the buttons of his white shirt, revealing a wider expanse of thick hair on his chest.

The table behind Amal was taken over by a woman of about thirty who was wearing shorts that exposed her white rounded thighs, while her blonde dyed hair was tied round with a red georgette handkerchief decorated with white jasmine, and another woman of about fifty the front of whose dress revealed a brown expanse of wrinkled bosom. Izzat clapped his hands energetically for the waiter who was actually close enough to have come at a mere sign.

'Three—three ice creams!'

Amal was horrified at her husband's sudden extravagance.

'Two's enough, Izzat,' she whispered, her face flushed. 'I don't really want one.'

Izzat gave no sign of having heard her. He kept repeating, 'Three ices—ice creams—mixed—got it?' in an excited voice.

When the waiter moved away, Izzat called him back again and said, stressing every syllable:

'Make one of them vanilla. Yes, vanilla. Vanilla ice cream!'

Amal relaxed, smiling triumphantly. 'Where is it all coming from?' her mother had asked her. 'Surely not from the fifteen pounds a month he earns? Have you been saving? No wonder, poor thing, your hands are all cracked with washing and you're nothing but skin and bone. What a shame he doesn't understand and appreciate you properly. He's leading you a dog's life while he gallivants around.'

Amal pursed her lips derisively. She and Izzat together, at last, really on holiday at a hotel in Ras al-Barr! A fortnight without cooking or washing or polishing, no more waiting up for him, no more of that sweltering heat. She bent her head back proudly as she swept back a lock of jet black hair from her light brown forehead. She caught sight of Izzat's eyes and felt her throat constrict: once again the fire was in those eyes that had become as though sightless, that hovered over things but never settled on them. He had begun to see, his eyes sparkling anew with that fire that was both captivating and submissive, which both burned and pleaded. That glance of his! She had forgotten it—or had she set out intentionally to forget so that she would not miss it? The fact was that it had come back and it was as if he had never been without it. Was it the summer resort? Was it being on holiday? Anyway it was enveloping her once again in a fever of heat.

Amal noticed Izzat's dark brown hand with its swollen veins and she was swept by an ungovernable longing to bend over and kiss it. The tears welled up in her eyes and she drew Midhat close to her with fumbling hands and covered him with kisses from cheek to ear, hugging him to her, and when the moment of frenzy that had stormed her body died down she released him and began searching for the spectrum of colours through her tears as she inclined her head to one side. She must not be misled: was that really the spectrum, or just a spectrum produced by her tears? . . . 'Tomorrow you'll weep blood instead of tears,' her mother had told her, and her father said: 'You're young, my child, and tomorrow love and all that rubbish will be over and only the drudgery will be left.' Amal shook her head as though driving away a fly that had landed on her cheek and murmured to herself: 'You don't understand at all . . . I . . . I've found the one thing I've been looking for all my life.' Her eyes caught the spectrum and she awoke to a metallic jarring sound as the glass of ice cream scraped against the marble table.

'Three ice creams, two mixed and one vanilla.'

'I'll look after the vanilla, old chap. Vanilla will do me fine,' said Izzat, carefully enunciating his words and giving a significant smile in the direction of—which direction? A suggestive female laugh came back in reply. In reply to the smile? Amal cupped the iced glass in her hands and turned round as she watched him. *White—vanilla—strawberry—pistachio—and the yellow ice? Would it be mango or apricot? Colouring, mere colouring. It can't be—it can't be.*

'Why don't you eat it?' asked Izzat.

She took up the spoon and was about to scoop up the ice cream when she put it down and again cradled the glass in her hand.

Izzat spoke to his son.

'Ice cream tasty, Midhat?'

'Tasty!'

'As tasty as you, my little darling.'

A second laugh rang out behind Amal. Her hands tightened round the iced glass from which cold, icy steam was rising, like smoke. She raised her eyes and reluctantly turned her head without moving her shoulder, slowly lest someone see her, afraid of what she might see. She saw her, *white as a wall, a candle, white as vanilla ice.* For a fleeting moment her eyes met those of the white-skinned woman in the shorts. Her lower lip trembled and she looked back at her glass, drawing herself up. She sat there stiffly, eating. The woman in the shorts took a cigarette from her handbag and left it dangling from her lips until the woman with the bare expanse of bosom had lit it for her. She began to puff out smoke provocatively in Amal's direction, but Amal did not look at her any more. She was a loose woman. Izzat hardly said a word without her laughing. Obviously a loose woman and he wasn't to blame.

Midhat finished eating his ice cream and began glancing around him listlessly, his lips pursed as though he was about to cry.

'*The Tongue*, I want to go to *The Tongue*.'

Amal sighed with relief: a great worry had been removed. This loose woman would be removed from her sight for ever more. She bent her head to one side, smiled, and said carefully as though playing a part before an audience,

'Certainly, darling. Now. Right now Daddy and Mummy'll take Midhat and go to *The Tongue*.'

She pushed back her chair as she gave a short affected laugh.

'Where to?' said Izzat with unwarranted gruffness.

'The child wants to go to *The Tongue*.'

'And where are we going after *The Tongue*? Surely we're not going to suffocate ourselves back at the hotel so early?'

Midhat burst out crying, trammelling the ground with his feet. Amal jumped up, clasping the child to her nervously. *Izzat? Izzat wants to—it's not possible—good God, it's not possible—*Midhat, irked by the violence with which he was being held, intensified his howling.

'Shut up!' Izzat shouted at him.

When Midhat didn't stop, his father jumped up and seized him from his mother's arms, giving him two quick slaps on the hand. Then Izzat sat down again and said, as though justifying himself:

'I won't have a child who's a cry-baby!'

Amal returned to her chair, and the tears ran silently from Midhat's eyes and down to the corners of his mouth. As though she had just woken up, the woman in the shorts said in her drawling husky voice:

'Come along, my sweetheart. Come along to me.' She took a piece of chocolate wrapped in red paper out of her pocket.

'Come, my darling! Come and take the chocolate!'

Amal drew Midhat to her. The woman in the shorts put her head to one side and crossed her legs. Smiling slightly, she threw the piece of chocolate on to the table so that Midhat could see it. Amal cradled Midhat's head against her breast, patting his hair with trembling hands. Midhat lay quietly against his mother's breast for a while; then he lifted an arm to wipe away the tears, and, peeping from under his arm, he began to steal fleeting glances at the chocolate. The woman in the shorts beckoned and winked at him, and Amal buried his head in her breast. *It's not possible, not possible that he would go to her—Izzat—Midhat— it's not possible that Izzat would want her.* With a sudden movement Midhat disengaged himself from his mother's grasp and ran to the neighbouring table. The lewd laugh rang out anew, long and jarring.

'Go and fetch the boy!' Amal whispered, her lips grown blue.

Izzat smiled defiantly. 'Fetch him yourself!'

'We're not beggars,' she said in a choked voice.

'Where does begging come into it? Or do you want the boy to turn out as timid as you?'

Amal didn't look at the table behind her where her son sat on the lap of the woman in shorts eating chocolate and getting it all over his mouth and chin, hands and shirt. She wished that she could take him and beat him till he—but what had he done wrong? The fault was hers, hers alone.

'Good for us; we've finished the chocolate and now—up we get and wash our hands,' the woman in shorts drawled in her husky voice.

Amal jumped to her feet, white-faced. The woman in the shorts went off, waggling her hips as she dragged Midhat along behind her.

Putting a hand on his wife's shoulder, Izzat said softly:

'You stay here while I go and fetch the boy.'

Amal remained standing, watching the two of them: the woman with Midhat holding her hand, the woman and Izzat following her. She watched them as they crossed the balcony of the Casino and—through glass—as they crossed the inner lounge and were lost behind the walls of the building, the woman's buttocks swaying as though detached from her, with Izzat following her, his body tilted forward as though about to pounce. For step after step, step hard upon step, lewd step upon lewd step. 'No, Izzat, don't be like that. You frighten me, you frighten me when you're like that, Izzat.' She had spoken these words as she dropped down exhausted on a rock in the grotto at the Aquarium. Izzat had been out of breath as he said: 'You can't imagine—you can't imagine how much I love you, Amal,' with pursed lips and half-closed eyes, heavy with the look of a cat calling its mate, a look that burned and pleaded. *Izzat and the other woman—and the same look that burned and pleaded . . . It can't be—It can't be.*

'A picture, Madam?'

Amal had collapsed exhausted on the chair, waving the old photographer away. 'No, Izzat—no, don't put your hand on my neck like that! What'll people say when they see the photo? They'll say I'm in love with you—No, please don't.' 'Here you are, Milady, the picture's been taken with my hand on your neck and now you'll never be able to get rid of me.'

'A postcard size for ten piastres and no waiting, Madam.'

'Not now, not now.'

The man went on his way repeating in a listless, lilting voice, 'Family pictures, souvenir pictures,' while behind him the bare-footed tombola ticket-seller wiped his hand on his khaki trousers. 'Why shouldn't yours be the winning one? Three more numbers and we'll have the draw. A fine china tea set for just one piastre. There's a bargain for you!' 'I'm so lucky, Mummy, to have married a real man.' 'A real man? A real bounder, you mean. Work! Work, he says—funny sort of an office that's open till one and two in the morning!' That's what Saber Effendi, their neighbour, had said, and Sitt Saniyya, pouring out the coffee, had remarked, 'You see, my poor child, Saber Effendi's had forty years in government service and there's not much that escapes him.'

Lifting Midhat on to his lap, Izzat said softly:

'The child went on having tantrums before he would wash his hands.'

Amal gave him a cold searching look as though seeing him for the first time. She bent her head and concentrated her gaze on a chocolate stain on Midhat's shirt. Izzat appeared to be completely absorbed by teaching the child to count up to ten. Midhat stretched out his hand and put it over his father's mouth. Izzat smiled and leaned towards Amal.

'You know, you look really smart today—pink suits you wonderfully,' he said.

Her throat constricted as she gave a weak smile. Again the old photographer said:

'A picture of you as a group, sir. It'll be very nice and there's no waiting.'

'No thanks,' said Izzat.

Amal spotted the woman in the shorts coming towards them with her swinging gait.

'Let's have a picture taken,' she said in a choked voice.

'What for?'

Aloof, the woman passed her, looking neither at her nor Izzat. She sat down and started talking to her woman friend.

Amal leaned across to Izzat, the words tumbling from her mouth:

'Let's have a picture taken—you and me—let's!' She pointed a finger at him, a finger at herself, and then brought the two fingers together. With a shrug of his shoulder Izzat said:

'Take your picture, old chap.'

When the photographer had buried his head inside the black hood, Amal stretched out her hand and took hold of her husband's arm; as the photographer gave the signal her hand tightened its grip. Waiting for the photograph, Izzat did not look at the woman, nor she at him. When the photographer came back with the picture, Izzat stood up searching for change.

Amal snatched eagerly at the photograph. She held it in her hand as though afraid that someone would seize it from her. *Izzat at her side—her lover—her husband*—The woman in the shorts pushed back her chair violently as she got to her feet. Passing near to their table, her eyes met those of Amal for a brief instant, fleeting yet sufficient—Amal let the picture fall from her hands. It dropped to the ground, not far from her. Without moving from where she sat she propped her elbows on her thighs and her head in her hands, and proceeded to gaze at it with a cool, expressionless face. The picture of the woman looking up at her was that of a stranger, a feverish woman grasping with feverish hand at the arm of a man whose face expressed pain at being gripped so tightly.

Slowly, calmly, Amal stretched out her leg and dragged the toe of her shoe, and then the heel, across the photograph. Drawing back her leg and bending down again, she scrutinized the picture anew. Though sand had obliterated the main features, certain portions still remained visible: the man's face grimacing with pain, the woman's hand grasping the man's arm. Amal stretched out her leg and drew the picture close to her chair with her foot till it was within arm's reach. She leaned forward and picked it up.

When Izzat returned with change the picture had been torn into small pieces which had scattered to the winds. The spectrum had disappeared and the sun was centrally positioned in the sky, while people were running across the hot sands to avoid burning their feet. Amal realized she had a long way to go.

Miracles for Sale

TEWFIK AL-HAKIM

THE PRIEST woke early as was his wont, preceded only by the birds in their nests, and began his prayers, his devotions, and his work for his diocese in that Eastern land whose spiritual light he was and where he was held in such high esteem by men of religion and in such reverence by the people. Before his door there grew a small palm tree planted by his own hands; he always watered it before sunrise, contemplating the sun as its rim, red as a date, burst forth from the horizon to shed its rays on the dewy leaves, wrapping their falling drops of silver in skeins of gold.

As the priest finished watering the palm tree that morning and was about to return inside, he found himself faced by a crowd of sad and worried-looking people, one of whom plucked up the courage to address him in beseeching tones:

'Father! Save us! No one but you can save us! My wife is on her death-bed and she is asking for your blessing before she breathes her last.'

'Where is she?'

'In a village near by. The mounts are ready,' replied the man, pointing to two saddled donkeys standing there waiting for them.

'I am willing to go, my sons,' said the priest. 'Wait a while so that I may arrange my affairs and tell my brethren and then return to you.'

'There's no time!' they all said as one voice. 'The woman is dying. We may well reach her too late. Come with us right away if you would be a true benefactor to us and a merciful saviour to the dying woman. It is not far and we shall be there and back before the sun reaches its zenith at noon.'

'Well, then, let us go at once!' the priest agreed with enthusiastic fervour. He went up to the two donkeys, followed by the

114

crowd. Mounting him on one of them while the husband of the dying woman mounted the other, they raced off.

For hours on end they pounded the ground with the priest asking where they were bound for and the men goading on the donkey, saying, 'We're almost there!' It wasn't till noon that the village came into sight. They entered it to the accompaniment of barking dogs and the welcome of its inhabitants, and they all made their way to the village hall. They led the priest to a large room where he found a woman stretched out on a bed, her eyes staring up at the ceiling. He called to her, but no reply came from her, for she was at death's door. So he began to call down blessings upon her, and scarcely had he finished when she heaved a great sigh and fell into a deep fit of sobbing, so that the priest thought she was about to give up the ghost.

Instead her eyelids fluttered open, her gaze cleared and she turned and murmured:

'Where am I?'

'You are in your house,' answered the astonished priest.

'Get me a drink of water.'

'Bring the pitcher!' shouted her relatives around her. 'Bring the water jar!'

They raced off and brought back a jug of water from which the woman took a long drink. Then she belched heartily and said:

'Isn't there any food? I'm hungry!'

Everyone in the house set about bringing her food. Under the astonished gaze of those around her the woman began devouring the food; then she got up from her bed and proceeded to walk about the house completely fit and well again. At this the people prostrated themselves before the priest, covering his hands and feet in kisses and shouting, 'O Saint of God! Your blessing has alighted on the house and brought the dead woman back to life! What can we possibly give you as a token of the thanks we owe you, as an acknowledgement of our gratitude?'

'I have done nothing that deserves reward or thanks,' replied the priest, still bewildered by the incident. 'It is God's power that has done it.'

'Call it what you will,' said the master of the house, 'it is at all events a miracle which God wished to be accomplished through your hands, O Saint of God. You have alighted at our lowly abode, and this brings both great honour and good fortune to us.

You must let us undertake the obligations of hospitality in such manner as our circumstances allow.'

He ordered a quiet room to be made ready for his guest and there he lodged him. Whenever the priest asked leave to depart the master of the house swore by all that was most holy to him that he would not allow his auspicious guest to go before three days were up—the very least hospitality which should be accorded to someone who had saved his wife's life. During this time he showed him much attention and honour. When the period of hospitality came to an end he saddled a mount and loaded it up with presents of home-made bread, lentils, and chickens; in addition he pressed five pounds for the church funds in the priest's hand. Hardly had he escorted him to the door and helped him on to the donkey than a man appeared, puffing and out of breath, who threw himself down beside the priest.

'Father,' he pleaded, 'the story of your miracle has reached all the villages around. I have an uncle who is like a father to me and who is at death's door. He is hoping to have your blessing, so let not his soul depart from him before his hope is fulfilled!'

'But, my son, I am all ready to return home', the priest replied uncertainly.

'This is something that won't take any time—I shall not let you go till you've been with me to see my uncle!' The man seized the donkey's reins and led him off.

'And where is this uncle of yours?' asked the priest.

'Very near here—a few minutes' distance.'

The priest saw nothing for it but to comply. They journeyed for an hour before they reached the next village. There he saw a house like the first one with a dying man on a bed, his family around him veering between hope and despair. No sooner had the priest approached and called down his blessing on the patient than the miracle occurred: the dying man rose to his feet calling for food and water. The people, astounded at what had occurred, swore by everything most dear that they must discharge the duties of hospitality towards this holy man—a stay of three full days.

The period of hospitality passed with the priest enjoying every honour and attention. Then, as they were escorting him to the gates of the village loaded down with gifts, a man from a third village came along and asked him to come and visit it, even if only for a little while, and give it the blessing of one whose fame had spread throughout all the district.

The priest was quite unable to escape from the man, who led the donkey off by its bit and brought the priest to a house in his village. There they found a young man who was a cripple; hardly had the priest touched him than he was up and about on his two feet, among the cheers and jubilation of young and old. All the people swore that the duties of hospitality must be accorded to the miracle-maker, which they duly did in fine style; three nights no less, just as the others had done. When this time was up they went to their guest and added yet more presents to those he already had, until his donkey was almost collapsing under them. They also presented him with a more generous gift of money than he had received in the former villages so that he had by now collected close on twenty pounds. He put them in a purse which he hid under his clothes. He then mounted the donkey and asked his hosts to act as an escort for him to his village, so they all set off with him, walking behind his donkey.

'Our hearts shall be your protection, our lives your ransom,' they said. 'We shall not leave you till we have handed you over to your own people: you are as precious to us as gold.'

'I am causing you some inconvenience,' said the priest; 'however, the way is not safe and, as you know, gangs are rife in the provinces.'

'Truly,' they replied, 'hereabouts they kidnap men in broad daylight.'

'Even the government is powerless to remove this widespread evil,' said the priest. 'I was told that gangs of kidnappers waylay buses on country roads, run their eyes over the passengers, and carry off with them anyone at all prosperous-looking so that they can afterwards demand a large ransom from his relatives. Sometimes it happens with security men actually in the buses. I heard that once two policemen were among the passengers on one of these buses when it was stopped by the gang; when the selected passenger appealed for help to the two policemen they were so scared of the robbers that all they said to the kidnapped man was: 'Away with you—and let's get going!'

The people laughed and said to the priest, 'Do not be afraid! So long as you are with us you will dismount only when you arrive safely back in your village.'

'I know how gallant you are! You have overwhelmed me with honour and generosity!'

'Don't say such a thing—you are very precious to us!' They went on walking behind the priest, extolling his virtues and describing in detail his miracles. He listened to their words, and thought about all that had occurred. Finally he exclaimed, 'Truly, it is remarkable the things that have happened to me in these last few days! Is it possible that these miracles are due solely to my blessing?'

'And do you doubt it?'

'I am not a prophet that I should accomplish all that in seven days. Rather is it you who have made me do these miracles!'

'We?' they all said in one voice. 'What do you mean?'

'Yes, you are the prime source.'

'Who told you this?' they murmured, exchanging glances.

'It is your faith,' continued the priest with conviction. 'Faith has made you achieve all this. You do not know the power that lies in the soul of the believer. Faith is a power, my sons! Faith is a power! Miracles are buried deep within your hearts, like water inside rock, and only faith can cause them to burst forth!' He continued talking in this vein while the people behind him shook their heads. He became more and more impassioned and did not notice that they had begun to slink off, one after the other. It was only when he reached the boundaries of his village that he came back to earth, turned round to thank his escort, and was rendered speechless with astonishment at finding himself alone.

His surprise did not last long, for he immediately found his family, his brother priests and superiors rushing towards him, hugging him and kissing his hand, as tears of joy and emotion flowed down their cheeks. One of them embraced him, saying, 'You have returned safely to us at last! They kept their promise. Let them have the money so long as they have given you back, father! To us, father, you are more priceless than any money!'

The priest, catching the word 'money', exclaimed: 'What money?'

'The money we paid to the gang.'

'What gang?'

'The one that kidnapped you. At first they wouldn't be satisfied with less than a thousand pounds, saying that you were worth your weight in gold. We pleaded with them to take half and eventually they accepted, and so we paid them a ransom of five hundred pounds from the Church funds.'

'Five hundred pounds!' shouted the priest. 'You paid that for me!—They told you I'd been kidnapped?'

'Yes, three days after you disappeared some people came to us and said that a gang kidnapped you one morning as you were watering the palm tree by your door. They swore you were doomed unless your ransom was paid to them—if we paid you'd be handed over safe and sound.'

The priest considered these words, recalling to himself all that had occurred.

'Indeed, that explains it' he said, as though talking to himself. 'Those dead people, the sick, and the cripples who jumped up at my blessing! What mastery!'

His relatives again came forward, examining his body and clothes as they said joyfully, 'Nothing is of any consequence, father, except your safety. We hope they didn't treat you badly during your captivity. What did they do to you?'

In bewilderment he answered: 'They made me work miracles —miracles that have cost the Church dear!'

The South Wind

ABDEL MALIK NOURI

SNAKE-LIKE, IT made its wary way through the dry desert, slowly traversing the brown arid wastes. Above, the sun burned hotly, filling the vast empty space with its searing rays. Everything was ablaze under it: the railway tracks that stretched into the desert, the black telegraph poles, the tins abandoned along the line, even the dust itself, that glittering salt-coloured dust covering the earth's surface as far as the eye could see.

The sides and benches of the carriages reflected slivers of light that wrung a hot sticky sweat from the compressed mass of bodies and enveloped everyone in a dazed, sickly drowsiness. Heads nodded and bodies quivered in rhythm with the jolting of the old railway coach. Life itself seemed greyish-white to them, like the mirage that gleamed on far horizons. The salty bitter taste on their lips was their only nourishment across this long, dozing desert.

All the way the wheels kept up their song which reverberated in Khudaira's lolling head: Allahu Akbar, Allahu Akbar, Allahu Akbar. A broad tongue of sunlight thrust down at her through the broken window, extending across to her blind daughter crouched beside her. Everything induced sleep, everything increased the feeling of heavy weariness. From time to time the wheels let out a long unpleasant grating sound and the coaches shuddered as they almost crashed into one another. Sometimes, on the side of the track, small, miserable-looking buildings made their appearance; alongside them loomed an occasional water hydrant, huge in its isolation, from which some of the passengers took a drink or washed their faces before hurrying back to their hard wooden seats. Khudaira, however, never left her place, for with each station the number of passengers increased and she was afraid of losing her seat: it was pilgrimage time and there were many travellers. Packed together, flesh to flesh, some were seated in the corridors, some on the carriage floor. Oh, if only she had had the time she too would have made a pilgrimage to Kerbela and been blessed by touching the dust covering the tomb of Holy Hussein! That would indeed have brought grace and blessings! Only last year Faheema al-Alwan had gone on the pilgrimage and everyone in the village had turned out to welcome her back, the women touching the train of her dress and kissing her hands and feet for good luck. Oh, if only she too could be so honoured, so favoured! It was indeed a great blessing to make a pilgrimage to the Lord of Martyrs and be blessed by the dust of his tomb! What rare fortune that would be! Allahu Akbar. Allahu Akbar. Allahu Akbar—

The limpid south wind crept in through the broken windows, its heat hitting the faces of the passengers. The flies clung tenaciously to moist faces, to hands and eyes and hair, hardly moving, finding rich nourishment in those hot, dusty bodies. Sleep so weighed down their heads that the passengers were hardly aware of the flies or of the dust that covered them, and all the while the wind blew in on their faces, sticky and oozing sweat.

Each time the train gave a jolt Khudaira moved restlessly in her place, wiped the sleep and flies from her sticky eyes, groped about for the fat red cock that crouched in her lap and began talking to her blind daughter about how they'd soon be arriving in the city. Then the train would start up again, its wheels once more taking up their incessant song inside her brain: Allahu Akbar. Allahu Akbar. Allahu Akbar—

He is the Almighty! Glory be to him! Who other is as powerful as He? He quickens the desiccated corpse. How, then, can He be incapable of bringing back sight to the eyes of the blind? Glory be to Him who descends not to earth and Whom no one can see! There He has His seat in the seventh firmament of Heaven, ever wakeful, looking down upon His faithful worshippers, sleeping neither by night nor by day. Who can deny His grace and His blessings? Who can deny those good works wrought by His righteous saints who spend their long lives in worship and seclusion from the world. Glory be to Him! Sheikh Muhyiddin was one of His most virtuous saints who, with His help, was able to open the eyes of the blind and cure the stricken. By merely putting a little of his saliva on a blind man's eyes, he could cause him to see the light and call out in joy to God Almighty, the Great, the All-powerful. Only a few days ago Wadha had called out to her:

'How unfair of you, keeping that beautiful young daughter of yours blind. Take her to the town before the Sheikh leaves.' This same Sheikh Muhyiddin had brought back the sight of Abu Ghuloum, known as 'the ass', who had put tincture of iodine in his eyes so that he might save his son from military service on the grounds of having to look after his helpless father. The whole village had given thanks to God in the name of the Sheikh and had gone out to welcome 'the ass' at the station on his return. Yet, even so, he was always bumping into people and cursing the way the world was crowded. Once, in the market, she had seen him with her own eyes tread on a dog's tail, at which the wretched animal had let out a yelp of pain; she had been standing at the shop of Jal'out the butcher, and he had told her that Abu Ghuloum was in fact still blind but that he knew his way to his house as he'd been living there for fifty years.

Then there was Musai'eeda. Her sight too had been restored by Sheikh Muhyiddin. They say that it had happened one evening just as the sun had gone down. When the Sheikh spat into her eyes, she had opened them and found darkness; then he had ordered her to raise them towards the sky, and with the help of God Almighty she had seen the canopy of the Heavens open and give forth a flaming light. She had fallen down at the Sheikh's feet kissing them fervently, and then fainted. Glory be to God in the Highest! But Musai'eeda had not returned to the village; she had married her relative al-Azzawi and he had taken her off to his people among whom, it was said, he already had three other wives.

'Alas, but what's it to us?'

Sheikh Muhyiddin was indeed a very great saint, his good works well known to all. From the countries of the world, from Sind and India and other parts, people came to him. God willing, His blessings on her and her daughter Khachiyya, on the whole of the Prophet's people, would be manifold. With God's help he would bring back the sight of the poor young girl who now crouched by her side as motionless as a rock. Perhaps she was asleep. How could one tell? Who was to know? Maybe she was asleep, poor thing, she who hadn't slept a wink all night; neither had she, her mother, nor yet Mizher's father. All night long he had tossed and turned on the rug, coughing violently. Khachiyya had said to her: 'Mother, hasn't dawn broken yet?' and the stars had still been shining in the black heavens, while from afar the cocks called to one another.

Suddenly Khudaira remembered the fat red cock nestling in her lap. She gazed at it tenderly and patted its hot back; then she sank back into monotonous melodic drowsiness. Allahu Akbar. Allahu Akbar—

How joyful Khachiyya had been the whole week! She had learnt that she would be going to the town with her mother so that Sheikh Muhyiddin could restore her sight. No longer had she seated herself in her usual place in the doorway morning and evening. She had not known what to do with herself and had spent her time coming and going, back and forth. Never before had her mother seen her in such good spirits, not at a betrothal party, a wedding or circumcision. Never before had she seen her thus. Poor darling. What was it that this sweet young girl lacked? The Lord had deprived her of light and it was within His power to restore it to her. That cousin of hers—that 'dog of a dog'—had not come forward to ask for her hand and now, poor thing, she had passed the age when she could get married. Never would she forget how that 'dog', leaning against the door of the reed hut with the dying sun's rays falling upon his light brown, shaven face, had said, 'Do you want me as a staff for your blind daughter?'

How cruel were these words to her and her old father! Khachiyya had cried for a long time, seated in her dark corner; no tears, though, had appeared in her eyes as she sobbed in silence, conscious of the disgrace she had brought upon her kinsfolk and family. All the other young girls of her age had married, all had produced sons, some already had two or three children.

As Khudaira moaned, the whirlpool of black memories almost carried her off with it, but then the flimsy coach suddenly began to shake and the wheels gave out a long painful screech. A dingy building came into sight at the side of the track: the train had come to a station. Who knows?—perhaps it had arrived at her destination. Khudaira remembered the journey she had made two years ago to this same town. She gave a short glance through the dust-covered window and dozed off again. The pilgrims were swarming into the crowded coaches, piling themselves on to the passengers, filling every empty space in the corridors with their bodies, their heavy luggage, and yet more flies. From here and there curses and shouts rang out, and a hand-to-hand fight developed at the top end of the long coach. Then again the train moved off; everything quietened down; the bodies arranged themselves in a hot, sticky mass, with the south wind blowing in on them from the dusty broken windows as hot as though it had leapt straight from the bowels of a furnace.

The cock, lying in Khudaira's lap, in the folds of her red dress stained with mud and flour, dreamed strange dreams. It had opened one eye with which to regard the red world of her dress, whilst the other remained closed under the heavy hand that pressed down on its back and part of its head. It had no desire to stir, for whenever it shifted or tried to move, the weight of the hand increased. Therefore it remained motionless, awaiting the hour of deliverance. Sometimes it regarded the passengers with its open eye, while inside its small head there revolved memories of a happy yesterday: the grain it had pecked from the open space by the reed hut, the vast expanse in which it was able to roam proudly, the shade of the palm trees, those small delicious tit-bits it would discover secreted in the golden discs of cow dung, the palm branch lying on the ground on which it sported every morning, and the broken strip of wattle wall which it would climb up and from where it would let out its strong crow, so full of youth's vitality. Finally, there was that desirable white hen which it had mounted several times a day, deliciously conscious of its vigour, puffed up with pride and self-confidence. It would dive upon the other cock, its rival, with all its might and main, bowling it over and all but killing it. Now, though, it had no idea where it was being taken or what was to be its fate. It knew nothing, was merely conscious of the strange joltings that startled it from time to time and of that heavy hand that almost prevented it from breathing. But why should it care? Everything has an end and everywhere one could find delicious grain and golden discs of dung, beautiful white hens and weak rivals with whom it was enjoyable to fight, grassy earth and a vast open space. Why worry?

The cock closed its open eye and began listening to the strange confused clatter of life around it. Khudaira's stomach moved regularly up and down and its small heart beat within the folds of her flimsy red dress under her coarse black *aba*. It felt a great, unbearable heat, a heat that almost choked it to death, but it was unable to stir or contemplate moving because of the weight of that heavy hand spread over it like a spider.

Khachiyya had leant her head, bound up in a black band, against her mother's shoulder and had fallen into a deep sleep. Khudaira was dreaming of the city and the miracles performed by Sheikh Muhyiddin. She recalled to mind the journey they had made by donkey that morning; it had been a difficult, tiring journey and it had brought a terrible pain to her back. When the donkey had been crossing the wide stream and its hooves had started to slip on the pebbles scattered about on the river-bed, she had been seized by fear; it had seemed that each moment it would fall, but she had been afraid to utter a word. Her eldest son, Mizher—may his eyes be spared—had chided her whenever she showed any fear. 'Why so frightened about that old bag of bones of yours? You're only an old woman like a worn-out pair of slippers.'

'God bless him, how nervous he is!' But he had a kind heart, as tender as a woman's. He himself had led her donkey when they had had to climb that frighteningly steep precipice. She had collapsed on the neck of the donkey, every limb in her body quivering in terror. She had been frightened, too, for Khachiyya, frightened that she would fall. Thank God it had ended all right. What a wonderful sense of relief had been hers as they threaded their way down the long pass between the orchards where the sun had again shone on them! The air had not yet become hot; it was still deliciously cool and she would have liked to go to sleep as she rode on the donkey. She had not slept the whole night; neither had Khachiyya, nor Mizher's poor father who, between speaking to her from time to time, had had violent spells of coughing. At the door of the reed hut, with the world still in darkness and stars shining in a black sky, he had bidden them farewell. By the time they had reached the station the sun had risen and was scorching them with its heat; they had drunk tea, seated on the floor of that bare ramshackle wattle structure which was the station. When the train arrived her son had handed over the money to her, as well as the spirited red cock.

'Look after it well and when you arrive sell it. They say a cock like this should fetch five *dirhams* in the town.'

This, of course, was to be Sheikh Muhyiddin's fee, the money she'd been given being scarcely enough for the train fare and a day's expenses. Sheikh Muhyiddin never accepted less than five *dirhams*. Wadha had told her that if she offered a single *fils* less the Sheikh would be angry and his magic wouldn't work. In this event her daughter's eyes would not be opened and she would return to the village as blind as she had left it—as had happened to many. The reason for this was that the money given to the Sheikh was used for repairing the graves of saints and it was thus improper to attempt to bargain. If only God would help her to sell the cock in the town for five or six *dirhams*; there were rich people there, 'people of good family and breeding'; one of them would surely buy the cock from her.

Allahu Akbar. Allahu Akbar, Allahu Akbar—

She had not slept the whole night. The south wind blew in on her face as she yawned and her heavy head dropped against the burning side of the coach. Her hand, spread like a spider over the back of the cock, relaxed its grip. The cock opened its eyes and looked round in surprise at the dozing passengers, then it too returned to its slumbers, its small head buried in the folds of the warm, protuberant stomach.

Khudaira smiled at the sweet dreams that were enacted behind her ulcerous eyelids. The flies drank the saliva at the corners of her mouth and gathered round her puss-congealed eyes, covering them with black, clammy wings, and all the while the train continued on its way like a wary serpent, above it the midday sun blazing down and filling with its scorching rays that vast, dead, empty void that stretched unendingly out.

Two years ago she had made the same journey. Then it had not been so crowded. There had been that soldier who had played *dabkeh* songs on a flute, and his companion, the dirty 'good-for-nothing' who danced like a woman. Yes, after tomorrow the two of them would return and, with God's help, Khachiyya's eyes would be opened; through Sheikh Muhyiddin's powers she would be created anew—she would see the sun, the passengers, everything. Poor thing, what had she seen of life? 'Blind, blind,' the boys shouted at her, running back and forth, tapping her on the head while she remained silent, saying not a word. Alone she would sit by the door from sunrise to sunset. Tomorrow a new life would open up before her, if only God would make it possible for her to sell the cock. Khachiyya's cousin would come forward like a cringing dog, but this time, merciful God, a hard bargain would be driven. Where would he find such a young and beautiful girl? Not if he were to search the whole district, not if he were to turn the whole world upside down: tall as the trunk of a palm tree, with her hair down to her knees and a nose as small and delicate as a date. Where would he find the like of Khachiyya? When her sight had been restored, poor darling, everyone would be dazzled by her beauty. How happy Mizher would be, his father and all the children! Mizher would be waiting for them at the station with the donkeys, then would follow that frightening ascent and the stream with the donkey's hooves slipping on the pebbles strewn along its bed. She would not be frightened, though; not this time. And all their friends and loved ones would come out to meet them, the women raising trilling cries of joy to the heavens, and then, in the evening, they'd make Abbas bread for distributing among visitors. If only God would grant them His help in reaching the town!

She was so very tired. Again she yawned. Allahu Akbar. Allahu Akbar—Mizher's father, too, had not slept. How sorry she felt for this old man! Between racking coughs he had told her, 'Bring a handful of dust with you from under the Sheikh's foot for good luck.

'And when, by God's grace, the girl opens her eyes, mind you don't let her look into the sun.

'And the cock, mind you take good care of it and sell it for five *dirhams*.'

A handful of dust. Yes, and two handfuls and more. Though precious, one has only to ask. And Khachiyya laughing under the sun. Allahu Akbar. Allahu Akbar. Allahu Akbar— The train rocking like a cradle, and the soldier blowing his flute and that dirty 'good-for-nothing' shaking his belly like a woman dancer, and the animals waiting in the shade by the tumbledown brick building, everyone joyful, and Mizher bringing them a freshly brewed pot of tea. All their loved ones would be out to greet them. Again she yawned. Oh! how tired she was! And all along the way the wheels sang out: Allahu Akbar, Allahu Akbar, Allahu Akbar, while the wind, heavy and sluggish, weighed down with dust, blew in on them.

Khudaira's head fell forward on to her breast and every part of her sank into sleep; her drugged limbs grew torpid and she snored in deep slumber. The cock raised its small head and looked around in wonder. The heavy hand had fallen from its back into the folds of that stiflingly hot, red dress. It lay in a world that was wholly red, wholly scorching. At times it felt as though it were about to catch fire. Terror enveloped it as it moved about in restless astonishment on Khudaira's lap, raising its small head and gazing out with its two yellow eyes at the squashed-up bodies around it exuding their hot, nauseating odour. Then its mind turned to melon seeds, wishing that it could peck some up with its beak. The smell of them crowded in on its nostrils and it longed for that delicious sound of tapping that its beak made on the ground when it ate seeds. In its crop lay aching hunger; it had not eaten since the early morning when it had pecked up some scraps of bread coated with dirt in that ramshackle wattle building. How it wished it could mount its crumbling walls and crow once more, so full of the vigour of youth, and thus proclaim its joy at the new day and call to its fellows, unknown and enfolded by vast distances. But the heavy hand was even then bearing down upon its neck when that giant black snake had made its appearance, emitting its heavy breathing to the skies and shaking the earth with its tread. The fear in its small heart had grown more intense and for the whole journey it had stayed tucked away in that red, flaming lap under that heavy senile hand, unable to stir. But now it stood erect on its two legs and brushed aside the torpor from its benumbed body. Now, in truth, there was nothing to hinder its movements; a new life, it appeared, was opening out in front of it despite that loose red dress that still rose and fell rhythmically, each time exuding a choking fog of intense heat. It also heard a strange sound issuing from the nostrils of its aged owner, which in its turn also increased the heat of the inferno pressing down on it. First it lifted its right leg and gently placed it on the massive thigh covered by the black *aba*. It took a deep breath. However, the position it was in was not comfortable, and after long consideration and looking about it several times and assuring itself of the safety of its position, it drew out its second leg and placed it next to the other, and so found itself standing up on the *aba*. What should it do now?

Once again it became frightened by those recurrent sounds—a moaning and whistling and a clamour—that emanated from the broken windows, the stifling wind, and from under that hollow snake which was taking it to it knew not where. In a state of intense terror, it tried to settle down again into its former position. It pushed its left foot backwards into the folds of the loose red garment, but quickly recollected the hellish, unbearable heat and the heavy hand that were to be encountered there. It returned to its original position on the top of the black *aba*, above the massive tremulous thigh. At that moment, however, the unpredictable coach began to sway and jolt violently, letting out a weird, high-pitched, ear-splitting whistle. Then, quite suddenly, as though it had hit up against a solid wall, it came to a stop. The cock felt a violent jolt, as though some one had pushed it from behind, and it found itself alone on the carriage floor. The door of the compartment was wrenched open and a tongue of sunlight darted in, momentarily blinding its two yellow eyes. But the sun soon retreated and was darkened, only a little of it remaining. Other bodies were climbing into the carriage: milling feet that trampled down everything in their path—feet—feet—nothing but people's feet. Frightened for its very life, the instinct of self-preservation took hold of the cock and it let out a series of short squawks like a frightened hen as it crouched in bewilderment among the feet.

The sun—the sun—all it wanted was the sun. As the sun's rays flowed over it again it found itself descending to another level, to hard solid ground which it discovered to its astonishment did not move as did that strange carriage, that frightening, hollow snake. For the first time since this accursed journey it felt itself free from every bond, from everything frightening. Now it was free to roam about in that vast limitless space before it with all its treasures and riches at the disposal of its beak; now at last it was returning, mighty and noble, to that state of nature which was free from mankind.

Joyfully it looked at its surroundings, its gaze travelling with a deep sense of contentment along the telegraph wires of the desolate station towards the group of palm trees—towards shade, water, female companionship, food.

Once again the train slowly crept along under the noon heat, loaded with all those heavy masses of warm, sticky flesh, with Khudaira smiling at the drowsy dreams that unwound behind the ulcerous eyelids. The south wind, heavy and limpid, blew in uninterruptedly on her face through the broken window, bringing to her and to Khachiyya seated beside her—to all the passengers— that sickly torpor which turns living creatures into beings that are but half alive.

A Space Ship of Tenderness to the Moon

LAILA BAALABAKI

WHEN I closed my eyes I was able to see everything around me, the long settee which fills one vast wall in the room from corner to corner; the shelves on the remaining walls; the small table; the coloured cushions on the carpet; the white lamp, in the shape of a large kerosene one, that dangled from a hole in the wall and rested on the tiled floor. Even the windows we had left curtainless. In the second room was a wide sofa; a table supporting a mirror; a wall-cupboard and two chairs upholstered in velvet. Since our marriage we hadn't changed a thing in the little house, and I refused to remove anything from it.

I opened my eyelids a little as I heard my husband mumble, 'It's light and we alone are awake in the city.' I saw him rising up in front of the window as the silver light of dawn spread over his face and naked body. I love his naked body.

Once again I closed my eyes; I was able to see every little bit of him, every minute hidden detail: his soft hair, his forehead, nose, chin, the veins of his neck, the hair on his chest, his stomach, his feet, his nails. I called to him to come back and stretch out beside me, that I wanted to kiss him. He didn't move and I knew, from the way he had withdrawn from me and stood far off, that he was preparing himself to say something important. In this way he becomes cruel and stubborn, capable of taking and carrying through decisions. I am the exact opposite: in order to talk things over with him I must take hold of his hand or touch his clothes. I therefore opened my eyes, threw aside the cushion I was hugging and seized hold of his shirt, spreading it across my chest. Fixing my gaze on the ceiling I asked him if he saw the sea.

'I see the sea,' he answered.

I asked him what colour it was.

'Dark blue on one side,' he said, 'and on the other a greyish white.'

I asked him if the cypress trees were still there.

'They are still there among the houses that cling close together,' he answered, 'and there's water lying on the roofs of the buildings.'

I said I loved the solitary date-palm which looked, from where we were, as though it had been planted in the sea and that the cypress trees put me in mind of white cemeteries.

For a long while he was silent and I remained staring up at the ceiling. Then he said, 'The cocks are calling,' and I quickly told him I didn't like chickens because they couldn't fly and that when I was a child I used to carry them up to the roof of our home and throw them out into space in an attempt to teach them to fly, and both cocks and hens would always land in a motionless heap on the ground.

Again he was silent for a while, after which he said that he saw a light come on at the window of a building opposite. I said that even so we were still the only two people awake in the city, the only two who had spent the night entwined in each other's arms. He said that he had drunk too much last night. I quickly interrupted him by saying I hated that phrase—I drank too much—as though he regretted the yearning frenzy with which he had made love to me. Sensing that I was beginning to get annoyed he changed the subject, saying: 'The city looks like a mound of sparkling precious stones of all colours and sizes.'

I answered that I now imagined the city as coloured cardboard boxes which would fall down if you blew on them; our house alone, with its two rooms, was suspended from a cloud and rode in space. He said that his mouth was dry and he wanted an orange. I concluded what I had been saying by stating that though I had never lived in any other city, I hated this one and that had I not dreamt that I would one day meet a man who would take me far far away from it I would have died of dejection long long ago. Pretending that he had not heard my last remark he repeated: 'I want an orange, my throat's dry'. I disregarded his request and went on to say that with him I paid no heed to where I was: the earth with its trees, its mountains, rivers, animals and human beings just vanished. Unable to wait further, he burst out at me, 'Why do you refuse to have children?'

I was sad, my heart was wrung, the tears welled up into my eyes, but I didn't open my mouth.

'How long is it since we married?' he asked. I uttered not a word as I followed him round with my eyes. He stiffened and continued, 'It's a year and several months since we married and you've been refusing and refusing, though you were crazy about children before we married; you were dying for them.'

He swerved and struck the settee with his hands as he burst out, 'Hey chair, don't you remember her entreaties? And you lamp, didn't you hear the sound of her wailing? And you cushions, did she not make of you tiny bodies that she hugged to herself and snuggled up to as she slept? Speak, o things inanimate. Speak. Give back to her her voice which is sunk into you.'

Quietly I said that inanimate things don't feel, don't talk, don't move. Angrily he enquired: 'How do you know they're dead?' I replied that things weren't dead, but that they drew their pulse beats from people. He interrupted me by saying that he wouldn't argue about things now and wouldn't allow me to escape solving the problem as I always did. Absent-mindedly I explained to him that the things around me, these very things—this settee, this carpet, this wall, this lamp, this vase, the shelves and the ceiling— are all a vast mirror that reflects for me the outside world: the houses, the sea, the trees, the sky, the sun, the stars and the clouds. In them I see my past with him, the hours of misery and dejection, the moments of meeting and of tenderness, of bliss and of happiness, and from them I now deduce the shapes of the days to come. I would not give them up.

He became angry and shouted, 'We're back again with things. I want to understand here and now why you refuse to have children.' No longer able to bear it, I shouted that he too at one time refused to have them. He was silent for a while, then he said, 'I refused before we were married, when it would have been foolish to have had one.' Sarcastically I told him that he was afraid of them, those others, those buffoons in the city. He used to beg for their assent, their blessing, their agreement, so that he might see me and I him, so that he might embrace me and I him, so that we might each drown the other in our love. They used to determine for us our places of meeting, the number of steps to be taken to get there, the time, the degree to which our voices could be raised, the number of breaths we took. And I would watch them as they secretly scoffed at us, shamelessly slept with the bodies they loved, ate three meals a day, smoked cigarettes with the cups of coffee and carafes of arak, and guffawed as they vulgarly chewed over stories about us and thought up patterns of behaviour for us to put into effect the following day. His voice was choked as he mumbled: 'I don't pay attention to others. I was tied to another woman.'

Ah, how can I bear all this torture, all this passionate love for him? He used to be incapable of confessing the bitter truth to her, that he didn't love her, wouldn't love her. Choking, he said that it wasn't easy, he wasn't callous enough to be able to stare into another human being's face and say to her, after nine years of getting up each and every day and finding her there, 'Now the show's over,' and turn his back and walk off. I told him to look at my right hand and asked him if my blood was still dripping from it hot on to the floor? 'You were mad,' he mumbled, 'mad when you carried out the idea. I opened this door, entered this room and saw you stretched out on this settee, the veins of your hand slashed, your fingers trailing in a sea of blood. You were mad. I might have lost you.' I smiled sadly as I pulled the shirt up to my chest, my face breathing in the smell of it. I said that my part in the play required that I should take myself off at the end, and the form of absence possible for me, the form I could accept and bear, was a quick death rather than a slow, cruel crawling, like that of the turtle in the film *Mondo Cane* that lost its way in the sands, held in the sun's disc, as it searched for the river-bank. He repeated sadly that he didn't know I was serious about him. I asked him sarcastically whether he was waiting for me to kill myself in order to be sure that I was telling the truth. I told him that I had lost myself in my love for him; oblivious to all else, I slipped unseen, like a gust of wind, through people's fingers, scorching their faces as I passed through the street. All I was conscious of was the weight of bodies, the height of buildings and of his hands. I asked him to draw closer and give me his hand which I craved to hold. He remained standing far off, inflexible, and at once accused me that after all that misery and triumph I was refusing to become pregnant from him, had refused again and again and again, and that from my refusal he understood I no longer loved him.

What? I cried out that he could never accuse me of that. Only

yesterday I was stretched out beside him and he gave himself up to
deep sleep while I was open-eyed, rubbing my cheeks against his
chin, kissing his chest, snuggling up under his arm, searching in
vain for sleep. I told him frankly that I was upset by the
speed with which he got to sleep, and by my being left alone and
awake at his side. He hastened to deny this, saying that he had
never been aware of my having remained sleepless. He believed
that I dozed off the moment he did. I revealed maliciously that it
wasn't the first time he had left me alone. I then related in full
yesterday's incident, telling of how he had been asleep breathing
quietly, with me stretched close up against him smoking a cigarette, when suddenly in the emptiness of the room through the
smoke, I had seen a foot fleeing from under the sheets. I moved
my own but it didn't move and a coldness ran through the
whole of my body. I moved it but it didn't move. It occurred to me
to shout. I moved it but it didn't move. I hurriedly hid my face in
his hair. I was afraid. He moved and the foot moved. I cried
silently. I had imagined, had felt, had been unable to tell the
difference between his foot and mine. In a faint voice he said:
'In this age people don't die of love'. Quickly seizing the opportunity I said that in this age people didn't beget children. In olden
times they knew where the child would be born, who it would be
likely to resemble, whether it would be male or female; they
would knit it woollen vests and socks, would embroider the hems,
pockets and collars of its dresses with coloured birds and flowers.
They would amass presents of gold crucifixes for it and medal-
lions with 'Allah bless him' on them, opened palms studded with
blue stones, and pendants with its name engraved on them. They
would reserve a midwife for it, would fix the day of the delivery,
and the child would launch out from the darkness and be flung
into the light at the precise time estimated. They would register
a piece of land in the child's name, would rent it a house, choose
companions for it, decide which school it would be sent to, the
profession it would study for, the person it could love and to
whom it could bind its destiny. That was a long, long time ago, in
the time of your father and my father. He asked, 'Do you believe
that twenty years ago was such an age away? What has changed
since? What has changed? Can't you and can't I provide everything that is required for a child?' To soften the blow I explained
that before I married I was like a child that lies down on its back

in front of the window, gazes up at the stars and stretches out its tiny arm in a desire to pluck them. I used to amuse myself with this dream, with this impossibility, would cling to it and wish it would happen. He asked me: 'Then you were deceiving me?'

Discovering he had changed the conversation into an attack on me so as to win the battle, I quickly told him that only the woman who is unfulfilled with her man eagerly demands a child so that she can withdraw, enjoy being with her child and so be freed. He quickly interrupted me: 'And were you unsatisfied?' I answered him that we had been afraid, had not travelled to the last sweet unexplored regions of experience; we had trembled in terror, had continually bumped against the faces of others and listened to their voices. For his sake, for my own, I had defied death in order to live. He was wrong, wrong, to doubt my being madly in love with him.

'I'm at a loss. I don't understand you', he muttered. I attacked him by saying that was just it, that he also wouldn't understand me if I told him I didn't dare become pregnant, that I would not perpetrate such a mistake.

'Mistake?' he shrieked. 'Mistake?' I clung closer to his shirt, deriving strength from it, and slowly, in a low voice, I told him how scared I was about the fate of any child we might cast into this world. How could I imagine a child of mine, a being nourished on my blood, embraced within my entrails, sharing my breathing, the pulsations of my heart and my daily food, a being to whom I give my features and the earth, how can I bear the thought that in the future he will leave me and go off in a rocket to settle on the moon? And who knows whether or not he'll be happy there. I imagine my child with white ribbons, his fresh face flushed; I imagine him strapped to a chair inside a glass ball fixed to the top of a long shaft of khaki-coloured metal ending in folds resembling the skirt of my Charleston dress. He presses the button, a cloud of dust rises up and an arrow hurls itself into space. No, I can't face it. I can't face it.

He was silent a long, long time while the light of dawn crept in by his face to the corners of the room, his face absent-minded and searching in the sky for an arrow and a child's face. The vein between his eyebrows was knotted; perplexity and strain showed in his mouth. I, too, remained silent and closed my eyes.

When he was near me, standing like a massive tower at a rocket-firing station, my heart throbbed and I muttered to him that I adored his naked body. When he puts on his clothes, especially when he ties his tie, I feel he's some stranger come to pay a visit to the head of the house. He opened his arms and leaned over me. I rushed into his embrace, mumbling crazily: 'I love you, I love you, I love you, I love you, I love you,' He whispered into my hair: 'You're my pearl.' Then he spread the palm of his hand over my lips, drawing me to him with the other hand, and ordered: 'Let us take off, you and I, for the moon.'

Zaabalawi

NAGIB MAHFOUZ

FINALLY I became convinced that I had to find Sheikh Zaabalawi.

The first time I had heard of his name had been in a song:

'What's wrong with the world, O Zaabalawi?
They've turned it upside down and made it insipid.'

It had been a popular song in my childhood and one day it had
occurred to me—in the way children have of asking endless
questions—to ask my father about him.

'Who is Zaabalawi, father?'

He had looked at me hesitantly as though doubting my ability to
understand the answer. However, he had replied:

'May his blessing descend upon you, he's a true saint of God,
a remover of worries and troubles. Were it not for him I would
have died miserably—'

In the years that followed I heard him many a time sing the
praises of this good saint and speak of the miracles he performed.
The days passed and brought with them many illnesses from each
one of which I was able, without too much trouble and at a cost
I could afford, to find a cure, until I became afflicted with that
illness for which no one possesses a remedy. When I had tried
everything in vain and was overcome by despair, I remembered by
chance what I had heard in my childhood: Why, I asked myself,
should I not seek out Sheikh Zaabalawi? I recollected that my
father had said that he had made his acquaintance in Khan
Gaafar at the house of Sheikh Kamar, one of those sheikhs who
practised law in the religious courts, and I therefore took myself off to his house. Wishing to make sure that he was still living
there, I made enquiries of a vendor of beans whom I found in
the lower part of the house.

'Sheikh Kamar!' he said, looking at me in amazement. 'He left the quarter ages ago. They say he's now living in Garden City and has his office in al-Azhaar Square.'

I looked up the office address in the telephone book and immediately set off to the Chamber of Commerce Building where it was located. On asking to see him I was ushered into a room just as a beautiful woman with a most intoxicating perfume was leaving it. The man received me with a smile and motioned me towards a fine leather-upholstered chair. My feet were conscious of the costly lushness of the carpet despite the thick soles of my shoes. The man wore a lounge suit and was smoking a cigar; his manner of sitting was that of someone well satisfied both with himself and his worldly possessions. The look of warm welcome he gave me left no doubt in my mind that he thought me a prospective client, and I felt acutely embarrassed at encroaching upon his valuable time.

'Welcome!' he said, prompting me to speak.

'I am the son of your old friend Sheikh Ali al-Tatawi,' I answered so as to put an end to my equivocal position.

A certain languor was apparent in the glance he cast at me; the languor was not total in that he had not as yet lost all hope in me.

'God rest his soul,' he said. 'He was a fine man.'

The very pain that had driven me to go there now prevailed upon me to stay.

'He told me', I continued, 'of a devout saint named Zaabalawi whom he met at Your Honour's. I am in need of him, sir, if he be still in the land of the living.'

The languor became firmly entrenched in his eyes and it would have come as no surprise to me if he had shown the door to both me and my father's memory.

'That', he said in the tone of one who has made up his mind to terminate the conversation, 'was a very long time ago and I scarcely recall him now.'

Rising to my feet so as to put his mind at rest regarding my intention of going, I asked:

'Was he really a saint?'

'We used to regard him as a man of miracles.'

'And where could I find him today?' I asked, making another move towards the door.

'To the best of my knowledge he was living in the Birgawi

Residence in al-Azhar,' and he applied himself to some papers on his desk with a resolute movement that indicated he wouldn't open his mouth again. I bowed my head in thanks, apologized several times for disturbing him and left the office, my head so buzzing with embarrassment that I was oblivious to all sounds around me.

I went to the Birgawi Residence which was situated in a thickly populated quarter. I found that time had so eaten into the building that nothing was left of it save an antiquated façade and a courtyard which, despite it being supposedly in the charge of a caretaker, was being used as a rubbish dump. A small insignificant fellow, a mere prologue to a man, was using the covered entrance as a place for the sale of old books on theology and mysticism.

On asking him about Zaabalawi he peered at me through narrow, inflamed eyes and said in amazement:

'Zaabalawi! Good heavens, what a time ago that was! Certainly he used to live in this house when it was livable in, and many was the time he would sit with me talking of bygone days and I would be blessed by his holy presence. Where, though, is Zaabalawi today?'

He shrugged his shoulders sorrowfully and soon left me to attend to an approaching customer. I proceeded to make enquiries of many shopkeepers in the district. While I found that a large number of them had never even heard of him, some, though recalling nostalgically the pleasant times they had spent with him, were ignorant of his present whereabouts, while others openly made fun of him, labelled him a charlatan, and advised me to put myself in the hands of a doctor—as though I had not already done so. I therefore had no alternative but to return disconsolately home.

With the passing of the days like motes in the air my pains grew so severe that I was sure I would not be able to hold out much longer. Once again I fell to wondering about Zaabalawi and clutching at the hopes his venerable name stirred within me. Then it occurred to me to seek the help of the local Sheikh of the district; in fact, I was surprised I hadn't thought of this to begin with. His office was in the nature of a small shop except that it contained a desk and a telephone, and I found him sitting at his desk wearing a jacket over his striped *galabia*. As he did not interrupt his conversation with a man sitting beside him, I stood waiting till the man had gone. He then looked up at me coldly. I told myself that

I should win him over by the usual methods, and it wasn't long before I had him cheerfully inviting me to sit down.

'I'm in need of Sheikh Zaabalawi', I answered his enquiry as to the purpose of my visit.

He gazed at me with the same astonishment as that shown by those I had previously encountered.

'At least', he said, giving me a smile that revealed his gold teeth, 'he is still alive. The devil of it is, though, he has no fixed abode. You might well bump into him as you go out of here, on the other hand you might spend days and months in fruitless search of him.'

'Even you can't find him!'

'Even I! He's a baffling man, but I thank the Lord that he's still alive!'

He gazed at me intently, and murmured:

'It seems your condition is serious.'

'Very!'

'May God come to your aid! But why don't you go about it rationally?'

He spread out a sheet of paper on the desk and drew on it with unexpected speed and skill until he had made a full plan of the district showing all the various quarters, lanes, alleyways, and squares. He looked at it admiringly and said, 'These are dwelling-houses, here is the Quarter of the Perfumers, here the Quarter of the Coppersmiths, the Mouski, the Police and Fire Stations. The drawing is your best guide. Look carefully in the cafés, the places where the dervishes perform their rites, the mosques and prayer-rooms, and the Green Gate, for he may well be concealed among the beggars and be indistinguishable from them. Actually, I myself haven't seen him for years, having been somewhat pre-occupied with the cares of the world and was only brought back to those most exquisite times of my youth by your enquiry.'

I gazed at the map in bewilderment. The telephone rang and he took up the receiver.

'Take it', he told me, generously. 'We're at your service.'

Folding up the map, I left and wandered off through the quarter, from square to street to alleyway, making enquiries of everyone I felt was familiar with the place. At last the owner of a small establishment for ironing clothes told me:

'Go to the calligrapher Hassanein in Umm al-Ghulam—they were friends.'

I went to Umm al-Ghulam where I found old Hassanein working in a deep, narrow shop full of signboards and jars of colour.
A strange smell, a mixture of glue and perfume, permeated its
every corner. Old Hassanein was squatting on a sheepskin rug in
front of a board propped against the wall; in the middle of it he
had inscribed the word 'Allah' in silver lettering. He was engrossed
in embellishing the letters with prodigious care. I stood behind him,
fearful to disturb him or break the inspiration that flowed to his
masterly hand. When my concern at not interrupting him had
lasted some time, he suddenly enquired with unaffected gentleness:
'Yes?'
Realizing that he was aware of my presence, I introduced myself.
'I've been told that Sheikh Zaabalawi is your friend and I'm
looking for him,' I said.
His hand came to a stop. He scrutinized me in astonishment.
'Zaabalawi! God be praised!' he said with a sigh.
'He is a friend of yours, isn't he?' I asked eagerly.
'He was, once upon a time. A real man of mystery: he'd visit
you so often that people would imagine he was your nearest and
dearest, then would disappear as though he'd never existed. Yet
saints are not to be blamed.'
The spark of hope went out with the suddenness of a lamp by a
power-cut.
'He was so constantly with me', said the man, 'that I felt him
to be a part of everything I drew. But where is he today?'
'Perhaps he is still alive?'
'He's alive, without a doubt. He had impeccable taste and it
was due to him that I made my most beautiful drawings.'
'God knows', I said, in a voice almost stifled by the dead ashes
of hope, 'that I am in the direst need of him and no one knows
better than you of the ailments in respect of which he is sought.'
'Yes—yes. May God restore you to health. He is, in truth, as
is said of him, a man, and more—'
Smiling broadly, he added: 'And his face is possessed of an
unforgettable beauty. But where is he?'
Reluctantly I rose to my feet, shook hands and left. I continued
on my way eastwards and westwards through the quarter, enquiring about him from everyone who, by reason of age or experience,
I felt was likely to help me. Eventually I was informed by a
vendor of lupine that he had met him a short while ago at the

house of Sheikh Gad, the well-known composer. I went to the
musician's house in Tabakshiyya where I found him in a room
tastefully furnished in the old style, its walls redolent with history.
He was seated on a divan, his famous lute lying beside him, con-
cealing within itself the most beautiful melodies of our age, while
from within the house came the sound of pestle and mortar and
the clamour of children. I immediately greeted him and introduced myself, and was put at my ease by the unaffected way in
which he received me. He did not ask, either in words or gesture,
what had brought me, and I did not feel that he even harboured
any such curiosity. Amazed at his understanding and kindness,
which boded well, I said:

'O Sheikh Gad, I am an admirer of yours and have long been
enchanted by the renderings of your songs.'

'Thank you', he said with a smile.

'Please excuse my disturbing you', I continued timidly, 'but
I was told that Zaabalawi was your friend and I am in urgent
need of him.'

'Zaabalawi!' he said, frowning in concentration. 'You need
him? God be with you, for who knows, O Zaabalawi, where you
are?'

'Doesn't he visit you?' I asked eagerly.

'He visited me some time ago. He might well come now; on
the other hand I mightn't see him till death!'

I gave an audible sigh and asked:

'What made him like that?'

He took up his lute. 'Such are saints or they would not be
saints,' he said laughing.

'Do those who need him suffer as I do?'

'Such suffering is part of the cure!'

He took up the plectrum and began plucking soft strains from
the strings. Lost in thought, I followed his movements. Then, as
though addressing myself, I said:

'So my visit has been in vain!'

He smiled, laying his cheek against the side of the lute.

'God forgive you', he said, 'for saying such a thing of a visit
that has caused me to know you and you me!'

I was much embarrassed and said apologetically:

'Please forgive me; my feelings of defeat made me forget my
manners!'

'Do not give in to defeat. This extraordinary man brings fatigue to all who seek him. It was easy enough with him in the old days when his place of abode was known. Today, though, the world has changed and after having enjoyed a position attained only by potentates, he is now pursued by the police on a charge of false pretences. It is therefore no longer an easy matter to reach him, but have patience and be sure that you will do so.'

He raised his head from the lute and skilfully led into the opening bars of a melody. Then he sang:

'I make lavish mention, even though I blame myself,
of those I have loved,
For the words of lovers are my wine.'

With a heart that was weary and listless I followed the beauty of the melody and the singing.

'I composed the music to this poem in a single night', he told me when he had finished. 'I remember that it was the night of the Lesser Bairam. He was my guest for the whole of that night and the poem was of his choosing. He would sit for a while just where you are, then would get up and play with my children as though he were one of them. Whenever I was overcome by weariness or my inspiration failed me he would punch me playfully in the chest and joke with me, and I would bubble over with melodies and thus I continued working till I finished the most beautiful piece I have ever composed.'

'Does he know anything about music?'

'He was the epitome of things musical. He had an extremely beautiful speaking voice and you had only to hear him to want to burst into song. His loftiness of spirit stirred within you—'

'How was it that he cured those diseases before which men are powerless?'

'That is his secret. Maybe you will learn it when you meet him.'

But when would that meeting occur? We relapsed into silence and the hubbub of children once more filled the room.

Again the Sheikh began to sing. He went on repeating the words 'and I have a memory of her' in different and beautiful variations until the very walls danced in ecstasy. I expressed my wholehearted admiration and he gave me a smile of thanks. I then got up and asked permission to leave and he accompanied me to the outer door. As I shook him by the hand he said, 'I hear

that nowadays he frequents the house of Hagg Wanas al-Damanhouri. Do you know him?'

I shook my head, a modicum of renewed hope creeping into my
heart.

'He is a man of private means,' he told me, 'who from time to
time visits Cairo, putting up at some hotel or other. Every evening,
though, he spends at the Negma Bar in Alfi Street.'

I waited for nightfall, and went to the Negma Bar. I asked a
waiter about Hagg Wanas and he pointed to a corner which was
semi-secluded because of its position behind a large pillar with
mirrors on its four sides. There I saw a man seated alone at a table
with a bottle three-quarters empty and another empty one in front
of him, there were no snacks or food to be seen and I was sure
that I was in the presence of a hardened drinker. He was wearing
a loosely flowing silk *galabia* and a carefully wound turban; his
legs were stretched out towards the base of the pillar, and as he
gazed into the mirror in rapt contentment the sides of his face,
rounded and handsome despite the fact that he was approaching
old age, were flushed with wine. I approached quietly till I
stood but a few feet away from him. He did not turn towards me
or give any indication that he was aware of my presence.

'Good evening, Mr. Wanas,' I said with amiable friendliness.

He turned towards me abruptly as though my voice had roused
him from slumber and glared at me in disapproval. I was about
to explain what had brought me to him when he interrupted me
in an almost imperative tone of voice which was none the less not
devoid of an extraordinary gentleness:

'First, please sit down, and, second, please get drunk!'

I opened my mouth to make my excuses but, stopping up his
ears with his fingers, he said:

'Not a word till you do what I say.'

I realized that I was in the presence of a capricious drunkard
and told myself that I should go along with him at least half-
way.

'Would you permit me to ask one question?' I said with a
smile, sitting down.

Without removing his hands from his ears he indicated the
bottle.

'When engaged in a drinking bout like this I do not allow any
conversation between myself and another unless, like me, he is

drunk, otherwise the session loses all propriety and mutual comprehension is rendered impossible.'

I made a sign indicating that I didn't drink.

'That's your look-out,' he said offhandedly. 'And that's my condition!'

He filled me a glass which I meekly took and drank. No sooner had it settled in my stomach than it seemed to ignite. I waited patiently till I had grown used to its ferocity, and said:

'It's very strong, and I think the time has come for me to ask you about—'

Once again, however, he put his fingers in his ears.

'I shan't listen to you until you're drunk!'

He filled up my glass for the second time. I glanced at it in trepidation; then, overcoming my innate objection, I drank it down at a gulp. No sooner had it come to rest inside me than I lost all will-power. With the third glass I lost my memory and with the fourth the future vanished. The world turned round about me and I forgot why I had gone there. The man leaned towards me attentively but I saw him—saw everything—as a mere meaningless series of coloured planes. I don't know how long it was before my head sank down on to the arm of the chair and I plunged into deep sleep. During it I had a beautiful dream the like of which I had never experienced. I dreamed that I was in an immense garden surrounded on all sides by luxuriant trees and the sky was nothing but stars seen between the entwined branches, all enfolded in an atmosphere like that of sunset or a sky overcast with cloud. I was lying on a small hummock of jasmine petals which fell upon me like rain, while the lucent spray of a fountain unceasingly sprinkled my head and temples. I was in a state of deep contentedness, of ecstatic serenity. An orchestra of warbling and cooing played in my ear. There was an extraordinary sense of harmony between me and my inner self, and between the two of us and the world, everything being in its rightful place without discord or distortion. In the whole world there was no single reason for speech or movement, for the universe moved in a rapture of ecstasy. This lasted but a short while. When I opened my eyes consciousness struck at me like a policeman's fist and I saw Wanas al-Damanhouri regarding me with concern. In the bar only a few drowsy people were left.

'You have slept deeply,' said my companion; 'you were obviously hungry for sleep.'

I rested my heavy head in the palms of my hands. When I took them away in astonishment and looked down at them I found that they glistened with drops of water.

'My head's wet,' I protested.

'Yes, my friend tried to rouse you,' he answered quietly.

'Somebody saw me in this state?'

'Don't worry, he is a good man. Have you not heard of Sheikh Zaabalawi?'

'Zaabalawi!' I exclaimed, jumping to my feet.

'Yes', he answered in surprise. 'What's wrong?'

'Where is he?'

'I don't know where he is now. He was here and then he left.'

I was about to run off in pursuit but found I was more exhausted than I had imagined. Collapsed over the table, I cried out in despair:

'My sole reason for coming to you was to meet him. Help me to catch up with him or send someone after him.'

The man called a vendor of prawns and asked him to seek out the Sheikh and bring him back. Then he turned to me.

'I didn't realize you were afflicted. I'm very sorry—'

'You wouldn't let me speak,' I said irritably.

'What a pity! He was sitting on this chair beside you the whole time. He was playing with a string of jasmine petals he had round his neck, a gift from one of his admirers, then, taking pity on you, he began to sprinkle some water on your head to bring you round.'

'Does he meet you here every night?' I asked, my eyes not leaving the doorway through which the vendor of prawns had left.

'He was with me tonight, last night and the night before that, but before that I hadn't seen him for a month.'

'Perhaps he will come tomorrow,' I answered with a sigh.

'Perhaps.'

'I am willing to give him any money he wants.'

Wanas answered sympathetically:

'The strange thing is that he is not open to such temptations, yet he will cure you if you meet him.'

'Without charge?'

'Merely on sensing that you love him.'

The vendor of prawns returned, having failed in his mission.

I recovered some of my energy and left the bar, albeit unsteadily. At every street corner I called out, 'Zaabalawi!' in the vague hope that I would be rewarded with an answering shout. The street boys turned contemptuous eyes on me till I sought refuge in the first available taxi.

The following evening I stayed up with Wanas al-Damanhouri till dawn, but the Sheikh did not put in an appearance. Wanas informed me that he would be going away to the country and wouldn't be returning to Cairo until he'd sold the cotton crop.

I must wait, I told myself; I must train myself to be patient. Let me content myself with having made certain of the existence of Zaabalawi, and even of his affection for me, which encourages me to think that he will be prepared to cure me if a meeting between us takes place.

Sometimes, however, the long delay wearied me. I would become beset by despair and would try to persuade myself to dismiss him from my mind completely. How many weary people in this life know him not or regard him as a mere myth! Why, then, should I torture myself about him in this way?

No sooner, however, did my pains force themselves upon me than I would again begin to think about him, asking myself as to when I would be fortunate enough to meet him. The fact that I ceased to have any news of Wanas and was told he had gone to live abroad did not deflect me from my purpose; the truth of the matter was that I had become fully convinced that I had to find Zaabalawi.

Yes, I have to find Zaabalawi.

The Gramophone

JABRA IBRAHIM JABRA

YUSUF TOOK hold of the zinc ingot and clamped it into the jaws of the vice. Tightening the vice, he took up a long file and rested it on the ingot; before proceeding to burnish it, however, he turned to me and said, 'Are you listening, Yacoub?'

'Yes,' I said and stepped over a heap of pieces of zinc to take a look at the glowing pot in whose fiery furnace the metal was being slowly melted down.

'Are you listening, Yacoub?' Yusuf repeated. 'Rest a while. You're still young and shouldn't overdo things. Hanna the boss is otherwise occupied'; and he gave me a wink to show how busy the boss was. Then he stretched out his thumb and forefinger as though holding a glass which, with an expressive gesture, he were raising to his lips. 'The boss is busy, but I wish I were with him right now. If only you knew, Yacoub, the sort of life I led in Egypt five years ago. Five years have changed my life. Every evening I would put on a smart, newly-pressed suit and a starched white shirt and off I'd go to some café or bar with two or three friends, then on to a cabaret. Money, all the money you could wish for. Drink and women—five years have changed my life.'

He then positioned the file on the ingot and got down to burnishing it, singing to the rhythmic movement of the file. I used to enjoy his singing as much as he himself did, his hands sometimes ceasing their work as his voice rose up in quavering notes to a pitch of ecstasy before dropping down into a husky whisper of pain, and it seemed to me that at such times his eyes filled with tears. His hands would then return to their work of burnishing or hammering. 'Five years,' he said, 'from prosperity to misery. By God, Yacoub, this is no life! Money, friends, and women: blondes, brunettes, tall and short. May God be praised for such wonderful variety.'

148

He cautiously produced a packet of cigarettes from an inner pocket, took one out and put back the packet. He lit the cigarette and blew out the smoke, one hand resting on the vice, and his far-away gaze recalling those days of affluence from between the wisps of smoke.

'Have a look at the pot would you, Yusuf?' I asked. 'Should I put in some more pieces of zinc?'

He gave it a glance from where he stood. 'Damn the pot,' he said. 'I told you the boss was busy. He'll be very late today. Have you got all the moulds ready in the sand?'

'Yes,' I said. 'They're all ready.'

Then, unexpectedly, Hanna al-Muwasiri, the boss, made his appearance. Though he tried to conceal the fact, his gait was unsteady; he was, however, in excellent humour and had no sooner stepped inside the workshop than he shouted out, 'Hey, Prince, hope you've polished them all. Do you think I don't know you, Prince? Don't I know you inside out? Hardly have I turned my back than you're going slow.' He sat down beside the sand we used for making the moulds. 'May God help Yusuf,' he said to me. 'He's gone grey, he's aged, look, look, Yacoub, look!' He lowered his voice and bringing his reeking mouth near to my ear, whispered: 'Be careful he doesn't see you. Ha ha, ha ha! God help you, Yusuf.'

Yusuf's trousers were torn and patched from top to bottom, in front and behind, no one remembering their original colour, not even Yusuf himself. They had become so transformed, so soiled and torn that they were kept together by little more than will-power and the leather belt he wore round his waist. One tear in the crutch had grown so large that no amount of patching could repair it and Hanna was drawing my attention to Yusuf's dangling private parts which were showing.

'Three hundred pounds I spent in a couple of months,' said Yusuf, blissfully unaware, ceasing his polishing for a while. 'By God, Hanna, three hundred pounds in a couple of months!' and he applied himself again to his work.

'Dream away, Prince,' said Hanna, 'but also put a little muscle into your work. We've got to cast these moulds before evening.' Then he turned to me and asked, 'Are the moulds ready?'

'Yes, master,' I said.

Despite his tipsiness he gave an expert look at the squares in the brown sand, his eyes travelling from one mould to the next. He then got up and glanced at the glowing melting-pot. He took off his coat and, undoing the buttons of his shirt, rolled up his sleeves. 'Come on, Yusuf!'

The job of pouring out the melted zinc occupied us for about a quarter of an hour. Those fifteen minutes, though, were as tiring as the rest of the day's work. I could see how the veins would stand out to bursting point on our arms, and as we raised the melting-pot with the long two-handled tongs, the sweat pour down our faces and into our eyes. At each mistake or error of judgment in pouring the molten metal into the moulds we would relieve the painful tension tormenting every part of our bodies by cursing and swearing.

Having finished our work and placed the pot into a corner to cool off, it seemed to me that Hanna had sobered up. He wiped his brow and face with an old rag, while Yusuf, seated on a box to rest, also dried his forehead. 'What about having a spot of supper?' he said.

Hanna, without saying a word, picked up a piece of soap and went to the far corner where we kept a large jar filled with water. He dipped a bowl into it and proceeded to wash his face and hands.

'Go and buy me a plateful of tripe,' Yusuf said to me, handing over a piastre which he took from a pocket by his belt. Hanna, lather still on his face and around his neck, called out: 'Yacoub, here's a piastre so that you too can buy yourself something to eat,' and he quickly ran his right hand over the towel, plunged it into his pocket and brought out a coin.

I went up from *The Pit* to *King David's Rise* where there was a man from Hebron who cooked stuffed tripe in two enormous cauldrons on a wood fire in the open air. The smell of the gravy, with its garlic, lemon, and pepper, quite apart from the smell of the tripe itself, was enough to whet all hungry appetites. He was always surrounded by a crowd of workmen from the smithies of *The Pit*, labourers, donkey-drivers, and taxi-men, some of whom were squatting on their heels or sitting cross-legged on the ground, while others were standing, all holding the plates of tripe in their hands, the whole place filled with the luscious smell. As I approached the cook who was ladling out pieces of tripe and care-fully measuring the helpings of gravy which he then poured into deep plates, I espied among those eating Abdul A'war, the magazine vendor, a heap of his wares at his side. He caught sight of me immediately and called out, 'Got the latest issue of *al-Dunya*?'

'No. Is it out?' I said, making my way towards him. Like a magician producing a rabbit from his sleeve, he extracted a copy of *al-Dunya* from the heap of magazines and passed it to me. As I handled it, sniffed the fresh ink and saw its many pictures, I was at a loss as to whether to return it to him and buy a plateful of tripe with my piastre or to add a further half piastre, buy the magazine and let my mouth water in vain.

'Let's have it!'

I took the magazine and handed over the one and a half piastres, then made my way back to the cook. 'One plate of tripe,' I said.

With practised skill and care he scooped up the prescribed amount and poured it into a plate which he passed to me. 'Mind you bring back the plate quickly,' he said.

I went down from *The Rise* to the foundry, carefully balancing the plate so none of the precious gravy would spill, the delectable magazine under my arm.

'Have some sense, my boy!' said Yusuf, seated on a wooden box.

'Where's the boss?' I asked.

'He's gone,' and he repeated the pantomime of raising a glass to his lips. 'Not a magazine again instead of food?'

'Here you are.'

He took the plate, reached out for a spoon lying among the files and hammers, and wiped it with his thumb. As I eagerly turned over the pages of the magazine and he sipped down the gravy, he bellowed at me, 'Are you in love, Yacoub? Is it your mind you're feeding or your belly? How do you hope to fill out and grow strong at your age if every time you get a piastre you buy some useless magazine that will profit you nothing instead of a divine blessing like this.'

Engrossed in turning over the pages of the magazine, reading the headings and gazing at the pictures, I made no reply. Though I was listening with but half an ear, he continued talking.

'Fortune lies in your arm. Nothing will do you any good except the strength of your arm. I suppose, from the rags I'm wearing, you think I never knew money and ease? Hundreds of pounds I've earned with this hand of mine. I really was a prince, Yacoub. "That's how the Prince wants it," they used to say. There's a fortune in this arm, but—women, blondes and brunettes, music, song and fun, long moonlit nights spent with—Ah, but you're too young, my boy. May God save you from rouged lips, eyes darkened with *kohl*, and plucked eyebrows.'

He sucked noisily at his spoon again and again, took up the stuffed tripe in his fingers and began gnawing at it, his words interspersing this activity.

'Here's an article entitled "Palace music in the Eighteenth Century",' I interrupted him.

'If you don't look out music can be dangerous,' he said, 'especially if you yourself have a talent for singing. The players of the lute, *kanoon*, and violin gather about you, the one with kohl-darkened eyes lies in your arms, the glass is passed round and the evening breeze enflames the fire in your heart—'

Suddenly he put the food to one side and struck himself on the chest with his fist. 'This accursed heart of mine, this bastard! It never reasons, never repents, until it brings ruin to its owner. You're still young, Yacoub, but you'll hear grown-ups say that women are all the same, that in the end there's no difference between one and another. Lies, I tell you, lies! Each woman has her own particular taste, her own flavour; each is a food which differs from every other. No single one can make up for what another one has to give. Don't be deceived by these rags, Yacoub. By God, I've seen a good bit of life!'

He stopped talking and I raised my eyes from the magazine and saw that he was looking at the door. I glanced in its direction and saw a woman walking slowly by, looking towards the foundry as though in quest of someone. Her cheeks were as red as roses, the rest of her face as white as flour; her eyes were thickly plastered with *kohl*. She continued on her way with her loose, swinging gait, holding a leather handbag. Yusuf rushed to the door, gazing out at her as she moved away, her buttocks swaying as she walked.

'Do you know who that was?' he asked at last.

'No.'

'That's Sobhiyya.'

'Sobhiyya?'

'God help the boss! She's on her way to Abu Shlomo's shop where Hanna is waiting for her. Abu Shlomo will serve him with arak in the back-room and then Heaven help you, Hanna. God protect us and protect this foundry!'

He took a packet of cigarettes out of his inside pocket, extracted one and returned the packet carefully. Lighting the cigarette and blowing out smoke through his mouth and nostrils, he said, 'As I told you, every woman has her own taste and flavour. May God be praised for such wonderful variety!'

On the following day Yusuf didn't turn up at the foundry. We had to prepare new moulds for some brass ingots which were rather complicated and Hanna the boss began digging up the previous day's ingots from the sand.

'So the Prince isn't going to turn up,' he kept on saying; 'so he won't turn up? Wallowing in his dreams and with us with work to do, responsibilities, money to pay out. So he's not turning up?'

At last he said to me, 'Go to his house and drag him along by the ears!'

Yusuf's 'house' was, to the best of my knowledge, in a road near to the workshop. On leaving work in the evening I would see him entering through a wooden doorway in amongst the blacksmiths' shops and he would then disappear from view. He had never invited anyone to pay him a visit. I opened the doorway and entered, greatly curious, but found no house there, only some steps belonging to a partially completed building. The steps terminated in a high platform alongside a wall with nothing above it but the sky; on one side of the platform was a wooden hut, little larger than a dog kennel. The planks of which it was made were crumbling and uneven; in many places nails protruded like tiny daggers, the result of the many previous uses to which the planks had been put.

'Yusuf! Yusuf!' I called as I arrived at the platform.

A weak, mournful voice answered me, 'Who is it? Come along in.' The door was no more than a piece of old sacking. On raising it I saw Yusuf stretched out under a blackened and threadbare covering, beside him a pitcher of water, some tin plates, a primus stove and several empty bottles, some lying on their sides. My eyes suddenly became riveted to the pile of records by a blue box which I immediately realized was a gramophone. There was no apparent connection between this bedraggled person and the records and gramophone.

'What is it? What do you want?' Yusuf muttered, opening heavy lids.

'The boss wants you at once,' I said.

He groaned and mumbled something to himself. When he raised the cover I saw that he was in his day-clothes.

'Can't I rest for a couple of hours without working?' he said. 'Can't I even have a rest?'

'God keep you from harm, Prince.' I said.

'And you too,' he answered, sitting up in his bed. 'By God, this is no life, Yacoub! It's no life at all.'

'But where did you get this . . . box?'

'The gramophone? Have I got anything left in life but it?'

'And you have records, too.'

'My wife ran away; my son, too, God strike him dead. He went off to Italy and became a monk, while I couldn't save a piastre like any decent human being.'

'Cheer up, old chap.'

'By God, this is no life,' he said, not looking at me, 'no life at all.'

I squatted down beside the records and began reading their titles, taking delight in their shiny touch. There were no more than ten of them and even these were broken or chipped at the edges. Yet to me, they represented a veritable treasure trove.

'Would you let me visit you sometimes to hear these songs?' I asked.

'You're welcome any day. Be careful with them, though. Nothing ruined me more than songs like these.'

I laughed in surprise. 'Songs?' I queried.

'What do you think I was doing in Cairo? I fell in love with Munira al-Turkiyya, whose records you see there. She had a voice of silver, of gold, as sweet as the waters of Paradise, and a face like a rose, a carnation. And then? She threw me out of her house with not a stitch on my back—pass me the pitcher, would you?'

I handed it to him and he poured some water into the palm of his hand and splashed it over his face. He repeated this two or three times and then said, 'A voice of gold, like the purest water.'

He produced a soiled khaki handkerchief from his pocket and wiped his face.

'Hurry up, Yusuf,' I said. 'We've lots of work today.'

He got up, took the packet of cigarettes from his inside pocket and lit one. 'Can't a fellow be ill for a while?' he said. 'By God, this is no life!'

As we made our way down the steps I said, 'Then you'll allow me to play some of your records?'

'Go ahead. But when you come, bring along with you a couple of glasses of arak. Eh, Yacoub?'

'And where would I get arak from?'

'No, you must, you really must.'

'All right.'

Our house had a small window through which there penetrated, in the evening, the sound of high-pitched songs coming from the gramophone of our neighbours, the family of Abu Abdullah. Whenever I heard the singing I would listen in delight despite the fact that our neighbours' stock of records was severely limited. Sometimes of an evening we would have a visitor and the shrill sounds would burst in through the window and we would remark in explanation, 'Our neighbours have a gramophone,' and our guest would nod his head as an indication of his awareness of our neighbours' importance, possessed as they were of a gramophone and records. Once I had ventured out with my mother to visit them and had seen the singing box, its jaws wide open and in it the shining disc of a record. How I had wished at that moment that they would play it! I was too shy to ask them, though, and the gramophone remained silent, while I returned home in a state of bitter disappointment.

It seems that the clearness of the night—the time was late spring —had put our neighbours into a merry mood, for they went on and on playing their records one after the other. I lay on my bed on the floor reading through the magazine. Though I was tired after the day's heavy work, the article on palace music in the eighteenth century so absorbed me that I was prevented from dozing off. The strange foreign names acted on me like a spell. I was unable to make up my mind whether the loud, high-pitched notes which I heard, and which sometimes resembled the shrieks of little girls, were the sort of tunes about which the article talked. I ended up by identifying the two in my mind. My head fell forward on my shoulder and in my sleep I saw Yusuf, dressed like a prince, lowering the needle on to a record on his gramophone, his face breaking into contorted lines as he sang in seeming agony. On waking up I exclaimed, 'By God, I'm off to Yusuf's hut.'

When my mother objected, saying, 'It's nearly eight—have you ever seen a boy of your age wandering round the streets at such an hour?' I answered, 'I'll be back quickly. Hanna the boss asked me to give Yusuf a message and I forgot to. Also, Mama, Yusuf's hu . . . house is quite close.'

The street, which during the daytime was filled with the ring and crash of blacksmiths' hammers, was now ominously quiet. I plucked up my courage and hurried to the wooden doorway which I pushed open. From the bottom of the steps I saw streaks of light emanating from between the planks of the hut. 'Yusuf!' I shouted.

He came out like a ghost and looked down at me from the platform. 'Who is it?' he asked, staring down. 'Yacoub?'

'Yes.'

'Come up.'

'Hey, where's the arak?' he asked when I had climbed up. His mouth gave off a smell of aniseed.

'How can I get hold of arak, old chap?'

'Doesn't your father drink? Haven't you a bottle of arak in the house from which you could steal me a couple of glasses? Is this the way to behave to a friend, Yacoub?'

Glancing into the interior of the hut to make quite certain that the gramophone and records were there, I said, 'I came to listen to some music with you.'

'All right, but—all right, come in.'

We sat on the ground and played one side of a record. Yusuf, however, was silent and listless, quite unlike his usual self. Then he seized hold of a bottle, raised it to his mouth and took a gulp. He made a wry face, and then sighed with satisfaction.

'Listen,' he said suddenly. 'Like to buy it?'

'What?'

'The gramophone.'

It had never occurred to me that such a thing was possible. 'But how?' I asked in astonishment.

'For two pounds.'

'Are you dreaming, Prince?'

'It and the records for two pounds, eh? I've got a scheme, an important scheme, and I must have money.'

'What is it?'

'What's that to do with you? Two pounds for the gramophone

and the records. Imagine it, Yacoub! You'd have music whenever you want, night and day—imagine it!'

He took me by the hand. I got up and we went down the steps together.

'I've got a scheme I must put through,' he said. 'I've saved a bit of money by living in this beggarly fashion, but I still need two pounds—and a little arak.'

'I only wish I had such an amount,' I said as I bid farewell to him at the doorway.

At noon on Saturday Hanna al-Muwasiri was in as high spirits as when he had just received a large sum of money. It appeared that the zinc and brass ingots we had made during the week had proved profitable and he certainly wasn't stingy in the bonus he gave to Yusuf and myself over and above our daily wage, which was paid on Saturday afternoons. 'We won't work this afternoon,' he said. 'What do you think, Yusuf? And what about you, Yacoub?'

'That's handsome of you, really handsome,' said Yusuf, his face bright with joy, and he tightened his belt to stop his torn, patched trousers from falling down.

'Buy yourself a book today,' Hanna said to me. 'Here's another ten piastres.'

'Thank you, master!' I exclaimed and went off home, my hand tightly clasping the piastres in my pocket.

My mother prepared me a hot bath (I used to bath in a tin basin placed on the kitchen floor) after which I went out to walk round the city's streets and stand listening at the doors of those coffee shops which played music. On my return at the end of the day I was surprised to hear a voice coming from my room: it was Yusuf talking to my parents about Cairo, Tanta, and Alexandria, while they listened entranced by the magic of his words. It was the first time he had paid us a visit. But what an astonishing change! I found him wearing a new pair of trousers, a clean shirt and a coat with not a patch to it!

When the coffee was brought Yusuf took up his cup and said, 'May God bless this boy of yours, Abu Yacoub. He has been endowed not only with brains but also with an excellent character. I say to him, 'My son, buy yourself something to eat' and he says 'I'd rather buy something to read.' In my youth I too used to devour books. Every book is a strange world in which the reader can live as though he is not of this infamous world. Is there anything better than reading in such a world as ours, a world to which one is ashamed to belong? Wherever one looks one sees nothing but morals degenerating, virtue being trampled underfoot, friends betraying one another, sons rebelling against their fathers, mothers plotting against their daughters, the sated swallowing up the hungry and the hungry wanting to prey on all and sundry. Ah, by God, a book is the finest companion, as the poet said. When I grew up, though, I became occupied with other things. With what? With the world. The world's a strange place, Abu Yacoub, a strange place—' and he sipped down the last of his coffee.

'As you live nearby, why don't you pay us a visit sometimes?' said my mother, no doubt won over by his flattering remarks about me.

'And why not?' he said. 'I would be honoured,' and he stood up. Suddenly I saw, in a corner by the door, the gramophone. I had not noticed it before, engrossed as I was in our visitor's conversation. Yusuf went towards the gramophone and picked it up by the handle. At the door he said goodbye to my father, then turned to me. 'Walk with me for a bit.'

I went out with him, wondering whether he was thinking of giving me the gramophone or lending it to me. We had no sooner reached the lane when he said, 'I didn't mention the matter in the presence of your father and mother in case they should be upset—I've brought you the gramophone.'

'For me?' I cried.

'For you to buy.'

'Oh,' I said, my hopes dashed. 'But where will I get two pounds from?'

'Do you think it's easy for me to part with it? This gramophone is all I've got left from the good old days. Though I've sold everything else, I swore to myself that whatever happened I wouldn't sell this gramophone. I lost my money and returned from Egypt and lived like an animal in that hut, yet even so I didn't sell it. But I've got important business tonight. I shan't sell it to you, though, I'll pledge it with you. Give me one pound and I'll leave it with you—it and the records of course. Just one pound and it'll remain with you till I return the pound. In fact

you needn't even return it to me then. Hang on to it till I happen
to ask you for it back.'

'But, Yusuf, I haven't got a pound.'

I plunged my hand into my pocket and felt around for the
silver coins I had, conjuring up to myself the supreme joy of gaining possession of the gramophone. Seventy-three piastres, however,
was all I had.

'Think up some way of getting hold of a pound, Yacoub.'

Suddenly I took out all the money in my pocket. 'It's all I
have,' I said.

He was taken aback at the sight of it in the palm of my hand; he
obviously hadn't expected to extract such a large sum from me.
He put the gramophone on the ground.

'All right,' he said, 'Give them to me and take it.'

I emptied the money into his hand. When I took back five
piastres he raised no objection.

'And the records?'

'Come and get them.'

In a state of great excitement at my profitable deal, I hurried
off to the hut with him. I was just about to leave when he stopped
me and said, 'I saw you had a heap of magazines at your house.'

'Yes.'

'Can you give them to me?'

'But they're old ones.'

'Never mind. Give them to me to look through.'

I used to collect all the magazines I bought in the belief that
one day I would read them again. I felt no reluctance, however,
in returning with Yusuf and giving him some of them, for I con-
soled myself with the thought that after several days I would get
them back. My parents greeted him on our arrival home and we
put the gramophone and the records to one side; Yusuf then took
up the entire pile of magazines in his arms.

'Are you going to read them all?' I objected. 'Take just a few
of them.'

He winked at me—in the way he had at the foundry—and
gave a hoarse laugh. With his chin resting on top of the pile of
magazines he said, 'What have I to do with reading at my age,
Yacoub? I'll sell them by the pound and get myself a few piastres.'
Then he added, 'Directly I take back the gramophone I'll pay
you the money I get for them—down to the last piastre!'

'That's all right,' said my father. 'That's all right. Take them, my good man.'

With his arms hugging the magazines Yusuf left.

'Does Yusuf drink?' my father then asked.

'Yes,' I said.

'It seems he started his evening at home before visiting us,' he said laughing. 'It's Saturday night, isn't it? It seems he's in dire need of money tonight.'

We then turned our attention to the gramophone and began playing through the records over and over again.

'All our neighbours will be surprised,' said my mother, smiling with pleasure. 'Umm Abdullah will say: "It seems that the Abu Yacoubs also have a gramophone." May God blind the envious eye!'

When, on Monday morning, I went to the foundry I found Yusuf there in his usual shabby clothes.

'Good morning, Prince!' I called to him cheerfully.

'Good morning,' he muttered mournfully without looking up. When I attempted to draw him into conversation he answered with terse distaste. Realizing that he had no wish to talk, I applied myself to my work.

A little later Hanna the boss came in. 'What have you been up to now, Prince?' he asked, removing his coat.

'They told you?' muttered Yusuf, glancing up at the boss with a sheepish look.

'Of course they told me.'

'They're a lot of bastards.'

Hanna gave a loud burst of laughter. 'You're a dirty old man,' he said. 'Isn't it enough that you drink?'

'Aren't I human, Hanna?' Yusuf answered with painful entreaty. 'Tell me, honestly, aren't I made of flesh and blood?'

'And couldn't you take a fancy to anyone but Sobhiyya?'

'It was Sobhiyya or no one.'

'How many ate and drank all night long at your expense?'

'Four, five—no, by God, six.'

'Just to please her?'

'Yes, but what was the use?'

Again Hanna gave a bellow of laughter. 'And she didn't let you!' he whispered, drawing close to him.

'Who told you so? I kissed her, I tell you I kissed her!'

'All right, I believe you, I believe you.'

After a while Yusuf turned towards Hanna and said, 'Boss, care to buy a pair of trousers? They're new, they've only been worn once.'

'Is there a coat to match.'

'No.'

'What's happened to the coat?'

'I sold it that evening. I hadn't got enough money so I sold it to Abu Shlomo. By God, this is no life, Hanna. Three hundred pounds I spent in two months: drink, good times, women and—'

'Enough of that,' Hanna interrupted him. 'Get on with your work. There are new moulds to be made today. Yacoub! How many kilos of zinc have we got left?'

'About thirty,' I answered.

'That's all right,' he said. 'Let's get to work on them.'

A House for my Children

MAHMOUD DIAB

I T I S N ' T possible that the idea occurred to me suddenly, for I had always dreamed of having a house. Though in my dreams its features were not sharply defined, it was characterized by a general enveloping air of warmth and serenity. When, therefore, the chance presented itself I grasped it as though my life depended on it.

While the idea was not a sudden one to me, it came as a surprise to my wife, who was unable to hold back her tears for excitement. I didn't in fact surprise her with it as an idea, which would not have caused her such excitement, but in the form of an actual contract for a vacant plot of land on a new housing estate in the eastern part of the city.

This was on the birthday of my children, Hala and Hisham. The former was four years old and the latter three. Born in the same month, though not on the same day, we used to celebrate their birthdays together.

On returning home that day my wife asked me:

'Have you forgotten that today's the children's birthday?'

'No, I haven't forgotten,' I said softly, attempting to conceal my restlessness.

'Don't tell me you're broke,' she said slyly.

'No, I'm not broke.'

'They've been waiting for you and yet I see you've come back without even troubling to buy them a piastre's worth of sweets,' she said, indicating my empty hands.

'I'm fed up with getting them only toys and sweets.'

Unable to prepare the way for the surprise any better than this, I produced a large envelope from under my arm and handed it to her.

'My present's in this envelope,' I said, and she took out the contract and ran her eyes over it while I watched her in an ecstasy of pride. Failing to understand what it was about at first glance, she raised her beautiful face enquiringly.

'What's this?' she cried.

'It's a house for them,' I said, smiling.

Hisham crept out from behind, and buried his face between my legs and gave a soft laugh. I bent over, picked him up and began kissing him, oblivious of the unexpected results my surprise had wrought in my wife.

From that moment great changes came over her. No longer did she bring up the old story of my love affair which she had found out about some days ago. Whether she had forgotten about it or merely pretended to have done so I don't know. She also became more tender and gay and there wasn't a relative or friend of hers to whom she didn't announce the news of the house we'd be building. In fact she no longer enjoyed talking to me about anything else.

We went, the four of us, to the plot of land the following day, in order, as she put it, 'to give it the once over.' We stood by one corner of it, she beside me, radiant with smiles, while Hala and Hisham ran races nearby, shouting and stirring up little eddies of dust.

My wife was outlining what the house would be like and went on unconsciously repeating herself, 'It'll be a single storey, won't it? But when the children get bigger we'll add another one. We'll surround it with a large garden. I'd love a house of mine to have a garden. I'll look after it myself. I'll fill it with flowers. What sort of flowers do you like, darling? Isn't it funny that for five whole years I've never known what flowers you liked?'

'I like jasmine,' I said.

'We'll cover the garden with jasmine,' she cried. Then: 'Living in a house like this far away from the smoke and din of the city is beautifully healthy for the children. My grandfather used to have a lovely house in Mansoura—it had an acre of garden. Imagine! By the way, you must make provision for a laundry room on the roof, also a servants' room—'

'What do you mean by a servants' room?' I cut her short. 'I've spent precious years of my life turning a dream into reality and I'd ask you not to turn it into a nonsense!'

'All right—and the garage, the house must have a garage.'

'But I don't own a car.'

'You'll have a car some time and where would you put it if the house didn't have a garage?'

She called out to Hala to bring back her brother, then she let out a shrill laugh and raced after her children with the gaiety of a young girl.

My thoughts wandered far afield as I watched the three of them in the middle of the plot of land. Only when my wife returned and was standing by me did I come to. She repeated what she had told me before, embroidering on it, while I replied to her in between my thoughts with 'yes' or 'no', without paying any attention to what she was saying.

I remembered an old house, far away in both time and place. The place was the town of Ismailiyya; as to the time, I am able to fix it in terms of my age, for at that time I was eight or nine years old. We owned a house in that town, a modest single-storey house surrounded by a small but beautiful garden. It did, not, however, possess a servants' room, for we had no servants; nor did it have a garage, for my father had never been in a private motor-car in his life. I remember that there was a trellis of vines in our garden, and two mango trees, a lemon tree, and a large hen house. I also remember that my father would not be in the house for a minute before he'd take up the hoe and wield it in the garden, the fence of which was covered in strands of jasmine. I don't remember when it was we came to own that house or when we moved into it. I do remember, though, that my father was extremely proud of it, while my mother regarded our coming into possession of it as a stupendous and historic event. She had thus made of it a set date by which she fixed the events of her life and those of the whole family. Many is the time I have heard her say:

'When we moved to the house I was pregnant with so-and-so—' or 'when we bought the house my husband's salary was so much—' and similar expressions which I still smile at when I recollect them.

I don't remember any particular happenings that occurred at home during that period other than the birth of one of my brothers, the fifth of us all and the third male child. No doubt the other incidents were all so commonplace that they have left no special impression on my mind. I do remember, though, that when evening came a group of our neighbours would turn up to see my father and they'd gather out in the garden and converse on various topics, while we children would play around them, and the breezes of spring would blow drowsily, made sluggish with the aroma of jasmine. It must be that it was ever spring in our house in those days, for I can scarcely imagine it now without games in the garden and the smell of jasmine.

Then some events occurred which did not immediately break the monotony of life. For this reason I can scarcely remember them now in detail though I do remember vague echoes of them, as for instance that I began hearing the word 'war', a word new to me, being repeated at home far more frequently than the word 'bread'; it was also constantly used by the grown-ups in our street without my understanding its meaning to begin with. There were other words I learned by heart despite their difficulty and strangeness because of the way they were repeated: 'The Allies—the Axis—the Germans—the Maginot Line' and others, all of which were mere words that I chanced to hear.

My father and our neighbours gathered in the garden would talk only about such matters. They would divide up into two opposing factions, one wanting victory for the English and the other praying that the Germans would win. My father belonged to the latter faction, and I, in my turn, prayed for a German victory. Often I would hear my father say, 'A German victory means that the English would get out of Egypt,' though Uncle Hassan, our nearest neighbour, believed that if the English got out of Egypt it would mean the Germans entering it. The grown-ups would carry on long animated discussions which would end on one night, only to begin again on another, while we children, in our games, would divide ourselves up into two groups, one 'the English' and the other 'the Germans'. I naturally belonged to the latter. We would then indulge in childish warfare which left us puffing and blowing to the point of exhaustion.

When it was time to go to sleep I would slip into bed and lie there for a time listening to the voices of the grown-ups in the garden. I would single out my father's voice among them and would then try to conjure up a picture of the Germans. I did not picture the Germans as being the same size as the English or as looking like them, but saw them as both larger and more magnificent.

One night the air raid warning sounded. That, too, was something new and exciting in those days. The lights in the street and the houses went out and darkness, weighted down with tense silence, ruled. Ghostly forms gathered at the doorways and the scent of jasmine was diffused more strongly than on any previous night.

'German aeroplanes!' shouted my father. Gazing up at the sky and listening intently, I was able to make out a disjointed humming that cut through the solid darkness at the horizon's end and drew nearer.

'Will they bomb the town?' I asked my mother in terror. 'No,' my father answered here in the tones of someone well-informed on such matters. 'Hitler wouldn't do that. They're merely making for the English camps.'

English camps surrounded our small town on all sides, indeed were almost touching it. We heard terrible explosions which I don't remember ceasing for an instant. An aeroplane burst into flames in the sky; then ghostly forms with heavy tread passed by announcing to the rushing people that the planes were laying waste the town and advising them to keep away from the houses.

Bands of phantom figures rushed out, running and stumbling in the street. Our parents got up and hurried us off with the terrified crowds towards the desert which stretched to the north-east of the city; there was no other place of escape.

That night seemed like nothing so much as the gathering of the dead at the end of the world. This was how father expressed it and my mother later repeated his words. People were pushing one another about crazily, barefoot in their night-gowns, calling out to one another in the midst of that solid darkness. 'Where are you, Muhsin? Where are the children? Did you close the door? Let the house go to hell! Hurry up, Lawahiz! Wait for me, father,' while the barking of dogs rang out in every direction. I cried as I ran, with three of my brothers and sisters—many were the children that cried in the midst of that solid darkness.

I am unable to say exactly how many people took refuge in the desert on that confused night. All I know is that the black desert was filled with them so that we were like people 'at an anniversary feast of some saint—at the anniversary feast of Sheikh Hitler,' as Uncle Hassan said ironically.

'Help me dig,' said my father to my mother in the voice of an expert on these matters. 'Dig, children! Hassan Effendi, make a hole for your children to protect them from the shrapnel.'

We dug a large hole in which my father fitted us tightly together, while explosions thundered in the town and the disjointed humming filled the sky and sudden flashes of light burst forth like lightning from time to time. Then the aeroplanes were circling above us.

'They're right over our heads,' shouted my father. My mother gave an anguished scream and threw herself on to us to cover us with her body. My father did likewise. Voices were raised throughout the desert ordering the people to be silent, followed by other voices telling them to shut up. I craned my neck, thrust up my head, and took a look, over my father's shoulder, at the sky in the hope of seeing a German in his aeroplane so that I might verify the picture I had stored up in my head of the Germans. However, my father violently pushed my head back into the sand.

'Why are they bombing us if it's the English they're fighting?' whispered my mother.

My father answered not a word.

'Aren't we their friends?' I asked.

'God's curse be on both of them!' my father shouted angrily.

The aeroplanes came so close to the ground that I could feel the reverberation of their engines shaking my body. Then sudden, fearful lights that whistled stripped bare the desert and were followed by shots that 'sprayed the people like rain' as Uncle Hassan's wife said the day we met her for the first time two years after that night.

The shouts that rose up from the ground mingled with the explosions coming from the sky, forming an inferno of clamour that still echoes in my ears despite the passage of years. When morning came my mother gave herself up to a fit of hysterics, as did all the women around us, and it was in vain that my father attempted to bring her back to her senses.

Eventually the slaughter came to an end, the aeroplanes dissolved from our skies and the explosions and all the other noises from the heavens ceased, making way for the crazed noises of the earth, until the blackness of night melted away before the first thread of daylight.

We got up out of our hole and followed our parents in utter exhaustion, our eyes tight closed as ordered by them lest we should see the carnage around us. We made our way to our house but didn't find it; nor did we find Uncle Hassan's house, nor a third house and half a fourth in the same street: they had all become heaps of rubble. On the heap that had been our house one of our geese roamed around in bewilderment; she was followed by one of her young of whom there had been five. There was not a trace of the scent of jasmine in the air.

Like someone in a daze my father stood looking first at the ruins, then at my mother who had been rendered speechless by the unexpected sight. The final and ghastly event of that day was to see my father crying, something I had never seen in all my life.

'A whole life's hard work gone in an instant,' my mother muttered through her tears.

'Thanks be to God,' mumbled my father, drying his tears, 'we weren't inside it.' Silence enveloped us for a while, then he said, 'You must emigrate into the country—' and in 'emigrate' I learned a new word that day.

'Let's go now to your aunt's house,' my father resumed, 'if it too hasn't been destroyed, until we arrange our affairs.'

The melancholy procession re-formed and off we went with miserable gait, 'as though at a funeral'—as I used to say whenever I recounted the story to my friends when I had grown up. Before moving away from the ruins of our house I saw my father pick up a protruding piece of stone and hurl it at the big heap of rubble.

'When the war ends,' I heard him say, 'we'll return and build it again.'

And the war ended . . .

My reverie was broken by a jog at my shoulder and my wife's voice saying, 'What's wrong with you? Aren't you listening? When shall we start building?'

The spectre of the ruins of our house still filled my head.

'Those people who invented all these terrible means of destruction,' I said, 'why didn't they think of inventing something to protect houses against them?'

Surprise appeared on my wife's face. She stared into mine with questioning tenderness. I smiled and added, sighing and waving my hand as though to chase away my thoughts, 'It doesn't matter, because I don't believe there'll be another war.'

Which only increased the signs of surprise on my dear wife's face.

Summer Journey

MAHMOUD TEYMOUR

BALIGH EFFENDI was a government official to whose good nature and kind heart both his superiors and those under him could testify. He used to perform the work entrusted to him in a satisfactory manner and had not taken a holiday, summer or winter, for many years. In the morning he would go off to his office, while his evenings were spent relaxing at a café.

A particularly hot summer set in and Baligh Effendi felt the need for a real rest; his incessant work had taken its toll and he no longer enjoyed his former perfect health. Hurrying off to his chief he diffidently asked if he might take a holiday. This request his chief gladly granted him.

Baligh Effendi was all smiles as he left his chief's office. No sooner, however, was he on his own than he found himself confusedly wondering where he would spend this holiday. Should he divide the time equally between his lonely, dismal home, where there was not a soul to sit with, and the café he frequented where the din and hubbub resembled a market auction?

A friend who had a bent for medicine advised him to get away from the capital; to choose some place where the weather and the surroundings would be different from the place where he had lived for so many years; only thus would he enjoy a proper rest and be restored to health.

Baligh Effendi decided to take his kind friend's advice and go off immediately.

There were but two choices before him; The first was to go to Hagg Rizk in Kafr Sufaita, the other to go and see Mr. Rashad in Alexandria. For a while he weighed up the advantages of being with his relative Hagg Rizk as against being with his friend Mr. Rashad, between life in the country and life at a summer resort, between Kafr Sufaita lying among villages and fields and Alexandria, the Pride of the Seas, surrounded by every delight and diversion. This business of weighing and comparing ended with his choosing Alexandria.

It would be a real surprise for his friend Rashad who would certainly never expect to have a visit from him. Why not give him a surprise? Hadn't Baligh Effendi more than once played host to his friend Rashad during his visits to the capital? Often he had stayed with him without being invited or without announcing that he was coming, and he had repeatedly told Baligh Effendi that he was welcome any time he liked at his home in Moharrem Bey. How eager he was to visit Alexandria where the fascinating beach life had been so alluringly described by his friend!

Baligh Effendi had never been to Alexandria nor had the pleasure of seeing the sea. The pictures he had seen in the papers, however, and the images he had built up in his mind from what he had heard, all came to him as he made his way to his friend's home in the district of Moharrem Bey, his heart filled with happy expectations.

After enquiring the way several times he arrived at the address just before noon. He found it to be one of those towering multi-storied buildings put up solely for reasons of gain in which the inhabitants are packed together like bees in a hive. His friend Rashad was living in one of the top flats.

Baligh went up the stairs carrying his suitcase stuffed with all sorts of presents. He reached the door of the flat completely out of breath, perspiration dripping from his brow. On pressing the bell a ringing noise echoed forth and presently the door gaped open to reveal a fat, flaccid woman with coarse features, sullen and scowling.

'It's forbidden,' she muttered, speaking as though forcibly wrestling the words from her mouth, 'to ring the bell, I'm telling you.'

'I'm sorry—I didn't know,' stammered Baligh in embarrassment. 'I'm Baligh, Mr. Rashad's friend—please tell him I'm here.'

He managed to bring a confused smile to his lips but the fat, flaccid woman paid no attention to it. Putting her index finger to his mouth she whispered:

'I would ask you, Baligh Effendi, not to raise your voice or make any noise. Madam hasn't had a wink of sleep for nights. Come along.'

With tortoise-like steps she advanced into the hall with Baligh following in her tracks. He stole a glance at her extraordinary frame and it seemed to him that her joints sank one into another like lumps of dough, making ever new and delightful shapes.

No sooner had she brought him to the drawing-room than she left him. The heavy, all-prevailing silence alarmed him as he sat down forlornly. He recalled the words with which the woman had received him and tried to make out what it was all about. From time to time he was able to hear strained whisperings, uneasy sighs, wary footsteps, and his discomfort increased yet further.

Suddenly a female cry, an anguished call for help, rang out. Baligh jumped up trembling. More cries followed, louder and more grievous, and Baligh began to pace about the room in utter consternation. Then quietness reigned in the flat and Baligh sat back in his chair mopping his face and fanning himself with his handkerchief, his ears pricked for any noise.

He heard the creaking of the flat door being opened and spotted his friend Rashad entering warily, bare-headed, with ruffled hair and twitching features. He greeted Baligh in an off-hand manner and followed up by asking eagerly:

'Isn't the delivery over?'

'What delivery?' Baligh answered him in confusion.

Several words and phrases formed themselves on Rashad's lips and revealed the unusual state of affairs that ruled in the household: Rashad was, for the first time, awaiting 'a happy event'. His wife had been having labour pains for two days and had been undergoing a most difficult delivery. Rashad's nerves had gone completely to pieces; unable to remain in the house for a second, he had spent the whole day wandering around aimlessly, only calling at the house for the latest bulletin.

At that moment the wife's voice was raised in a reverberating scream and Rashad began striking his head with clenched fists.

'I'll go mad!' he burst forth in a choked voice. 'I shall go raving mad—I can't—I can't stand any more.' He slipped out of the door of the flat and hurled himself down the stairs like a wild animal on the run.

Baligh remained standing in the centre of the room in a daze. He thought of leaving the house at once and saving himself from this torment that surrounded him. His glance fell upon the suitcase a few steps away, bulging with presents and almost bursting in impotent rage. It occurred to him to stay on for a while, that maybe the worst had passed, but immediately he heard the wife let out a scream:

'I'm dying . . . I'm dying.'

Baligh found his hand taking hold of the handle of the suitcase and his feet propelling him towards the door. Suddenly he found himself face to face with the fat woman.

'Rashad Effendi's left the house, more mad than sane,' she said, giving him a sideways glance. 'There are only some ladies here and the midwife's asking for certain necessary things. What's to be done? What's to be done?'

The midwife emerged, the piles of flesh imprisoned within that short white piece of cloth called a dress wriggling and writhing, doing everything possible to make good their escape.

She approached Baligh, head held high and sleeves rolled up as though entering a wrestling ring. In a hoarse commanding voice she began enumerating to him her requirements.

'These things must be brought at once,' she ended up. Baligh, staring at the vast bare arms with the bulging muscles, hastily answered:

'You'll have everything you want in just a matter of moments!'

He ran off towards the door, to return after a while with a large parcel containing bottles and other purchases from the chemist's. No sooner had he arrived back at the flat than he almost fell down from exhaustion. On reflecting about the whole business he began to feel irritated. He soon pulled himself to-gether, however—after all, wasn't it reward enough that he had satisfied his conscience and behaved gallantly at a moment of distress?

As he entered the hall that vast arm with the bulging muscles stretched out towards him and quickly took the parcel, disappear-ing with it into one of the rooms. No sooner had it vanished than the fat woman emerged.

'There's a visitor in the drawing-room,' she said weakly, as though about to give up the ghost, and she began pushing him before her. The visitor was a neighbour who had heard the news and had come to make enquiries and present his congratulations. Baligh welcomed him warmly, thinking that he could make use of him at this critical time. The visitor, however, no sooner made his greetings than he departed with the usual good wishes for health and strength.

A steady stream of visitors followed. No sooner had Baligh bidden one goodbye than he was receiving another. He felt he was most eloquent in the way he described the state of affairs, especially when he knew nothing more of the heroine than a voice, like the stifled whistle of a train, giving vent to its complaints and seeking help.

Chaos broke out in the house with people coming and going, with voices raised in exasperation, while the cries for help that came from the heroine's room were unceasing, though at times louder than others. The whole house had been electrified into alertness and Baligh felt himself to be its pivot. He was possessed of a feeling of great pride as people went hither and thither at his bidding.

The buxom midwife with the vast arm and bulging muscles came up to him.

'The situation's difficult,' she said, her hands on her waist. 'I must have someone to help me . . . Get a doctor.'

Baligh was unable to answer a word. Where would he get a doctor from, he who till today had never set foot in the place? He was about to explain to the midwife his thoughts on the matter when she thrust a piece of paper at him.

'Here are the names of some dependable doctors. Get one of them for me at once. Don't forget that in your hands lies the fate of two human beings.'

With the midwife's words ringing in his ears, Baligh Effendi took the paper and rushed out of the house. He soon saw a taxi which he stopped. In it he tore off up hill and down dale, scarcely arriving at one address than it rushed him off to another—on one occasion he was informed that the doctor was out on a call, on another that the doctor was enjoying an afternoon siesta and wasn't to be disturbed. After some delay he made his way back to the house with a doctor whose name was not contained in the list but had been produced by the taxi-driver.

The doctor applied himself to his work with due energy and diligence. In his neat white smock, red rubber gloves and white cap, he had skilfully arranged that a lock of his wavy hair should show up lustrously against his forehead.

The pace had taken its toll of Baligh. He had been uninterruptedly on the go, receiving neighbours asking for news, giving orders raucously to the fat and flaccid woman, obediently taking orders from the muscular midwife and listening to the man in the white cap who was so delighted with his lustrous lock of wavy hair, and between whiles rushing up and down the stairs seeing to the household's requirements.

Suddenly a piercing cry rang out from the mother's room: the awaited newborn proclaiming its arrival, a piece of flesh weighing no more than a few pounds which could turn the world upside down for days and nights on end. Baligh felt a tremor of excitement run through him as the members of the family—both those he knew and those he didn't—bore down upon him to exchange joyous congratulations; even the fat and flaccid woman, beside herself with happiness, embraced him and implanted two resounding kisses on his cheeks. As for the midwife with the muscular arms, she kept up an incessant chatter about the heroic manner she had gone about her job and how she had managed to rescue the child and its mother from the jaws of imminent death. After a while the man with the white cap made his appearance holding in his hands the newborn babe so well wrapped up that none of it was visible save two beady eyes and a screaming mouth.

The doctor thrust the howling bundle at Baligh, who took it from him in some confusion and began walking round and round with it. Things eventually quietened down and the doctor took his leave, Baligh accompanying him to the door and pressing some notes into his hand.

When Baligh had finished saying goodbye to the doctor he went up again to the flat to find the whole place immersed in silence. He strolled into the drawing-room, and looking at his watch found that it had gone full circle and that it was now midnight. Feeling as though his limbs were giving way under him, he slumped into a chair. With a wide yawn that convulsed his whole frame, he got up and changed over to a comfortable sofa. It wasn't long before he was in a deep sleep of exhaustion.

After a while Baligh felt two hands shaking him insistently. He raised his head in alarm, his eyes blinking, to find himself looking at the spectre of a man twisting about and screaming in front of him like a juggler at a fair.

'Congratulate me, my friend,' he was saying. 'Your arrival has brought me luck—I'm the father of a baby boy!' Baligh made an effort to open his eyes as he wiped away the saliva running down the corner of his mouth.

'Congratulations, old chap—congratulations,' he muttered hoarsely. In no time he had fallen back on the sofa, his snores as loud as the lowing of an ox.

The Election Bus

TOUMA AL-KHOURI

IT WAS the election season. Like eggs whipped up into a froth, the villages were in a turmoil of excited activity, their alleyways as busy as beehives. Buses rushed continually up and down in droves, transporting voters from towns and villages, from every farm, hamlet and homestead.

Old men in their nineties, the infirm, those scarce up from the operating table, the blind and the halt, all were being brought along to vote. And why not? A single vote could well bring defeat to a candidate and put another in his seat in Parliament.

All means of transport, old and new, were being employed for this purpose; from donkeys on hire to the peasant woman's ox, to mules and camels, to lorries and buses and every conceivable kind of wheeled vehicle.

And little wonder, for while some of the mountain roads were as good as motorways, others, in process of being resurfaced, were as jagged as bayonets for kilometres on end. Some were still under construction, others scarcely existed at all, only too often requiring a guide to show one the way. On these, animals were the sole means for transporting voters, ballot officers, and clerks. There were also villages which could only be reached 'by descent', like inspiration from above, either by parachute or helicopter; or else one had to slip out of the country like a hashish smuggler and make one's way back again from a neighbouring country, partly on horseback, partly on foot, travelling for at least a day and a night.

Mahrousa, Abu Fahl's new bus, was making its way towards the northern province, the majority of the voters it carried being by origin from that district. Despite the fact that the walls inside bore such spells against the evil eye as 'The envious prevails not' and 'This do I owe to my God', it did not escape the comments of certain envious people, male and female, because of its being so profitably crammed with passengers.

The person who started it was Umm Suleiman, the widow of Salloum al-Ja'eetawi who, miraculously escaping when his bus had crashed down into the valley, died shortly afterwards from sheer grief.

'Abu Fahl must be making a thousand liras a day.'

'If not, how would he be having a two-storey house?'

'And orchards of cherry trees, peaches, and apples.'

'Don't forget the new building in Beirut.'

Umm Suleiman, her resentment smarting under these searing comments, was unable to control herself.

'And what's it to do with us?' she interrupted, putting an end to the conversation.

'May God bestow His blessings on one and all.'

'Amen,' intoned the others, shamefaced, quite forgetting that it was she who had started it all.

Mahrousa continued along the side of the valley with its passengers laughing and exchanging pleasantries.

The turnings were many, and the road narrow and suspended in mid-air with fearsome chasms and deep valleys on either side.

The passengers, most of whom were from the coast, were, though alarmed, held spellbound by the grandeur of the scenery. Some of them, frightened to gaze down, closed their eyes in a pretence of sleep, hoping that they might be snatched away—at one bound, as in a dream—to the opposite side of the road where the going was safe and easy. A few took pleasure in contemplating the little hillocks and bushes bordering the road as they glorified the Creator aloud: Allah! Allah!, as though to ingratiate themselves with Him, albeit indirectly, so that He might protect them from the disaster of falling headlong into that abyss from which one would arise only on the Day of Judgement. Yet others, as though in defiance, pretended to laugh—a laugh that was a cross between a curling of the lips and a smile at pistol-point—craning their necks out of the windows and pointing down into the depths below, their hearts in their mouths.

Mahrousa, occupied in making its way along the shoulder of the valley, bellowed and hooted, striking terror into the hyenas in their lairs and the coveys of crouching partridges.

The feeling of discomfort was dispersed at long last when the bus left the valley ridge for the spacious breast of the hill, where the road widened out like the palm of a hand and the passengers heaved a sigh of relief and returned to their former hilarity; one cracking jokes, another humming some Western tune, while a third broke forth into a plaintive *mawwal*. In a matter of minutes the bus was transformed into a regular orchestra; one group singing, another clapping, a third stamping. Those finding the atmosphere not to their liking silently mumbled or inwardly cursed—the only other choice being to bash their heads against the wall.

Along the route there were numerous halts: a passenger wishing to make a purchase, a mother with a child wanting to make water; some wishing to get down to quench their thirst from the waters of a nearby spring reputed to be efficacious for gall-stones; a woman seeking a lift for a short distance, a mere stone's throw (a throw of several kilometres). But it was no trouble, the bus was spacious enough, and the driver's heart even more so. The new passengers were quite content, standing or sitting, while those who had seats on someone else's lap (or with someone else on theirs), bore up with patience, especially after hearing a young 'tough', with slanting tarboosh and upturned moustache, declare in a deep gruff voice, as he made room beside him for a young girl with a face like a full moon, 'Think nothing of it, fellows. We're all one happy family.'

Another, giving up his place to a girl-friend of the first girl's and spread-eagling himself above her like a protective umbrella, commented: 'Elections happen only once every four years. Make room for them, you people.'

No sooner was *Mahrousa* overlooking a village loyal to the candidate than it proclaimed its arrival with blasts on the horn. When they learned that Zarzour Bey himself was in the village they burst out in unison:

'We're all for you, Zarzour Bey,
We're all for you, Zarzour Bey.'

Loud voices sang out in harmony accompanied by clapping, stamping, and slaps on the sides of the bus with hands and sticks; this was immediately followed by the ululations of women from high up on the balconies, on the roads and from the flat roofs of the houses.

The Bey looked down majestically at the procession, his

appearance rendered yet more radiant by his being dressed in spotless white. This alone was quite enough to give rise to a series of reverberating bangs from every sort and kind of weapon dating back to Napoleon Bonaparte and before.

Just as a single rooster raises its voice and is joined by the cocks of the quarter together in answer, so did a single shot suddenly turn the whole village into a battlefield.

> 'We're all for you, Zarzour Bey,
> We're all for you, Zarzour Bey.'

The voices alone were enough to bring down the seven walls of Jericho, to say nothing of the accompanying ululations of the women and the spluttering of Hotchkiss and Tommy guns.

The voices of the passengers rang out with this refrain, while bullets whistled into space; the sound carried from valley to valley, bringing terror to the birds of the air and the beasts of the forest, till a bend in the road cut *Mahrousa* off from both eye and ear.

The way was a long one and the passengers grew weary with so much standing and sitting, so much going up hill and down dale. One of them, therefore, amused himself by starting to sing the plaintive notes with which the singer of popular ballads warms up; it was soon taken up in chorus and accompanied by much clapping. In no time at all the whole bus had broken into song: from the driver to the young girl sitting alongside him, to his assistant who stood indefatigably the whole way by the door, to the old man of seventy at the rear, resting on his stick with his foreign-style hat pushed back on to the crown of his head, to the young boys and girls squatting by the windows, to the children seated in their elders' laps.

The *Mu'anna* and the *Muwwal*, the *Karradi*, the *Itaba* and the *Abu Zallouf*, none were missed out. The first was sung by an old man with hoarse, touching tenderness, while the *Abu Zallouf* was performed by a young girl with hair done like a boy's. The duet of the *Karradi* was between the driver and his assistant; all thrust and parry, it brought tears of laughter to the eyes of all.

Every kind of song was tried out; all, in one way or another, incomplete or mutilated. All talents were used to the full: those who knew a line by heart sang it, while those who knew no more than half joined in with that. The really accomplished were those who could go through a whole song on their own without help. No matter whether one's voice was melodious or rotten as old wood, all ears listened and all hands clapped appreciatively.

It then occurred to one of them, carried away by all the singing, to dance a *dabkeh*.

'Make room for him, everyone, make room for him.'

Sufficient space was made available in the gangway by those who had occupied it sitting three or four to each seat made for two; some of the passengers sat on each other's knees, others on the backs of the seats or on the backs of those sitting down. Those of both sexes who were standing were thrown tightly together, propping each other up by shoulder, waist, or back.

The dancer was an accomplished performer and caused great delight. Without warning a bottle of arak was whipped out. Its owner took a gulp, after which it was grabbed by various hands. Its odour—no lavender ever smelt so aromatic!—was quickly diffused through the bus. Nostrils dilated and appetites opened up as bottles and flasks were produced and passed round.

Someone objected when he saw the driver steering with one hand and emptying the remains of a flask down his throat with the other. Guffaws of laughter rang out on every side, the driver joining in with a hearty bellow.

'A whole barrel of arak couldn't make Abu Fahl drunk!' commented the driver's assistant.

'To Abu Fahl's good health,' called out a young man, holding a bottle of arak in the air.

'To Abu Fahl's good health,' shouted others in reply, downing their glasses with abandoned laughter.

At the back the short, slender form of the old man stood up.

'Hey, we don't want to get ourselves killed,' he shouted, waving his hat. 'Don't get the driver drunk.'

His husky voice went unheard except for a young man sitting nearby who burst out laughing, then turned to a friend beside him and whispered: 'This fellow's mighty keen not to die!'

The others glanced in the direction of the old man. Finding that he was twitching nervously and mumbling to himself with rage, the young man stood up and shouted, winking to the driver:

'Step on it, driver, you're doing fine—
Up to one hundred and ninety-nine!'

Clapping, he went on repeating the phrase, with his head swinging on his thin neck like a pendulum, back and forth between the driver and the old man. The latter was beside himself with rage and kept muttering:

'Where has this fiend sprung from?'

The whole bus then took up the refrain, punctuating it with handclaps:

'Step on it, driver, you're doing fine—
Up to one hundred and ninety-nine.'

The driver did 'step on it' and *Mahrousa* seemed to take flight— as indeed did the heart of the old man—intoxicated by the arak, the petrol and the rhythmic singing punctuated by piercing handclaps. Not a bus, not a car, not a lorry, not a living creature did it allow to stand in its path—all were overtaken as it thundered on in a cloud of dust which rose up from its wheels and formed a halo about its head.

In vain did the old man fume with rage, in vain raise his stick menacingly, wave his hat threateningly: it merely increased the driver's ardour, the passengers' singing, and *Mahrousa*'s headlong flight.

The dancer, flushed and sweating, continued to dance to each new song, while under him the bus gambolled over the potholes and swayed drunkenly at the bends and corners.

The arak went on circulating among the passengers and it wasn't long before stomachs, sharpened by drink, were demanding food. From baskets, bundles and suitcases food in prodigious quantities was shared out in a great pooling of resources. Into each and every stomach there came to rest a portion of the many different foods that were to hand: tinned sardines, canned meat, sausages, and small pork chippolatas, rounds of *kubbeh*, fried and grilled salted meat, pieces of charcoal-broiled mutton, boiled eggs, baked potatoes, fried aubergines, cheese, sour cream, tomatoes, cucumber, and black olives.

Then came the fruit course, handed round in as many forms as the munificent climate of the country provides; from grapes and figs, bananas and peaches, to plums and cherries and apples and pears.

When the bundles and baskets were depleted, the stock of songs exhausted, and jaws had wearied of munching and throats grown hoarse with undiluted arak, the radio was given full play to delight the passengers with a variety of songs from countries near and far. Some yawned, others lay back in a stupor, some nodded sentimentally, others slept. *Mahrousa* alone continued to roar and hoot and gambol along the old pitted, winding road, rocking the sleepers, jogging up the food in their stomachs, and jolting the intoxicated and the drowsy.

With the contents of his stomach whisked about by *Mahrousa*'s dance over the potholed road, one passenger was unable to stop himself stretching his head out of the window and vomiting noisily. Those seated behind him tried to duck without success; it was those who were dozing, however, who fared the worst.

The bus filled with protests and laughter as one wiped his nose, another his hair, a third his front, a fourth the pocket of his coat or shirt. Several quarrels and fights almost broke out—and indeed would have done so had it not been for the intervention of a few good-hearted types who patched things up as best they could before they got out of hand.

It was natural, in order to bring about a change in an atmosphere charged with animosity and the fumes of vomit, that something be done to restore to the hearts of one and all their former gaiety—even though nothing could be done about the soiled suits and frocks—and so succour was sought in the radio's latest popular songs:

> 'By your eyes, talk to us.
> Were it not for them we would not have come.'

Everyone bestirred himself at the sound; those who were asleep woke up; the torpid came to life again; those who had been stretching and yawning burst into a fit of renewed animation; faces that had been angry and frowning beamed with joy. Once again those passengers who made up the chorus began with renewed energy to accompany the singer on the radio with their own singing and clapping:

> 'You let us half-way down the well,
> Then cut the rope behind us.'
> Oh my. Oh my. Oh my.'

All were wholly engrossed in the music and singing, all that is except for the driver whose attention was being distracted by the 'sweet young thing' beside him. He was, it would seem, head over heels in love with her, which love he expressed by side-long glances through lids rendered heavy with arak, food and pre-cipitate passion. 'The sweet young thing' had never in fact been sweet, but the passing scenery enveloped everything in beauty, even her. The driver had never actually been particularly keen on her type, but the road was a long one and their two legs did keep touch-ing whenever *Mahrousa* rounded a sharp bend.

Meanwhile the chorus was absorbed in repeating the words:

> 'You let us half-way down the well,
> Then cut the rope behind us.'

The driver availed himself of the opportunity to extend his love-play beyond mere oglings to a distending of the neck and a stretching of pursed lips, and he swung the bus round the bends so that he might snatch a kiss from the cheek of 'the sweet young thing'. 'The sweet young thing' made no objection but laughed contentedly as she submitted to this barefaced flirting (which passed unnoticed save by a married man at the back and a bachelor behind him).

The married man, his appetite whetted by the driver's love-play, implanted a furtive kiss on the elbow of the lady on his right instead of on the cheek of his wife who sat on his left. From the one he received a slap, from the other a few caustic words, and thus the matter ended. The lady's husband, being drunk, remained blissfully unaware of the incident, otherwise the con-sequences might well have been unpleasant.

The bachelor, roused by the scenes on either side of him, was unable to contain himself.

'And the best of luck!' he shouted, swallowing his saliva and firing his pistol in the air. As though he had been the only one to notice the shot, the driver urged *Mahrousa* on to even greater efforts, at which the old man at the back protested at the top of his voice:

'Take it easy, my dear sir, take it easy,' but as before his voice was drowned in the singing and general hubbub. And once again that 'fiend' just to spite the frightened old man, started up his former refrain:

> 'Step on it, driver, you're doing fine—
> Up to one hundred and ninety-nine.'

And the driver stepped on it.

This time, though, he should have stepped on the brake and not on the accelerator. He was in the process of overtaking a Fiat car and was negotiating the bend on the left-hand side of the road at a frenzied speed when he met head-on with a lorry taking the corner on its right-hand side.

Despite the spell that was written up above *Mahrousa*'s windscreen: 'Drive on, for God's eye watches over you,' God, it seemed, had on this occasion no wish to watch over it with His eye. This was to be explained no doubt by the simple fact that the wording read 'Drive on' and not 'Fly on.'

After flying through the air, *Mahrousa*, gazelle-like, bounded down one terrace, a second and a third, then landed on its back, returned again on to its front, then again on its back, and thus it remained with its front wheels rotating as though kicking out at the air.

While the air reverberated with a variety of groans and moans, screams and curses, the radio, alone of the occupants to escape unscathed, loudly chanted away:

> 'You let us half-way down the well
> Then cut the rope behind us.
> Oh my. Oh my. Oh my.'

As though in protest at the dissonant chorus which accompanied its tune on this occasion, the radio stopped abruptly. The silence was followed by a scraping sound, followed immediately by the appearance of the seventy-year old man dragging himself from under the bus.

As he turned his gaze on the bus, his head clasped in his hands, and saw it lying prostrate, the picture of the Bey on its front standing upside down, he was overcome with a fit of hysterical laughter and started dancing, clapping and singing:

> 'We're all for you, Zarzour Bey,
> We're all for you, Zarzour Bey.'

Which refrain the poor fellow still sings over and over again as he passes his days in the asylum to which he has since been confined.

Summer

ZAKARIA TAMER

H ER BODY was beautiful and warm. She tried to put it out of reach of his hands the moment he sat down beside her on the couch, but his arm had been quick to encircle her waist tightly. Her body was full and rounded and the softness of her flesh sent a convulsive shudder through his limbs. Though the girl's eyes were captivating, irresistible, they contained a pathetic appeal. With lowered gaze she said, 'Let me go, Majid—please.'

His face was near to hers. His lips approached hers and touched them lightly, just sufficiently for him to feel their delicate softness. At that moment he was overwhelmed by a strange sensation that almost brought him to his knees before her, letting his head drop into her lap, his breathing heavy.

'Let me go, Majid—please. I want to leave.'

How could he let her go? Often he had implored her to visit him, and now here they were alone in a room with the door barred. How could he let her go?

'I love you, Itaf,' he said in a low, trembling voice.

'You're lying,' she said coyly. 'You don't love me.'

He was unable to define exactly the nature of his feelings for her: did he love her or did he merely desire her body?

He kissed her lips greedily and asked: 'Why would I kiss you like this if I didn't love you?'

Though she knew the answer, though she saw it in his eyes, in the strange, hungry look that made her terrified, she was unable to answer his question. Some obscure thing within her body began to awaken, producing a hard core of alarm deep inside her. She wished she could close her eyes for a moment, then open them again suddenly and find herself in a street thronged with people or in her room with the sound of her mother's voice calling out from time to time.

She was unable to prevent a long sigh escaping from her lips as Majid's rough hand touched her body, a hand intoxicated by the smoothness.

'Let me go, Majid,' she said. 'Someone may see us.'

'We're alone.'

'The window's open.'

A woman standing on the balcony of the building opposite laughed and said to a woman standing beside her: 'Did you see what happened? Majid, our neighbours' son, has taken a girl into the house—his parents are away—and here he is closing the window of his room despite the heat.'

Under the balcony a policeman's whistle blared out, followed by the screech of brakes as a car came to a sudden halt. A woman's face peered through the window enquiringly at the policeman.

The policeman stared back at the beautiful, radiant face. A moment of silence passed before he said: 'You were speeding.'

'I confess it,' she answered in a sweet, gentle voice that stirred within him a mysterious tenderness.

A strange smile played in the policeman's eyes as he waved her on. The car drew away from him and he followed it with his gaze till it disappeared. The beautiful face, the voice, the smile, all these things had reminded him of the previous night when he had quarrelled with his wife, of how he had got into bed and moved up close to her and she had not stirred. The bitch! She knew how to take her revenge on him, if he kept her short of funds, by presenting him with a cold, passive body.

The sun cast its flames above him; the street was deserted. He was seized by a strong yearning to be at home, stretched out in the coolness of his room with his wife beside him.

The sun was cruelly hot and the sweat poured clammily from his body. He stared at a girl who came out from the dark mouth of a building and made towards the nearby grocer's shop.

The grocer raised his head from his book of accounts and wiped away the sweat from his face with the palm of his hand. He stared at the servant-girl who had entered and now stood before him. She was so close to him that had he leaned forward slightly his face would have been touching her breasts. They were so fully developed that he felt in awe of them. Many a time had he sought to laugh off this feeling of his and had tried to respond to her many advances, but each time the sensation of awe was too strong for him and he had been frozen in his tracks. Why was it that he always remembered her whenever his teeth bit into a ripe, juicy apple?

'What are you sitting there for like the dead?' shouted the servant. 'Are you ill? Get up and give me what I want.'

He continued staring at her for a moment, then stretched out an eager, trembling hand towards her massive breasts. Without moving the servant gave him a broad smile.

'Are you in a hurry?' he asked.

'They're waiting for me.'

'Will you come this evening?'

She tossed her head and laughed softly, then stretched out her fingers and gave his lower lip a sharp pinch.

The sun blazed down crazily: the cool breeze was dead and the street semi-deserted.

Itaf rested her head on Majid's chest. 'My father will kill me if he finds out,' she said.

'Do you regret it?'

'No, I don't. When shall we get married, Majid?'

'We shall get married soon, my darling.'

Majid took refuge in silence. Itaf got to her feet and said: 'I'm going—I'm late.'

Majid accompanied her to the door. Coldly he held her to him, kissed her. She was happy, her face radiant with joy. She kissed him passionately before closing the door behind her.

He went quickly back to his room and threw himself into a chair. He felt that the threads that bound him to life had suddenly been broken, leaving him at odds with everything around him.

Itaf's question bore down into his very depths: When shall we get married?

He shied away from such a question. She had given herself to him and was now asking for the price: marriage. Everything in his city had its set price; no one gave anything for nothing. All were merchants of a new and superior type, lurking everywhere behind their various masks. How he loathed this type of human being! He loathed them savagely and now he had discovered that Itaf was one of them.

'When shall we get married?' she had asked him.

'We shall get married soon,' he had replied at once, doltishly.

What was to be done? His mind refused to think about it. It

had turned into a lump of solid stone. Depressed, he rose from the chair, put on his coat, and left the room to go out to the street.

The street was his great refuge. He walked slowly, heedless of the savagely scorching rays of the sun.

'When shall we get married?' Itaf had said.

'We shall get married soon,' he had replied at once, doltishly.

Previously he had dreamed of marrying Itaf, but now everything had changed. If only she had yielded to him as evidence of her love! But that loathsome question had sprung forward brutally demanding its price of marriage. It had destroyed everything.

What was to be done? Majid came to a stop and leaned back against a garden wall. What was to be done? Should he marry her? Should he pay the price? There was nothing within him but disgust. He would not marry her—let tomorrow bring what scandals and calamities it might!

Majid spat savagely on the ground, then continued on his way with heavy tread. Before him the asphalt with its tired brown face panted under the hot sunlight.

Note on Authors

Yusuf Idris was born in 1927 in an Egyptian village. He studied medicine, practised for a while, then became a government health inspector. Now devotes himself entirely to writing and journalism. Has published seven volumes of short stories and is regarded as Egypt's most original exponent of the genre; his wide knowledge of the highly expressive colloquial language of Egypt is often used in the dialogue of his stories. However grim his subjects may be— and death is one of his favourite—his essentially Egyptian sense of humour is ever-present. Many of his stories have been translated into Russian and other Eastern European languages. More recently he has interested himself in writing for the theatre— pungent comedies in the colloquial language with political overtones.

*　　　*　　　*

Walid Ikhlassi comes from Alexandretta in Syria where he was born in 1935. Now lives in Aleppo where he lectures at the University on agricultural economy. Has published two volumes of short stories, a short novel, and two plays.

*　　　*　　　*

Abdel Salam al-Ujaili was born in Rakka, a small Syrian township on the Euphrates, in 1918. Studied medicine at Damascus University and practises in his home town. Has interested himself in politics and has been M.P. for Rakka. Recently held ministerial posts, including that of Minister of Culture. Though devoting only his leisure time to writing, he is regarded as Syria's leading exponent of the short story. Of his thirteen published books, six are volumes of short stories.

Ghassan Kanafani, at present living in Beirut, where he is the editor of a daily newspaper, was born in 1936 in Acre, Palestine. Has published three volumes of short stories, a short play, and two short novels. Most of his writing deals in one form or another with the tragedy of Palestine. For six years he worked as a teacher in Kuwait. Recently he has published the first serious attempt in Arabic at a detective novel.

*   *   *

Shukri Ayyad, in his forties, was born and spent his childhood in the Province of Menoufiyya, U.A.R. He studied Arabic literature at Cairo University and took a doctorate. Made an early name for himself as a writer of short stories of which he has published two volumes. Has undertaken translations into Arabic of fiction and critical works. Recently served as Cultural Counsellor at the U.A.R. Embassy in Rio de Janeiro. Is now an assistant Professor of Arabic at Cairo University.

*   *   *

Fouad Tekerli, born in 1927 in Baghdad, has published only one volume of short stories (in 1960). Studied law at Baghdad University, worked in the Ministry of Justice and became a judge in Baghdad. Recently spent some time in Paris doing research work.

*   *   *

Yusuf Sharouni was born in the province of Menoufiyya, U.A.R., in 1924. Having studied philosophy at Cairo University, he worked for several years as a teacher in the Sudan. Has published two volumes of short stories, and some critical writings. For the last few years has worked at the Supreme Council for the Arts, Literature and Social Sciences in Cairo.

*   *   *

Abdel-Moneim Selim was born in the province of Rosetta, U.A.R., in 1929. Studied law at Cairo University and worked for a time as an Inspector of Taxes. Has published two volumes of short stories and a collection of plays. At present is living in London where he is the correspondent for an Egyptian weekly.

*   *   *

Taieb Saleh was born in 1929 in the Sudan. Studied at Khartoum University and later at Exeter University. Spent twelve years in the Arabic Section of the B.B.C. in charge of the drama department. The present story was published in a quarterly Arabic magazine, edited by the compiler of the present volume, and the translation first appeared in *Encounter*. Has recently finished a novella entitled *The Season of Migration to the North*, which is being published in Beirut, together with a volume of his short stories. Now works in Khartoum as Technical Adviser to the Sudan Broadcasting Service.

*   *   *

Yahya Hakki, born in 1905, studied law and served for some years in the diplomatic service. Has travelled widely in Europe and speaks English, French, Italian, and Turkish. Specializes in the short story and the novella—his *Lamp of Umm Hashem* deals with great sensitivity with the problem of an Egyptian, religious and conservative, who is educated in England and is then faced, on his return, with choosing between the Western and Eastern ways of life and values. Has published several volumes of short stories, also a study of the early short story in Egypt. At present he works as editor of the cultural magazine *al-Megalla*.

*   *   *

Latifa el-Zayat, born in 1926, is Assistant Professor in the English department at Einchams University, Cairo. Her novel, *The Open Door*, showed her as a writer of great sensitivity, interested in the techniques of fiction; the dialogue in the novel—as in the present short story—is written in the colloquial language. She has written on T. S. Eliot and Ford Madox Ford.

*   *   *

Tewfik al-Hakim was born in 1902 in Alexandria. Studied law in Cairo and later in Paris, and was for some years in government service in the provinces before devoting himself wholly to writing. Is better known as a novelist, essayist and playwright—of which he is Egypt's leading exponent—than as a writer of short stories. His novel *The Maze of Justice*, an amusing picture of life in the country districts of Egypt, is one of the few Arabic novels available in English translation. Has published nearly fifty books. A recent play, 'The Tree Climber', has been translated into English by the compiler of the present volume and was published last year by O.U.P.

*   *   *

Abdel Malik Nouri, an Iraqi, was born in 1921 on board a ship on its way through the Suez Canal. Studied in Baghdad, then at the American University in Beirut, and took a degree in law from Iraq. Worked as a lawyer and published his first volume of short stories in 1946. He has since published two more volumes. He is at present living in a village in Lebanon.

*   *   *

Laila Baalabaki, in her early thirties, was born and lives in Beirut. She made an instant name for herself with the publication of her first novel *I live*, which was translated into French and other European languages. Since then she has written another novel and a book of short stories, besides prolific journalistic writings as a columnist in Beirut's leading weekly magazine. Noted for her outspokenness, the present story, when it appeared in Arabic, led to her being prosecuted (unsuccessfully) by the police.

*   *   *

Nagib Mahfouz was born in Cairo in 1911 and took a degree in philosophy from Cairo University. Began writing historical novels in the thirties then, in 1945, wrote the first of a series of novels in which he has recorded contemporary Egyptian life with great skill, detail and wry humour. In 1956 and 1957 he published his trilogy, in 1,200 pages, about an Egyptian middle class family during the period between the two world wars. His more recent novels are shorter, often allegorical in tone, and show an increasing preoccupation with technique. He is at present employed as Director of the official Cinema Organization. Though primarily a novelist—certainly the most successful in the Arab world today—he regularly contributes short stories to *Al-Ahram*, Egypt's leading daily newspaper.

*   *   *

Jabra Ibrahim Jabra was born in 1919 in Bethlehem, Palestine. He was educated at the Arab College in Jerusalem and Exeter College, and took his degree in English literature at Cambridge University. He also had a year and half doing post-graduate work at Harvard. He lectured on English literature in Jerusalem and later at the University in Baghdad, where he has now settled, having taken Iraqi nationality. He is extremely versatile, having published poetry (in Arabic and English), novels, short stories and literary criticism; he also paints. His translations into Arabic include Faulkner's *The Sound and the Fury* and a new rendering of *Hamlet*. In 1960 he published a novel (written in English) entitled *Hunters in a Narrow Street* (Heinemann). Like most Palestinians he has a deep yearning for his lost motherland which is expressed in much of his writing. For the last few years he has occupied a senior position in the Iraq Petroleum Company.

*   *   *

Mahmoud Diab was born in Ismailiyya, U.A.R., in 1932. He took a degree in law and works at the Conseil d'Etat in Cairo. He has published a volume of short stories and two plays, the second of which, *The Storm*, was well received by critics when staged recently in Cairo.

*   *   *

Mahmoud Teymour, born in 1894, is regarded throughout the Arab world as the pioneer of the Arabic short story. Coming from an Egyptian family of Turkish origin many of whose members, including his father, were famous in the field of letters, he has devoted his life to writing and in particular to the short story, of which he has published numerous volumes. He has also written plays, criticism and travel books, and is actively interested in the problems of the development of the classical Arabic language. His stories have been widely translated and the present compiler published a selection of his stories in a small edition in Cairo in 1946 under the title *Tales from Egyptian Life*. Until recently he was editor of an Egyptian magazine devoted to the short story.

*   *   *

Touma al-Khouri is Lebanese and is in his forties. He took a degree in philosophy and works as a schoolmaster in Beirut. Besides three volumes of short stories, he has published several plays.

*   *   *

Zakaria Tamer, still in his twenties, was born in Damascus, is largely self-educated and for some years worked in a locksmith's. His first volume, *The Neighing of the White Steed*, was published in Beirut. He was recently employed for a short time in Jeddah in the Saudi Arabian television service, but is now back in Damascus working as a journalist. He has published in all three volumes of short stories.

*   *   *

Denys Johnson-Davies, the translator of these stories, was born in Vancouver in 1922, began studying Arabic at the School of Oriental Studies, London University, in 1937 and later took a degree at Cambridge. He spent the war years in the Arabic section of the B.B.C. and from 1945 to 1949 lived in Cairo where he lectured at the University. Publications include a textbook on Arabic translation, two original novels and a play—Tewfik al-Hakim's *The Tree Climber*—translated from the Arabic and published last year in O.U.P.'s Three Crown series.

DATE DUE

OCT 2 8 '85			
			PRINTED IN U.S.A.